A Man of Sorrows

A Man of Sorrows

~

Michael A. Greenberg, M.D.

Authors Choice Press
San Jose New York Lincoln Shanghai

A Man of Sorrows

Authors Choice Press
an imprint of iUniverse.com, Inc.

For information address:
iUniverse.com, Inc.
5220 S 16th, Ste. 200
Lincoln, NE 68512
www.iuniverse.com

ISBN: 0-595-19422-2

Printed in the United States of America

To My Three Fathers

Acknowledgements

Family, patients, colleagues, friends, and editors contributed to this book and to my life during the long process of its birth. You know who you are and I am grateful to each of you.

Prologue

"Hypothermia isn't the worst way to die," Kevin Hargrove said to the empty Heineken bottle abandoned on the graffiti-covered breakwater at Montrose Harbor. "Especially if you're anesthetized with a *really* expensive scotch." Kevin kicked at the emerald glass, but missed and turned his peat-soaked attention to the lights of Chicago's skyline reflected in a cold Lake Michigan. Here, just a little over a year ago, Matthew Harrison and he had sat and talked from dusk until the sun rose over the Michigan side of the lake. Next morning, Matthew left for somewhere on the West Coast. The two men shared a bottle of scotch that night, too. The all-nighter was intimacy of the kind guys share when they've been through war or some other personal hell together. They had survived Matthew's disastrous first year of medical residency.

Kevin raised the bottle and toasted Matthew's life. The October wind raised a small chop on the lake. The moonlight dancing on the black water reminded Kevin of the darkened lecture halls in medical school where he had first learned the inevitable victory of death. The best lectures–standing room only–were those in forensic pathology. For two days, the entire medical school enrollment, whatever friends and family members they could pass off as fellow students, and those residents who could sneak away from their ward duties, gaped at bizarre slides of murders and suicides. From the cherry red faces caused by carbon monoxide poisoning (like freezing to death, not a physically painful way to go) to the guys who accidentally hanged themselves while masturbating (the restriction of oxygen to the brain was said to greatly intensify an orgasm), they sat fascinated by the myriad pathways to the morgue, never believing that at some point in their lives they too would make the journey. Some of the students and housestaff made crude comments about the victims. Others ostentatiously ate lunch during the bloody lectures.

Reaching down with his hand to test the temperature of the water, Kevin wondered what color coffin his mother would choose for him and how the mortuary artists would undo his body's grotesque bloating. He pushed the thought from his mind, and took another swig of scotch. A layer of frost formed inside his body. He stood up and shivered as he buttoned his coat against the inner and outer chill. "I'm not here to drown, old buddy," he said loudly to the water and the lights. He waved the bottle. "I'm here to celebrate my successful new medical practice and my wonderful life. And to thank *you*, Matthew Harrison." He took one last long drink and tossed the bottle toward the water. It fell short and shattered on the rocks. "Typical," he laughed.

Standing on the edge of the rocks, on the spot where Matthew had once jumped into the water, Kevin thought of how Matthew had taught him about a different kind of immersion, one in which you don't know whether you're being baptized or sinking to an agonizing death. Shivering and cold, tears running down his cheeks, Kevin stood there in silence through the sunrise of the next day, waiting for the Heineken bottle to tell him which of them had won.

1

Kevin Hargrove was chief resident when Matthew Harrison entered the medicine residency program at the Illinois Research Hospital. He was a kind of Father Superior–a shepherd for the terrified novices. From the moment he met Matthew, he sensed that something special moved within him. Most men, including Kevin, become doctors because they're good in science and want to make a decent living. But Matthew was different from the other residents with whom Kevin lived and worked. He became a doctor solely to help others.

Kevin struggled for everything that came naturally to Matthew. He envied Matthew's passion and his gifts. To Kevin, Matthew seemed graced.

Illinois Research Hospital was as antique and senile as the saddest of its Medicare patients. The goose-shit green paint throughout and the colorless linoleum floors beaten down by generations of residents appeared to be the only things holding the building together. Each floor had a central nursing station where piles of battered stainless steel patient charts and stacks of unfiled laboratory reports hid laminate counters worn through to the wood. Every chart and report was there except the ones the residents needed. A disintegrating cardboard box filled with books, stethoscopes, and personal items lost by generations of medical students slumped in a corner of the floor. Above the desk was a sign that read "Cows May Come and Cows May Go, But The Bull Goes On Forever." Sanford Buckman, the departmental chief, decided it was funny and could stay. At least, Kevin thought each time he looked at the sign, Buckman can take a joke.

The morning of his first encounter with Matthew, Kevin had spent most of the night at the hospital undoing a senior medical student's near fatal mistake. Misunderstanding the directives given to him by a sleep-deprived first-year resident, the student had allowed an elderly woman to go into cardiac failure.

Kevin stabilized the patient, then showed the responsible resident and student where they had erred. Returning to his routine, he was on the way to review the overnight lab reports when he discovered Matthew on his knees in the corridor next to an old black man in a wheelchair. The patient, whose senile dementia would be obvious even to a first-year medical student, was shouting a stream of barely coherent obscenities in a high pitched voice, as if some long dead relative, or maybe the crisp young doctor, had mortally offended his pride. His cloudy old eyes searched vainly for the source of his agitation.

Matthew looked up at Kevin with a blinding smile. "My first day. I didn't want to be late." He looked at his watch. "Matthew Harrison. First-year in medicine."

Kevin wondered how this man could keep his composure in the midst of the cacophony. "I'm Kevin Hargrove. You have time. What's the story with this guy?"

"You're the Chief Resident," Matthew said. He rose and extended his hand.

Kevin looked down at the pool of urine at the base of the old man's wheelchair and eluded Matthew's grasp. It was too early in the day for contact with bodily fluids. "You're on the fifth floor," he said. "The class-room is on six."

"Thanks," Matthew said, laughing easily. He turned and grabbed two foil-wrapped alcohol pads from a medicine cart stationed a few feet away. He tore them open, cleaned his hands, and dropped the waste in a trash receptacle attached to the side of the cart. "I knew something was-n't right with him," he said, pointing at the old man whose yelling had not diminished. "His Foley bag broke. I slipped on the flood and bumped his wheelchair." He squinted at Kevin, like an athlete assessing the next easy hurdle. "Do I need to fill out an incident report?" he asked, taking a bright yellow Parker Duofold from his shirt pocket. Kevin thought that a pen like that would have seemed presumptuous or out of place with most men of their age and status. In Matthew's hand, how-ever, it looked like the most natural thing in the world.

"If we did an incident report each time we disturbed a patient, the world's forests would disappear in a week. Leave him," Kevin said evenly.

"But he's so confused." Matthew returned the pen to his pocket and gently put his hand on the old man's shoulder. The verbal fusillade stopped instantly; the man closed his mouth, shut his eyes, and breathed deeply.

The silence reverberated in Kevin's ear. "You better leave now or you *will* be late. You need your photo ID before this morning's meeting. I'll take care of him." But it was clear the old man had already been cared for.

Matthew nodded, walked down the hallway, and disappeared up the stairwell. Kevin turned to give the patient a quick once over. What he saw stunned him. He felt the small hairs on the back of his neck rise and his heart race. The man's eyes were lucid, and he looked at Kevin as if he had awakened from a deep sleep. Kevin grabbed the patient's chart from the back of the wheel chair, flipped though its pages, then snapped his penlight out of his pocket.

"I must be losing it," he said to himself, shining the beam in the old man's eyes for a second and then a slightly panicked third time. "This guy had bilateral cataracts so obvious a Cub Scout could have diagnosed them." Kevin's sweating hand lost its grip on the chart. It dropped into the urine, the splatter barely missing his leg. "Damn," he muttered aloud. Carefully picking the chart up by a dry corner, he grabbed a handful of paper towels from the same medicine cart Matthew had used and gingerly wiped down the chart's metal covers. After washing his hands in the nursing station sink, he returned to take one last look at the old black man. The harsh ring of a phone in a nearby patient's room broke his trance. He turned and left to join Matthew and the other residents for the morning departmental meeting. Had he stayed just a few seconds longer, he would have heard the old man ask a passing nurse for a glass of water—the first coherent sentence he had spoken in ten years.

Kevin stood before his new charges, arms folded, nervous but outwardly cool. He saw Matthew slip into the classroom, walking directly in front of Sanford Buckman to take the only remaining seat. Buckman looked at his watch for an extended moment and then directly at his new resident. Not being roasted over the coals was the first and only break Matthew got from Buckman.

Per Buckman's precise instructions, Kevin had already distributed packets of department rules and guidelines to the new residents. Buckman went through his usual first day routine of reading every rule in the handout. Most of the residents listened as though God were speaking. Matthew appeared to be daydreaming until Buckman began his tirade in earnest, that is. Kevin noticed Matthew's head jump when the chief slammed his fist down on the desk. Buckman was a big man, aging but strong with the fierce gaze of an eagle—and just as lethal.

"You can blame the lawyers, the greedy public looking for a malpractice windfall, or the insurance companies, but it's doctors who are the cause of our current crisis in medical care. Doctors who, like you, were once residents. Some who don't pay attention to their patients. Others who overlook important details. And those who are just plain sloppy and lazy. It's my job to make each of you part of the solution instead of adding to the problem." His voice raspy and resonant, Buckman had everyone's attention now–even Kevin's, who was a regular audience for Buckman's tirades, when he grilled Kevin on the performance of the residents, the state of the patients, and the outcomes of the housestaffs' procedures. But soon Buckman slipped off his high horse and continued with the same sermon he had been preaching to generations of students. Kevin had heard it twice before, which didn't make it any less true or terrifying.

"Look to the person on your left and your right. That adds up to three, right? I'm reasonably sure you can count that high. Now, one of you, either you or one of the other two, will not finish your residency here."

The room of incipient doctors shifted uneasily. Kevin had to grin. Buckman's fierce routine never failed to unnerve his brood of green new charges.

"One in every three people who earn an M.D. degree shouldn't be a physician. And in my program we weed them out."

Buckman paused.

The fear in the room made it hard to breathe. Buckman had voiced the doubt inside these young doctors–that they would never measure up, no matter how hard they worked or how many letters they had after their names.

"Incompetent doctors put patients in premature graves." Buckman slapped his palm on the desk in righteous emphasis. How many of these anxious residents, Kevin wondered, had already heard the sad story of Sandra Herrington? She had been accepted into the training program two years ago, despite what everyone recognized immediately as deep emotional problems. Fearful of making a mistake, and even more obsessive-compulsive than the average doctor, she repeatedly asked Buckman the same questions about the most basic patient management issues. Tiring of her behavior, Buckman told her she was "too fragile for a medical life." He harassed her continually. Too fearful to quit the program, she was found in her garage, her car running, an angry note blaming Buckman taped to the dashboard. Buckman waltzed through the investigation and refused to cancel a lecture scheduled the same time as Sandra's funeral. He was a heartless bastard.

Buckman took a breath and relaxed. His voice grew suspiciously soothing as he continued. "Two out of three of you will be a credit to the profession. If you manage to complete your residency here, if you live up to my standards, you will be among the best-prepared physicians in the country. I take care of my residents. My kids are well-placed and successful." He smiled in a way that was more frightening than his temper had been.

Kevin knew the state of the residents' minds during this speech: numb panic. Most of them had not slept well in the past few days, anxious because their responsibility for patient care had just taken a quantum leap. It happens every July 1st, the New Year's Day of training programs—the most dangerous day to be a patient in a university hospital in the United States. All over the country, the scene is repeated in one dreary green corridor after another—in lofty urban teaching institutions, fancy Sun Belt medical centers, and even in some smaller and more humble community hospitals. Sleepy-eyed, unprepared first-year residents, magically transformed into medical doctors only a few short weeks ago when their deans handed them diplomas, now assume their responsibility as caretakers of the still-well, sick, and dying. They understand how little they actually know so early in their training; everyone is afraid of harming patients. Buckman hates deaths on his watch. Kevin has seen him tear into any resident whose bad luck it was to have been assigned a dying patient.

Buckman was spent, his well-rehearsed inaugural speech completed. He looked older and more tired than he did when Kevin had heard the speech the first time, two Julys ago; his eyes were dull and his face seemed to collapse in on itself when he stopped speaking. Kevin watched as he added, "We'll start hospital rounds now. Don't forget the reception tonight. We always have one hundred percent attendance. Understood?"

Everyone did.

Kevin cornered Matthew as he was about to leave the room. "Are you okay?" he asked.

"Sure. Why?" Kevin thought he heard hesitation in Matthew's response. "You seemed jumpy during the meeting. You still seem on edge. Not the unusually calm guy I met earlier today on the fifth floor."

Matthew smiled. "Nothing's wrong," he said. "Except Buckman's style."

"You'll learn how to get along with him," Kevin said.

Matthew's smile darkened. "I sure as hell hope so."

2

Kevin caught a big break later that day. The Friday afternoon "gripe session," Buckman's attempt to be one of the ordinary guys, was canceled. Officially an opportunity to generate solutions for patient care problems, the meeting was actually Buckman's way of gathering intelligence from the resident staff. They met in his gritty office, curtains drawn against the light, dusty bookshelves piled with reprints of his papers, and a human skeleton said to be either Buckman's first wife or the asphyxiated bones of Sandra Herrington. "A sudden change in Dr. Buckman's schedule," his secretary said. This had been happening a lot lately, and it put smiles on everyone's faces, especially Kevin's. All too frequently, a not-so-bright resident would open his big dumb mouth about an issue that was really none of his business anyway–usually to score brownie points with the Chief–and give Buckman another opportunity to, as he was so fond of saying, "rattle the residents' cage."

Fabricating a bullshit reason, Kevin called Buckman at home to be sure he was there. After light speed rounds to make sure nothing was brewing that could explode in the next hour or so, he made a quick phone call, received his assignment, and slipped into a cab. Kevin told the driver to take him to the Sears Tower. He was on what had, over the past year, become regular missions of mercy.

"I'm glad I could get my physical today," Jon Nathanson said.

"It works for me," Kevin said, checking his watch. "This should take just a few minutes. I've got a bunch of new ducks in the water today."

Nathanson, like many of the overstressed young lions of capitalism that Kevin had examined for million dollar insurance policies, ignored his comment; it was clear that whatever he did was, in his estimation, more important than what Kevin did. Nathanson was Kevin's age, but at least fifty pounds overweight, despite two squash racquets resting like hunting trophies on a chrome and leather couch in his upper floor office–the kind with a three-million dollar view. His taupe wool trousers, held up by leather suspenders, broke perfectly on a pair of Prada shoes. Even his aftershave smelled like money.

"Are you an intern?" Nathanson asked.

"Roll up your sleeve, please, so I can take your blood pressure. Actually, I'm Chief Resident."

"How much do you boys make these days?" Nathanson asked.

"Not enough. Can you get that sleeve up just a bit higher?" Kevin went ahead and told him his base salary.

Jon whistled through his front teeth. "My watch cost more than that." He grinned. "But I suppose you'll be shopping for a Lexus soon–unless managed care squeezes your salary even more."

Kevin did his best to ignore the comment. "When was your last regular physical?" he asked as he recorded Nathanson's blood pressure–190 over 120–on a piece of scratch paper. Jon laughed and said that he didn't remember. Kevin told him that his blood pressure and weight were both elevated enough to be potential problems.

"What'll it take to buff the numbers, Doc?" Nathanson asked.

"Buff the numbers?" Kevin parroted, his face a mask of innocent sincerity. He detested guys like Nathanson and had been invited to play their game enough times that he was no longer shocked by their arrogance. But he also knew that one angry call from any of these jerks to his insurance agent could derail his gravy train.

"How about three hundred?" Nathanson asked.

"You only weigh two thirty," Kevin said. He stared blankly at Nathanson's porcine face.

Small beads of sweat appeared on Nathanson's forehead. "Look, Doc, let's be honest with each other. I need the insurance coverage as part of a contractual obligation." His smile thinned. "And you need the money or you wouldn't be here. I'll give you three hundred dollars to change the figures enough to make this work. I'm sure it's done all the time."

"I'm sorry," Kevin said, digging deep for his most empathetic voice. "That would be fraud." He put his hand on Nathanson's shoulder. "Relax. It'll cost you more, but you'll get your policy. And I promise not to say anything about the bribery attempt or you'd never get coverage."

Nathanson pushed Kevin's hand away as if he had been smearing dog shit on the shoulder of his three hundred-dollar shirt. Kevin gave him his I'm-really-a-nice-guy smile. "You're not the first to try. And I give the same advice to everyone with your numbers: Eighty-six the beer or the Scotch or whatever it is you drink. Take up jogging. A large insurance settlement can buy dozens of Brioni suits, but you can only wear one after you're dead." Kevin packed up his instruments, left Nathanson steaming, and returned to the hospital. He'd been gone less than an hour. With no one, especially Buckman, the wiser, he now had a hundred dollars more to pass on to his mother, who needed it.

Kevin's little ducklings didn't notice his short absence and waddled through the day with only minor damage to the patient population of the hospital. At six o'clock, he left for home. Matthew fell in step beside him; he lived in the apartment below Kevin, it turned out, with his wife, Eileen.

"Are most of the residents married?" Matthew asked.

"You are," Kevin responded. "Why?"

"My wife needs friends. We're alone here–except for Susan Olivera."

"You know Susan?" Kevin asked.

"From med school."

The hospital offered resident housing at very attractive rates. Chicago's medical center was bordered by eighty-year old Italian neighborhoods, fast sliding into multiracial poverty. The run-down apartment buildings sold cheaply to the hospital by fleeing whites. A few coats of paint, new locks on the doors, a truckload of tacky furniture and the interns and residents called it home, or at least a rest stop on the way to better and usually more suburban things. The buildings were walking distance from the hospital–convenient for a chief resident who had to run over on a moment's notice to smother the fires that continuously broke out among its patient population–mostly inner city welfare types, piss-poor protoplasm inviting disease. They made great practice material for doctors-in-training–a daily melange of stab wounds, AIDS, heart and kidney failure, and leprosy. Most of the housestaff couldn't wait to graduate and open their own practices in the suburbs where the patient population smelled good and had gold MasterCards.

"Got a few minutes?" Matthew asked Kevin as they reached their building. "I'd like you to meet my wife."

Kevin checked his watch. "Sure. The reception doesn't start until eight."

Matthew's apartment was almost identical to Kevin's, except Matthew had a wife to keep it clean. Matthew had met Eileen, an education major, in college. Being lucky got him a second bedroom. They had a collection of family photos and a Japanese scroll painting of pine trees purchased on a San Francisco vacation. Brick and board bookcases, made from fantastic old bricks Matthew found in the neighborhood, held a Bang and Olufsen system, much better, thought Kevin, than his Aiwa. That was the benefit of two salaries–Eileen had found a job at a day care center.

Matthew sat with Kevin on the couch in the living room, tired from his first day. Eileen brought them a pitcher of iced tea. "If you were any more beautiful, I don't think I could stand it," Matthew said, taking the glass from her hand.

"Don't stop there." She smiled at him, then at Kevin, who took the bait. His return smile added his name to her list of admirers, which, Kevin imagined, was probably a long one. After an infinite moment, their eyes disengaged and Eileen began to flit around the apartment like a nervous mother bird, unsure if the latest breeze had disturbed the order of her nest. She plumped the pillows behind both men. Kevin's gut felt hollow. He wanted someone to care for him, to tell him how much to drink, and to be there when his eyes opened with the morning light spreading like a stain across his bedroom wall. Her medium length hair, the rich gold of a Kansas wheat field, framed a face that needed only the barest touch of lipstick to achieve aching perfection. Her eyes were gray-blue, not the virginal clarity of watercolor, but the muddy, opaque quality of tempera.

Eileen ran her fingers over the immaculate bookshelves, checking for any rogue dust that might have escaped her earlier efforts. She smoothed the wrinkles from her Laura Ashley dress, a floor length deep blue floral with just the tiniest border of lace around the plunging neckline. Matthew rose from the couch, slipped his arms around his wife and hugged her. He frowned. "Were you smoking today?" he asked.

"Five," she said. "Just a few drags from each."

"You promised," he said gently.

"I've had a hard day."

"I know," he said, tightening his embrace. "But I love you."

"And I," Kevin interjected, "know when I'm superfluous."

Matthew shut the door after Kevin left and decided that there was only one way to end that day's debate about cigarettes, which he knew he would not win. He and Eileen had enough time before the reception to tear off each other's clothes and fall on the bed–but not before Matthew turned on the stereo and slipped Peter Gabriel's "Passion" CD into the player. They woke a half-hour later, the rich fullness of the music spilling into the emptiness of their bodies, an energetic yin and yang that danced in the honey-hued light of the summer evening casting shadows on the bed and its two naked lovers. Matthew turned to Eileen. "Are you awake enough to answer a question?"

She opened her eyes. "I think so."

"Can we stay home tonight?"

She yawned, smiled, and moved her fingers mindlessly on his chest. "We can make love again after the reception."

He shifted his body from underneath her hand. "It's not about sex, Eileen. Can we?"

She sat up. Matthew felt her mood shift. "I don't think so, Matthew. It's required."

"Let's be crazy. Just once."

"What's this about?"

"I don't know."

"Until you do know, Matthew, we're going."

"Okay, then. I'm sick."

"Tell me the truth, Matthew. What's wrong?"

"Nothing."

"Then get out of bed and get going."

He sighed. "I klutzed my way through the morning and then was almost late for Buckman's meeting. Oh, Jesus, Eileen, this sounds so juvenile." He sighed again. "He won't miss us."

"Trust me. He will. I'm going to shower." Eileen left the bed for the bathroom.

"Fuck Buckman. Fuck his whole stinking program." Matthew followed her and ran the hot water at the sink to shave while she showered.

"You sound like my father," Eileen said from behind the frosted plastic shower curtain.

"Buckman scares me," he told her while he ran the razor over his face. "I know I've made it through worse than him, but...ouch!" Eileen, now out of the shower, had jostled his arm reaching for a hairbrush. A half-inch gash on his chin began to bleed profusely.

"Matty, I'm sorry."

"It's okay." He placed his index finger on the cut. When he removed it seconds later, the cut was completely healed leaving only the blood that had run down his neck.

Eileen, standing behind him, their faces reflected together in the mirror, gently touched his shoulder. "How did you do that?"

Matthew heard her voice from a distance, as if he were standing in a tunnel. He broke from her touch and turned away. "Are you done with the shower?"

Eileen reached out again, turned his head to her face, and touched the spot on his chin where the cut had been. "It looked worse than it was," he said. But he knew the truth.

She stared at his chin, accepting his explanation, kissed him on the cheek, and went to get dressed. Matthew looked long and hard at the place he had cut himself. He began to tremble, remembering the pain he felt at the age of eighteen.

"Please," he whispered to the pale ghost that stared back at him from the mirror. "Go away."

3

The student union, a three story concrete box, sat directly across from the hospital. Its brute simplicity contrasted with the carved gargoyles and dark stone of the main building of the Research. The residents spent their breaks and lunch hours there. It was only fifty yards from the Research, but was so dissimilar in architectural style that it felt light years away from Buckman and the patients.

Three restaurants served heart-unhealthy food, the smell of grease competing with the stench of formaldehyde and phenol from the large and very noisy groups of first-year medical students fresh–or less than fresh–from their cadavers. The bookstore in the basement (used books were cheaper three blocks away) had a good selection of magazines, including foreign language periodicals for homesick residents.

Hidden upstairs was the neo-Gothic Founder's Room with its dark, distressed oak paneling, burgundy wool carpet, and heavy leather furniture. Oversized oil portraits of famous sons, Buckman sure to be among them one day, lined the walls. It was rumored to be easier to obtain a crypt at Pere Lachaise than to hang there.

Matthew, strikingly handsome in the blue wool blazer he had added to his standard J. Crew uniform, held Eileen's hand and followed the crowd toward the sounds of the string trio overshadowed by loud voices and laughter. Terrazzo floors, inset with brass medical center logos, reverberated with the unmistakable click-clack of high heels. Typical of all medical center social functions, residents discussed medicine. Their spouses attempted small talk, bored with the usual medical chat and humor. Faculty groups engaged in more lively conversation, their relationships having developed intimacy over time.

Eileen looked sharply at Matthew when Stensen, a morbidly obese, sloppily dressed resident, smiled through layers of nicotine and instructed Matthew to sign the register. Another Buckman regulation. Matthew blanched like a teenager required to check in with Mom and Dad.

"Clearly, please, so your name can be read," Kevin said with veiled sarcasm, sneaking up behind them.

"I told you we couldn't miss this," Eileen whispered to Matthew. She shot Kevin a glance that said she was a player.

Matthew returned her triumphant smile with a boyish grin. "You win," he said. "Do you want to hang with us, Kevin? Or are you on duty?"

"It's a party for everyone. Except maybe Buckman. And even if I was working, do you think I'd miss an opportunity to be with a beautiful woman—even a married one?"

The first familiar face Matthew and Eileen encountered after joining the party was another first-year resident, Nick Shulman, a friend of Matthew's since college. A year younger than Matthew, Nick was short and dark, his face a long-abandoned battlefield of acne scars, his head prematurely bald. Just this side of pudgy, he seemed uncomfortable, as if outclassed by his expensive wardrobe.

Nick greeted Kevin with a polite handshake, Matthew and Eileen with warm hugs. "Are you ready to dump this *goy* for me, Eileen? Jewish guys make the best husbands."

She pushed him away with the coyness of a debutante, "But not the best lovers, Nicky. And besides," Eileen said with a smile, "you can't afford me."

Nick turned to Matthew. "Why so quiet, bud?"

"Cocktail parties bore me."

"We can find a sports bar."

Eileen took Matthew's hand. "He doesn't do bars anymore," she said with the finesse of a lioness protecting her kill. "He's nervous. New residency. New Chief."

"Buckman scares the shit out of me too," Nick said.

"A realistic fear," Kevin said. "Bucky's unpredictability is more dangerous than his anger. We find ways to avoid him or to make end runs around him. When he gets involved with a patient, our scutwork triples."

"Matthew's used to a grind," Eileen said. "Surgeons earn good money, but work their tails off from their first day of training."

"Can I get a drink?" Matthew asked.

"Unfortunately, just punch," Kevin said. "You must be special. Buckman never takes transfers from surgery. Did you get cut?"

"I decided I liked medicine more," Matthew said.

"Bucky should have given you *some* credit for the two years," Kevin said.

"Can we change the subject?" Matthew asked, looking peeved.

"People leave training programs for lots of reasons," Nick said. He laughed nervously. "Buckman spelled it out for us this morning."

Matthew dropped Eileen's hand and grabbed Nick's wrist–hard. "Do you need a fucking garden hose to clean out your ears, Nick? Let's talk about something else."

Eileen gracefully pried Matthew's hand from Nick's arm and spoke softly but forcibly through gritted teeth. "Maybe *you* need the hose for your *mouth*, Matthew. I don't appreciate the language and other people might not either."

An awkward silence enveloped the group for half an eternity. Eileen studied Kevin's face as if looking for a reaction to Matthew's behavior.

"Hey, bud, Susan's here tonight," Nick said, playfully punching Matthew in the arm, breaking the tension.

Eileen's eyes swept the room. "Really? Where?"

"Probably cornering some poor schmuck about past life regression," Nick said. "I'll go find her."

Nick left for only a few moments, and returned with Susan Olivera. "Like I said. She was trying to get Buckman to co-sign orders for crystal therapy. Ayurveda too. The curanderos are coming out at midnight."

Ignoring Nick, Susan gave Matthew and Eileen warm hugs. Susan had graduated medical school a year after Matthew, but was now a year ahead of him because of his detour in surgery. She was one of the few residents who openly supported alternative medicine. Susan was thirty, divorced from some guy she wouldn't talk about, three years older than Kevin but a year behind him in the program because she had earned an R.N. before going to medical school. She had worked a short stint as a charge nurse on a cancer unit at a suburban hospital.

Susan was Kevin's personal sexual fantasy. Her long ebony hair and the way it reflected the light made his hands want to loosen it from its tight bondage. The bulky clothes and thick owl glasses she wore couldn't hide the sensual body beneath and only gave her a sense of mystery, like one of those tightly wound brightly colored paper "surprise balls" you buy in Chinatown gift shops. As you unwind the long strip of paper, small inexpensive charms and toys are exposed. The joy, of course, is in the process of discovering what's hidden inside the ball. In the end, you're left with a few disappointingly ordinary plastic trinkets and a mess of paper to deal with, which was where the aptness of the simile ended. With Susan, Kevin expected he'd find a collection of unexpected treasures.

Susan smiled warmly. "It's good to see old friends. Even Nick. Sorry I haven't phoned, Eileen, but I took extra call for a guy with the flu. And I had some outside stuff to do also."

"Moonlighting?" Nick asked.

Susan looked at Kevin for a split second, then back at Nick. "No," she said. "Something personal. Besides, Buckman won't let us moonlight. He's made it crystal clear that residency is a full-time job."

Before Kevin could change the subject, Nick did it for him. "Raising the dead with aromatherapy? Secret homeopathic practice?" he asked. "I know the department's into it, because there's so little alcohol in the punch. You have to take the dose on faith. Our new-age healer knows all about faith. Hope and charity too. Don't you, Susan?"

"You're such an ass, Nick," Susan laughed.

Eileen took Nick's arm. "Let's eat," she said. "I'm starved. They all walked over to the buffet table, Nick talking non-stop to a silent Matthew.

"Food of the gods," Kevin said stuffing a miniature eclair into his mouth.

"How can you eat that?" Susan asked. "You tell patients to avoid what you're doing. It's hypocritical."

"I'm a pragmatist, not a hypocrite," he said. "Less for them—more for me."

Eileen asked Kevin where he planned to practice when he graduated.

"I'm not sure yet," he said. "But I want to stay in Chicago."

"Girlfriend?" she asked.

"I wish. My mother lives here."

Nick put his arm around Matthew's shoulders. "Matthew and I are going to open a practice together. Right, bud?" Matthew looked uncomfortable.

"Really?" Susan asked.

"It's a match made in heaven," Nick said. "Matthew can cover the Jewish holidays so I can go to Temple and check out everyone's new clothes. And I can work on Easter so he can get in a round of golf and tell the patients he's in church."

"Get serious, Nick," Matthew snapped, pulling out of Nick's grasp. "You're such a dickhead."

Matthew's response froze the group into a second icy silence. Eileen shot Matthew an angry glance. Ignoring her disapproval, Matthew turned and saw Buckman. "It's your idea anyway, Nick. I'm not sure what I'm going to do and it's three fucking Buckman years away."

"Maybe less, Buddy," Nick said in what Kevin thought was an act of self-immolation.

Matthew's intensity increased. "Can you shut the fuck up?" Faces from other groups turned.

Eileen dug her fingers into Matthew's forearm. "This is the last time I'm going to ask…"

"Let's kiss Buckman's ass and get the hell out of here," Matthew said.

Nick, Matthew, and Eileen left to pay their respects to Buckman. Kevin watched until the three were out of earshot. "Is he always this angry?" he asked.

Susan raised her eyebrows. "This isn't like him."

"Do you know why he quit surgery? Do I have to worry about this guy?"

"No. He's cool, Kevin. A really nice guy. Usually."

"Not tonight," Kevin said.

Buckman was isolated in the corner of a room, deep in an animated discussion with the head of ophthalmology. A beautiful young woman in an expensive black cocktail dress stood at his side.

"They look intense," Eileen said. "Maybe we shouldn't break in."

Ignoring Eileen's suggestion, Matthew walked directly up behind Buckman.

"Excuse me, Doctor Buckman…" Buckman blanched, seemed caught off guard by the intrusion.

"I'm Matthew Harrison. This is my wife, Eileen. And Nick Shulman."

"I'm Francie Buckman," the young woman said delicately. "His daughter."

"Doctor Harrison, unlike surgeons, we start our rounds at six-thirty sharp in the morning."

"Yes sir," he said, offended by Buckman's deportment in a social setting.

"That doesn't mean you slide in at the last moment as you might have done in the operating room."

"I understand, Dr. Buckman." Matthew stared directly into Buckman's dark, menacing eyes for a full half-minute, losing his orientation in place and time. Then Matthew blinked, severing the connection. His forehead was damp with sweat even though the air conditioning had been on full blast.

Buckman was dazed. He shuddered slightly, breaking the spell and regaining his composure. "Thank you, Harrison. See you tomorrow."

"Nice to have met you, Francie. Good to have seen you, Doctor B." Nick said.

Buckman's face became granite. "Dr. Shulman, don't ever refer to me in the familiar again. I'll let this one slide, but never again. Do you understand?"

"Sorry, sir. Just the informality of the recept…"

"Do you understand the concept of never, Doctor Shulman?"

"Understood, Doctor Buckman."

"Excellent." He turned and smiled at Eileen. "Nice to have met you, Mrs. Harrison. Have a nice evening. Oh, and one favor please. Could you ask Dr. Hargrove to join me for a moment? I noticed you were with him before you joined me." He shot Matthew a final quizzical glance and turned his back.

"What was that?" Nick asked.

"A staring contest," Matthew answered, disconcerted.

Five minutes after Kevin was found and sent to talk with Buckman, he returned to find Nick, Susan, Matthew, and Eileen still keeping to themselves. He told Nick that Buckman had made a last minute change in the schedule, putting him on call that night.

"That bites," Nick said.

"Get used to it," Kevin said. "Bucky does this regularly. And don't call him Dr. B. again. That's probably why he picked you."

"Point taken," Nick muttered. "But why the sudden switch?"

"Bucky's making the on-call guy work on a paper for the *New England Journal*. Pig out here, Nick. On-call food sucks."

Susan excused herself to check a patient in the hospital. Kevin explained to Matthew and Nick that Buckman's rounds were called "The Kingdom of Fear" because of his reputation for knowing the shittiest little detail about every disease known to mankind. Bucky loved to pimp the housestaff with his knowledge. Nobody knew the answers to his questions, unless they happened to have read the 1946 volume of *The Journal of Obscure Diseases* that day.

"If he's so awful, how do the residents learn anything from him?" Eileen asked.

"Elementary physics," Kevin responded. "Shit rolls downhill. We learn from each other. Junior med students from seniors, seniors from first year residents and so on up the ladder. Bucky shares his secrets with the senior residents and we pass them down the line."

Eileen was upset. Kevin assured her that he would take care of Matthew. "It's not as bad as it seems," he said. "You know about the party later?"

"Yes," Matthew said. "Pizza or something like that."

"Something like that," Kevin echoed. "And the secret initiation to the fraternity."

"Shit," Nick said. "I get doubly screwed."

"We'll pass," Matthew said. "I left keg parties and paddling back in college."

"I'm kidding about the initiation," Kevin said. "You should meet the other senior residents. Learn how to survive Buckman. Drink good beer."

"I think it would do you good to go," Eileen said. "Your chief resident told you to do it."

"Your wife's smart," Kevin said. Eileen smiled. "We stick together. Cover each other's asses. We'll show you the ropes."

4

Tim Davidson's apartment reeked of pizza and beer. It was located a few blocks from where Kevin and Matthew lived, the only hospital apartment large enough and clean enough to fit all the residents. He shared it with another third year, Phil Edelstein. The decor was Spartan; sports pages tacked on the walls covered stains and cracks the paint could not.

Everyone was present (one hundred percent attendance required) except the guys on call. Chairs had been borrowed from the clinic waiting room. Smashing Pumpkins was on the CD player. Phil held court, telling a story.

"...so Buckman asks me in front of the patient where the x-ray report is, and I tell him the truth. Hey, Stenson you pig, don't spill your fucking beer on the couch. I live here."

He shot his roommate a goofy conspiratorial smile and continued. "Nobody in the hospital can find the chart. Meanwhile, the patient goes wild and chews out Bucky's ass." The roomful of residents laughed. Even the first-year residents, still relative strangers to each other and to the seniors, had begun to loosen up. "Bucky couldn't say a word to the guy.

He wasn't an ordinary guy with a big mouth. He was a fucking federal judge."

Johnson, a second year resident, sitting on the floor, broke in, "I'd give my right nut to see Buckman eat shit. Is there a video?"

"Sure," Kevin said, "But only third year residents get to see it. Unless you're willing to take extra call…"

"Don't *touch* me!" Susan shrieked. The room quieted. A sea of confused faces turned toward her, standing next to Bill Herrera, a first year resident. She seemed nervous and was smoothing the shoulder of her blouse.

"But, I thought…" he stammered. "You said…"

"You thought wrong," she replied angrily.

"I'm sorry," he said, appearing confused. "I didn't mean to…"

Everyone was silent. It was as if a gun had gone off and Susan was holding it. She stood there, looking as uncomfortable as if she had walked into the room naked and blown lunch in the middle of the floor. "I'm sorry if I overreacted," she finally said, regaining her composure and breaking the spell. "Phil, please go on with your story."

Phil looked at her and shrugged. He chugged the remainder of the bottle in his hand and continued. "What I saw is nothing to what Kevin knows. Tell 'em Kev."

Kevin had enough ethanol in his blood to unlock his lips and he wanted the room to forget whatever had happened with Susan. The dog, tell them about the fucking dog, his thick brain told him. "It was about two years ago. The chief of physical therapy had a dog that got sick–majorly ill–really suffering."

His canine whimpering brought encouraging laughter.

"This pup had a belly more swollen than Mrs. Fletcher in 603 and, like her, slept sitting up. But unlike Mrs. Fletcher, the dog had connections. He was the *cousin* of the chief radiologist's dog. So, while Mrs. Fletcher waits five days for her liver scan, Fido gets sneaked into the hospital during a staff meeting."

"This dog," someone shouted from the corner of the room, "did *not* belong to an HMO."

"Family pets are entitled to professional courtesy," Kevin said. Everyone laughed. "The two chiefs brought in a vet and vet nurse and ran a liver scan with some unused isotope–leftovers can't be traced, you know."

"Bucky should only know."

"Yeah, Cardone, he eventually did. There was only one tiny problem, however–the dog coded on the table–stone çold dead–and nobody jumped at the chance to do mouth to muzzle."

"Tell 'em about the guy who tried to make you during his insurance physical," Phil said.

Kevin's heart skipped three beats and then began to race. He shot Edelstein a shut-your-mouth-or-die look. Hoping that nobody had caught his comment, Kevin continued with the dog story, telling how they drew blood and urine from the poor dead animal and did an autopsy on the table. "The pup had angiosarcoma. For the non-medical significant others present, that's a type of liver cancer. The fluid in the dog's chest forced him to sleep upright. When they put him out and laid him down, the plural fluid pressed on his heart and killed him."

"Tell 'em about the guy," Phil insisted.

"You're drunk, Phil. You mean the smartassed medical student…"

"Smartassed student? Nah, I meant the guy in the office…"

Kevin cut him off in mid-sentence. "Some brilliant med student presented the case to Buckman on teaching rounds. Showed him the lab results–Polaroids of the x-rays taken by the vet and–get this–he told Bucky it was a patient who died during a procedure. The chief went crazy. Danger, Will Robinson–malpractice and all that stuff. Buckman went through a complex differential diagnosis and couldn't figure it out."

"And?" somebody asked.

"Something didn't compute. But the student, being really smart, told Buckman that he hadn't asked to *see* the patient. And then he produced a photo of a cocker spaniel."

Kevin took a long swig of beer and moved over to where Phil was sitting. Just as he was about to open his mouth, Kevin clamped his hand as hard as he could on Phil's shoulder.

"Bucky tried to trash the guy's future," Kevin continued, his fingers digging painfully into Edelstein's shoulder muscles. "The student didn't give a shit. He had a pathology residency sewn up." He dragged Phil out of his chair, down the short hallway and shoved him into the bathroom.

"What the fuck do you think you're doing?" Kevin asked, his hand balled into a fist two feet from Phil's face.

Phil managed to focus his eyes. "I'm *sorry,* Kevin. It was too much beer and two straight nights on call."

"You better learn when to shut your mouth, Phil, or you can be on call two solid fucking *years* in a row."

"I *said* I'm sorry, Kevin. What the hell do you want from me? All the seniors know. We cover for you, don't we? But even if *we* never slip, sooner or later something's going to leak."

"Not if I can help it."

Kevin pushed him out the door and proceeded to piss the last three beers down the toilet, angry that his professional future had been compromised by Phil's stupidity.

As he finished, zipped, and turned to face his imaginary Buckman and deny that he had been moonlighting during clinic hours, a combination of blood alcohol and a slippery ceramic floor sent Kevin crashing into the medicine cabinet. He fell helpless against the lower half of the mirror, which splintered into a hundred sword-like shards. Three of them sliced neatly into the back of his right hand. It was like a dream. It didn't hurt, but he knew it would.

Reflexively, he grabbed a washcloth from the bar next to the sink. Pulling the pieces of glass out of his hand, he held the cloth firmly over the cuts and watched in slowly mounting horror as it turned bright red.

The voice outside the door was Matthew's. "Are you okay, Kevin?"

"Get out of here."

"I heard a crash."

"It was nothing."

"You're a bad liar, Kevin. Open the door."

What the hell, Kevin thought to himself as he turned the lock. I need help. Matthew looked at the mirror and then at Kevin's hand.

"Let me see," Matthew said. As if it were the most natural thing in the world, Kevin offered Matthew his hand. Matthew removed the washcloth and examined the still bleeding cuts, then asked Kevin to move his hand to check if any tendons had been severed. Matthew took Kevin's hand again. "They're clean, but they need sutures," was all Kevin heard Matthew say. The room filled with an indefinable emptiness. When after what could have been an eternity or just a few seconds, the void vanished, Kevin saw that Matthew appeared as glazed as he felt.

Matthew was still holding Kevin's hand, but the cuts had disappeared. Kevin looked at his hand and lost consciousness. Matthew caught him.

"Don't touch me," Kevin said, waking on the floor where Matthew had placed him after cleaning away pieces of broken mirror. Every pore of his body opened and began to sweat. Kevin saw the washcloth at his side, picked it up and looked at it, his heart racing, his mind praying to every god in the universe that this was all a drunken fantasy, that the fabric was not soaked with his blood. His hand crushed it into a ball, as if he could make the whole episode disappear if only he could no longer see the sanguine truth of what had happened.

Kevin slowly stood up. They both stared silently at his hand. It was no longer a part of him, but an object, a grail, a dog that did *not* code on the exam table, a healed thing. Matthew spoke first. "Kevin…don't say anything to anyone."

"Are you kidding?" Kevin said, acutely present to his bewilderment, "Who do you think I'm going to tell?" Kevin's body was doing a seven point six on the Richter scale.

"I'm serious, Kevin," Matthew said, grabbing him firmly by both his shoulders. "You have to keep quiet." Kevin stood frozen in his grasp, unable to move and yet not wanting Matthew to touch him again—ever. Their mutual fear filled the small bathroom.

Kevin pulled away. "What happened?"

"I have to get out of here," Matthew said. Kevin's sweat-soaked hand stopped Matthew's before it reached the ancient white porcelain knob.

"Just tell me what you did," Kevin said, fighting to control the shakes.

"I don't know," Matthew said. "I can't help it."

"This isn't the first time, is it?" Matthew dropped his eyes to the floor. "It isn't, is it?" Matthew remained silent. "Tell me, goddamn it. I'm the chief resident."

Matthew raised his eyes to meet Kevin's. "Why the fuck do you think I quit surgery?"

"You closed cuts like this?"

"Twice."

"*Twice*? And nobody said anything?" Kevin asked.

"One was a drunk in the clinic. He didn't even know he was cut. The other was a lady who swore she wouldn't tell anyone. I got the hell out of there before it happened again."

Kevin knew he couldn't push him. He had to take control of the situation. He told Matthew to sit on the edge of the tub and chill while he wiped up the small amount of blood in the sink and cleaned the glass from the sink and floor, careful to avoid being cut again by their razor sharp edges. Then Kevin stuck the washcloth in his pants pocket, grateful that he had worn black, in case the blood should be absorbed through the material. "No evidence, no crime," he said.

"Yeah, right, Kevin."

"No cut. No blood. Nothing happened."

But they knew that something had happened. A bond of complicity and fear had been formed between them–or rather forced upon them. The blood and the washcloth had indelibly twisted their lives together in a conspiracy–two doctors terrified of the power of a true healer.

5

The three of them walked home. Kevin was dazed from overdoses of both Matthew and Heineken. His life felt unreal, measured by the thirty second intervals before he put his hand in his pocket again and felt the washcloth, now stiff with his dried blood. The feeling of disconnection was enhanced by the pink sodium streetlights that made night feel like day. A few slow moving cars of black and Hispanic youths cruised them, their radios blasting angry rap. Eileen moved closer to Matthew, her eyes dancing from shadow to shadow. She moved with fluid grace, as if her essence carried no weight. Kevin understood how any man would be attracted to a woman that beautiful.

Matthew was withdrawn, ignoring Eileen's repeated requests to speed the pace. "You two are on another planet," she said. "Did I miss something tonight?" They turned a corner and Eileen let out a small cry of alarm. Matthew ignored her question, shifting his attention to the reason for her distress, an unconscious derelict who lay half in the street, half on the curb. He smelled bad and looked worse. Eileen grabbed Matthew's lapel.

"Let's go, Matthew."

"He's probably just a drunk, Eileen. I'll get the cops."

"No," she said, gripping him tighter. "Leave him."

"Kevin and I'll move his legs out of the street."

"I said leave him!"

"But, Eileen, his legs…"

"Don't touch him."

Matthew seemed puzzled. "What's wrong with you? He can't hurt us."

"If you won't take me home, Kevin will." She turned to Kevin, her eyes pleading for escape.

Much as Kevin wanted to be her Galahad, he told Eileen that Matthew was right, that they at least owed it to the guy to save his legs.

Matthew gently pulled her hands from his jacket. "He's a human being, Eileen."

"He's disgusting," Eileen said. "Move him and let's get out of here."

Matthew and Kevin pivoted the man to relative safety. He stared at them drowsily and didn't resist. Kevin did a quick assessment. His pupils were okay and his pulse was strong. As Kevin moved his coat, a pint of cheap bourbon fell from his pocket and rattled on the sidewalk without breaking. "Tomorrow's breakfast," Kevin said. Then a blue and white rounded the corner and after a short exchange, the three continued their walk home in silence. Eileen refused Matthew's hand.

Matthew stopped and looked into her eyes. "My grandfather almost died on the street," he said. "People thought he was drunk and ignored him. It was an insulin reaction."

"This guy's not your grandfather, Matthew. He's a filthy bum. How could you touch him and then touch me?"

"I'm a doctor, Eileen. I touch people for a living."

Touch? Kevin thought. The image of Matthew touching his hand filled his head. His hand slipped into his pocket and felt the cloth.

"He reeks, Matthew. Who knows what's crawling on his body?"

"He probably hasn't showered in a year," Kevin said. "But I'll take a chance on a few lice rather than leave a man's legs in the path of a bus. Even a bum. I agree with Matthew."

"You're taking a shower," she said to Matthew.

They arrived home, still in silence, Matthew and Eileen not touching. Kevin was surprised Matthew invited him in, but accepted the invitation and took a seat on one of the blue tweed chairs in their living room. Eileen, capable of creating frostbite from twenty paces, and Matthew sat at opposite ends of the couch.

Matthew moved toward her. She pushed him away. "How could you say that he was *just a drunk*?" she asked.

"The guy was harmless," Matthew said. "not Hannibal Lecter. I know about alcoholics. I've treated enough. We've been though this before."

She didn't respond.

Kevin thought he should leave, but felt a voyeuristic pleasure in observing their domestic intimacy.

"It's your rule," Matthew said. "Nobody goes to sleep until an argument is finished."

"Matthew, I *hate* drunk people."

"I know," he said gently, moving next to her. She had softened enough to allow him to put his arm around her. "But you didn't see the guy drink. I told you. He could have been a diabetic. Or had a stroke."

"Not him. At the party. And you too, Kevin."

"Me?" Kevin asked. "I'll cop to a few beers, but I'm light-years away from drunk. Maybe I should leave."

Eileen rose and asked him to stay. "My father's an alcoholic," she said.

"Oh," he responded.

Matthew rose from the couch and took her hand. "I don't like to talk about it," she said. "But I didn't want you to think I was a heartless bitch." She smiled.

"Don't worry," Kevin said. "The information won't leave this apartment."

"Thank you, Kevin," she said sweetly, touching his hand. "I'm sorry I reacted so badly."

Matthew suggested that it would be a good time for everyone to get some sleep. "Sleep sounds good," Eileen said. "You can hold me all night," she said to Matthew, taking his hand. "*After* you shower."

Hold me, Kevin thought, as he lay sleepless in bed, staring at his intact hand, afraid to turn off the lights. He wondered if Matthew was awake too, or if he was safely asleep, wrapped in Eileen's arms after an hour of sweaty sex. Lucky bastard, Kevin thought. He wanted someone to hold him during the long and lonely hours of the night. Finally, after hours of watching the agonizingly slow pirouette of his bedside clock's second hand, the shakes hit his body full bore. "I have to forget this," Kevin said to his pale and sleepless face in the mirror while he shaved. Yesterday's cold coffee was his breakfast after he brushed his teeth and got dressed for morning rounds. He took one last look at his hand. "I don't have the slightest fucking clue what this is," he continued in his terrifying monologue. He took a deep breath.

6

At 6:15 on the second morning of Buckman's rounds, Matthew arrived on the sixth floor looking worse than Kevin. His eyes were red and swollen and one of the collar buttons on his perfectly ironed blue pin-point oxford cloth shirt was undone. Kevin pointed out his flaw. Matthew strolled over to the nurses' station mirror and fiddled with the button.

As if they had been buddies for years, Matthew told Kevin about a dream that had kept him awake most of the night. Matthew said he was tumbling down a high waterfall, desperately grabbing for rocks and tree trunks, terrified of being swept away.

Kevin looked down at his hand and the shakes began again. "I don't place much stock in dreams," he said. His palms begin to sweat and he willed the tremors to stop. "But flesh and blood," he continued, his voice quavering, "that's another matter…"

Matthew's red eyes swept the area around them. "I thought you agreed that *never happened.*"

"Right," Kevin said, hardly daring to look Matthew in the eye. "But that's what *I* dreamed about last night. Only I was fucking *awake* for my dreams." His heart accelerated for the ten-thousandth time in the past twenty-four hours as he heard the crunch of the mirror and felt his blood drip into the sink. His gaze dropped back to his hand's seamless surface. "I've been haunted all night."

"Just one night?" Matthew asked. "You're damn lucky."

"Once in a *lifetime* is too much," Kevin said.

"Good morning, doctors. We'll begin rounds in a minute." Buckman started on time. Even on Saturday. "First a question: What is the most common cause of pancreatitis in Trinidad?"

"Is he for real?" a first-year resident whispered.

Yeah, Kevin thought. We're dead. And this is hell.

"Nobody?" Buckman's beady eyes searched the room for what seemed like hours. Kevin hated not knowing the answer, detested having to avoid Bucky's gaze, feeling not good enough. It was pure torture. As he measured the time Buckman took until he gave up in his quest for an answer, Kevin dreamed of the day when he would be out from under him. Buckman's record was two minutes. "I thought not," Buckman continued with a smile. "The answer, doctors, is scorpion bites. Look it up. Remember it. And now a special question for Doctor Shulman. Doctor Shulman, are you here and awake this morning?"

"Yes, sir."

"Last night you admitted a patient with abdominal pain and a presumption of peptic ulcer disease. Is that correct?"

"Yes, Doctor Buckman. Mrs. Compton. Room 611."

"Very good. You remember where you left her. And you referred to her by name, not by diagnosis. Now, Doctor Shulman, you ordered a STAT blood count for her. Did you not?"

"Oh, shit."

"What was that, Doctor Shulman? Did you order the STAT test?"

"Yes, sir, I did."

"Thank you. What were the results?"

Nick's glance at Matthew revealed that Buckman had his nuts in a vice and was slowly tightening it. Matthew, sympathetic to his friend's panic, responded with a pained look.

"I didn't get the results."

"You didn't get them?"

"I'm sorry, sir, but two other patients were admitted from the E.R. at the same time, and in the confusion of my first night on call, which was a last minute assignment, the test slipped my mind and…"

"Thank you, Dr. Shulman," Buckman said, silencing him. Buckman let almost a minute pass in absolute quiet. His eyes moved from resident to resident. Not just Nick, but half the room was sweating and squirming. Kevin felt genuinely sorry for Nick and ashamed that he had stuck him with the last minute call. But, he thought to himself, we all have to learn sometime. Nick will be a better doctor for this lesson. And, he added as an afterthought, better him than me.

"Doctor Shulman."

"Yes, sir."

"Tell me, if you can, the meaning of the word STAT."

"Immediately, sir. Right away."

"Correct, Doctor. And when you order a test STAT, you obtain the results STAT, not the next day. Do you understand?"

"Yes, sir."

Buckman got louder. "For your information, the lab drops everything they're doing to get those results immediately. And that translates into inconvenience for everyone, not to mention the additional cost of a STAT test which is almost double. If everyone ordered tests STAT, the concept would lose its meaning, wouldn't it?"

"Yes, sir."

"And, Doctor Shulman, did you consider your patient? Do you think anyone ill enough to warrant a STAT test might benefit from those results? Or be harmed if an incompetent physician fails to obtain vital data?"

Matthew, wishing he could rescue Nick, shook his head in disbelief at Buckman's abusiveness. "Excuse me, Doctor Harrison? Our ex-surgeon?"

"Yes, sir." Matthew snapped to attention. He felt Buckman's stare penetrate his skin.

"Do you have a comment to share with us?"

"Sir?"

"You looked as if you had an opinion regarding my discussion with Dr. Shulman."

"I think you made your point, sir."

"Do I detect sarcasm, Dr. Harrison?"

Although he was glad to have given Nick a breather, Matthew wished he hadn't moved his head. He did not want to tangle with Buckman. "No, sir."

"I believe, Dr. Harrison, you went to school with Doctor Shulman in Peoria. Do they teach residents in that halfway house of medicine to order STAT tests and ignore the results? Do they order STAT tests so irresponsibly in surgery?"

Matthew struggled to remain calm and submissive. "No, sir."

"That's correct, Dr. Harrison. Even in Peoria a STAT test is only ordered for a damn good reason. And you check the results the same night."

Nick, unwilling to let Matthew take the heat for his mistake, spoke up. "You're right," he said weakly. "I'm sorry, Doctor Buckman."

Buckman raised himself to his full height. He looked like an Old Testament prophet in tweeds. "Sorry means nothing in medicine, Shulman. Sorry keeps funeral homes in business. Do it again and you'll learn the real meaning of sorry. Nobody on my service screws up twice. Do I make myself clear?"

"Yes, sir," Nick responded.

"Harrison?"

"Crystal, sir."

Buckman handed the chart to a medical student. "Let's make rounds."

The rest of the morning Bucky tormented Nick and Matthew with an endless barrage of esoteric questions. Occasionally one of the two answered a question correctly, earning a moment of praise from the chief, followed by a cynical postscript to the commendation.

At the end of rounds, everyone reassembled in the classroom. "That's it for today," Buckman said. "We're indebted to Doctor Shulman for teaching us the meaning of STAT, but, to his credit, he knew where his patient was. Stop smirking. This is serious. Yesterday we had a problem in the hospital. A patient scheduled for an emergency procedure was abandoned on the wrong floor. Fortunately he was not on my service."

Oh shit, Kevin thought. Buckman's going to make this my problem. "Whoever is responsible," Buckman continued, "will be looking for a job driving a taxi where dropping a fare off at the wrong address isn't usually lethal."

Kevin looked around the room, silently praying for the universal innocence of the resident staff.

Buckman looked at each of their faces. Then he paused and settled his eyes on Matthew for a long moment before returning his gaze to the room in general. "I said stop the smiles. The patient was an elderly, senile black gentleman in a wheelchair and while he was waiting helplessly for us to do our jobs, he went into shock and died. Keep track of your patients. That's all. Good morning." He turned and left the room.

Kevin recalled the old man's eyes. His heart rate soared past the Dow Jones Average. Matthew turned white and rushed from the room. "Shit," Kevin whispered to himself. "This problem needs concrete shoes–STAT." Kevin followed Matthew into the men's room, fifty feet down the hallway. He pushed the door open to find Matthew hacking and coughing, his dry heaves echoing in the cavernous old bathroom.

"I'm fucked, Kevin. Really fucked," Matthew said bending over the sink to scoop a handful of water to rinse out his mouth. "I'm sorry."

"You bumped his wheelchair," Kevin said.

"I'm a fucking curse."

"You didn't *kill* him."

"I know *that*," Matthew said. "But everything I touch turns to shit."

"Not everything," Kevin said, holding up his hand, feeling genuinely sorry for him.

"Maybe I should quit this program while I'm still ahead," Matthew said despondently. "Maybe I should fucking quit medicine altogether." He opened his mouth to continue, but choked on the words.

"Listen to me, Matthew," Kevin said. "I'm sorry the old man died. I'd be more concerned if he dropped dead during grand rounds and you pulled a Lazarus act on him."

"It doesn't matter how he died. Buckman's going to find out it was me who bumped him. He'll be pissed one of his residents was even remotely involved."

"Buckman's not going to find out shit. Not unless you tell him. *I'm* certainly not going to. And besides, you weren't legally a resident until morning rounds started. Just keep your mouth shut. About the old guy. And about my hand. And cut the attitude with Buckman. It's stupid."

"He's such a prick."

"But he's the head prick around here."

Matthew smiled. "I guess I should thank you for covering for me. I'm not the kind of resident you dream of having on your service."

"I don't know what I think about you," Kevin said. "Not yet."

Kevin liked Matthew even if he terrified him. Or maybe he was just curious about him. But thinking about his hand and replaying the incident with the old man, Kevin had begun to sense that he was more connected to Matthew than either of them realized. And he had begun to feel afraid.

7

At noon that day, just outside the main door of the hospital, Susan and Kevin were engaged in a heated emotional discussion about a patient she had admitted, a middle-age man with renal carcinoma who Kevin had just transferred off the service. She was bending his ear about the patient's high blood calcium and elevated liver enzymes when Kevin dropped the news on her that Buckman had already agreed to the transfer.

"You dumped him," she said, turning red.

Kevin assumed his choirboy face. "I would never do that, Susan."

"Save the charm for Buckman," Susan said cynically. "And the lies for somebody who knows you less well than I do. Patients going sour get transferred to other services. You'll do anything to buff the morbidity and mortality numbers. Nobody dies on *our* service."

"If I admit you're right, Susan, will you leave me alone?"

"If you get Mr. Foster back."

"Can't do. Buckman looks at the stats more than the patients. It's my ass in a sling if either slips. But you're wrong in this case. Foster belongs on the renal service."

"He does not."

"Get off it, Susan. The renal guys asked Bucky personally for Foster."

Matthew exited the front door into the blinding midday sun. Preoccupied, he passed by Kevin and Susan.

"Matthew?" Susan asked loudly enough to stop and make him turn, "Are you avoiding us?"

"Sorry," he said squinting. "I didn't see you."

"How are you doing?" Kevin asked.

"Is something wrong?" Susan asked.

"It's a greeting, not an actual question," Kevin said, regretting his choice of words. He worried that Susan had sensed what was asked but not actually said. Matthew smiled, said that he was fine, and that he wanted to spend his lunch hour taking a walk.

"The three of us are going to lunch," Susan said, firmly, "and you can tell *me* how you're doing. Are you coming, Kevin?" She shot him a saccharine smile. "Or are you going back inside to dump–I mean transfer–the rest of my patients?"

Susan's pager beeped. "Just a second," she said, picking up a house phone located on the wall just outside the main door to the hospital. She spat a Spanish curse and hung up.

"Who was that?" Matthew asked.

"A relative in Cook County Jail," she said.

"A convict?" Matthew asked.

"We all have family members we wish we could trade in for a clock radio," Susan said, sounding annoyed. "It's time to eat."

"Is that the same guy who calls you every couple of weeks?" Kevin asked.

"I'm hungry," Susan said, taking Matthew's arm. She led them two blocks from the hospital to a storefront with signs in the window advertising the restaurant's signature dish: polish sausage with fries for $2.29. An eight-foot plastic hot dog, overflowing with condiments, hung above the door. The place was a yellow and red Formica shrine to the god of grease.

Susan looked at the pained expressions on both their faces. "Maybe I should order a cheeseburger to prove I'm no saint."

Susan led the way in and found a booth. The table's thick chrome edge collected tiny bits of food from former patrons. Kevin slid into the heavily worn yellow Naugahyde seat and delegated Susan to get lunch for the three of them. He handed her a twenty and told her what he wanted to eat. "My treat," he said.

"Now I know something's wrong," she said.

"Payback for the Foster transfer."

"Hardly," she said. "But I accept." Matthew asked for a Coke. She left to order the food.

As soon as Susan was out of earshot, Matthew became visibly agitated. "I'm sorry, Kevin. I can't let go of my feelings about the old man."

"For Christ's sake," Kevin said. "Get over it. You didn't kill the guy. He just died. Ask Susan. I'm sure she'll agree."

Susan returned with a cigarette burned plastic tray from which she unloaded a salad for herself, the Coke for Matthew, and a large gyros with fries for Kevin. She also had a fistful of wet napkins.

"Are you going to give me a sponge bath?" Kevin asked.

"I've been here before," she said, using them to clean the table. She tossed the wad of wet paper into a nearby waste receptacle and slid into her seat. "Tell me, Matthew. What's eating you?"

"Nothing. Honest."

Kevin took a big bite of greasy gyros. "This stuff's orgasmic."

She ignored Kevin. "Do you forget how many times I saved your ass in med school–not to mention Nick's?"

"So?" he asked.

"I know you too well."

Matthew sat in silence. "Tell her," Kevin urged again.

"What happened to Doctor Wonderful?" Susan asked.

Kevin grinned. "Doctor Wonderful?"

"His nickname in med school," Susan said. "He got along with *everyone.*"

Kevin smiled between bites of his sandwich. "Wait until the other residents find out who's working with them."

"Thanks a hell of a lot, Susan. I'm telling you," Matthew repeated. "It's Buckman."

Susan assumed that Matthew was talking about the STAT incident and assured him that what he was feeling about Buckman was par for the course, that everyone got the Chief's treatment sooner or later. "He's a department chief," she said. "It takes a big ego to climb to that position and well-padded balls to stay on top."

"I can take his abuse," Matthew said. "That's not it." He dropped his eyes to the floor.

"Are you going to tell her or should I?" Kevin asked.

Matthew took a deep breath. "It's the old man. The one Buckman was talking about. I was there."

"Tell me about it," Susan said.

Matthew told his version of the old man in the wheelchair, painting a picture so paranoid that Kevin began to wonder who the guy under the perfect exterior really was. Here was a gifted human being, a smart, good looking, happily married young doctor who had the power to heal people, a medical school graduate who was acting like a first class neurotic.

"Matthew," Susan said, "nobody dies because someone bumps their wheelchair."

"I *know* that. I'm not an idiot. But I *deserted* the old man."

"You said you were scared of Buckman. I don't see the connection," Susan said.

"I didn't stay with him because I was afraid of being late for Buckman's morning rounds."

"I told you to leave," Kevin said.

"No," Matthew said. "That's not me. I know the collision didn't kill him. But by abandoning him, I may have contributed to his death. If I'd stayed longer, I might've been able to do something when he went into shock." Kevin breathed a sigh of relief. Matthew was right in a quirky kind of way.

"Matthew, listen to me," Kevin said. "The man was eighty-seven years old and in end-stage renal failure. His number was up. You're too hard on yourself. And, Doctor Wonderful, it was only your first day. You weren't responsible for running the entire hospital and saving all its dying patients. I left him too–very much alive and stable."

Matthew was absentmindedly fingering his wrists. "I thought Buckman was staring at me. Like he knows I was there."

"He wasn't staring at me," Kevin said, "and I was there too."

"Buckman stares at everybody," Susan said. "That's one way he breaks you down. I've seen you stand up to attendings and senior residents tougher than him during medical school. His delivery might be shitty, but his message is often correct. Like Nick and the STAT test."

"He didn't have to impale Nick. Or me."

"He didn't."

"I mean about Peoria."

"You're taking this personally. He likes to test people–to know what they're made of."

Susan placed her hand on Matthew's. She recoiled. "Your hand, Matthew."

"What?" he asked.

"It's hot. Really hot."

Hot hands? Kevin thought. And suddenly the thing he had been struggling with since the episode in Tim Davidson's bathroom became crystal clear. It was the searing heat from Matthew's hands as they touched his that was the last thing he felt before the fog took over, a sensation so shockingly out of place in his reality that he had repressed it.

"I'm terrified of the bastard," Matthew said. "It's just a gut feeling, but I think he has it in for me."

"You don't understand him," Susan said. "You've been here two days. He wouldn't have accepted you into the program–especially as a transfer–unless he knew you had the right stuff."

"Understand him?" Matthew repeated cynically.

"Why he's so angry–such a perfectionist."

Kevin knew where Susan was heading and decided not to stop her. "It's about his daughter, Francie," Susan said sadly. "She's got metastatic melanoma. It's not very advanced yet, but it's hopeless."

Very few residents knew the closely guarded secret that Susan had shared with Matthew. Buckman had sent his twenty something daughter, Francie, everywhere: Sloan Kettering, M. D. Anderson, the best hospitals in Europe, but the answer was always the same. Buckman and his wife had been about to sign divorce papers but had put the process on hold for Francie. They slept in separate bedrooms.

"Can't you see, Matthew?" Susan asked. "Buckman's insistence on perfection in his residents is twisted because he's unable to fix the one case he really cares about."

"What's worse," Kevin added, "is that Francie blames her father for her illness."

Francie had shown her father an ugly mole growing on her upper right thigh. Overwhelmed with a writing assignment from a prestigious medical journal, Buckman had taken only a cursory look at his daughter's problem before passing it off as insignificant. A few months later, when Francie got the courage to risk another attempt at showing the lesion to her father, it was too late. The tumor had spread. Francie, once a healthy young woman, became her father's worst nightmare.

"I met her at the reception. Why didn't she show the mole to her mother? Or another doctor?" Matthew asked.

"Who knows?" Susan said. "I wasn't there and I can't judge another doctor's actions. Whether or not Buckman overlooked the melanoma or why Francie didn't press the issue doesn't really matter now, but it explains Buckman's attitude and his insistence that we know every possible diagnosis in the world—including Trinidad."

Matthew looked puzzled. "How do you know all this? Why such a big secret? Or is this all rumor?"

"It's fact," Kevin said. "Straight from a source in Buckman's office. If the secret gets out, Susan gets nailed." Kevin told Matthew that Francie's oncologist, Dr. Finnigan, the head of the department and a colleague of Buckman's, was sympathetic to non-traditional care and had asked Susan to work with Francie.

"You're treating her without Buckman's knowledge?" Matthew asked. "Isn't that risky? Or dumb?"

"I'm not treating her—not exactly," Susan said. "I've given her some books to read. Stuff about patients who have beaten cancer. And I've directed her to some healers. Francie has little to lose at this point. She needs hope. She's reaching for anything that might help."

"Buckman would kill you if he knew," Matthew said.

"No shit, Matthew," Kevin responded. "Buckman would kill a lot of us if he knew our secrets."

"Why are you doing it?" Matthew asked.

"Because it feels right," Susan said. "I only shared this with you for your own good. To help you understand the man."

"Are you okay with this, Kevin?" Matthew asked.

"Not really," Kevin said. "But as long as my name isn't anywhere on the chart, they can do whatever they want. Or whatever Francie wants."

Matthew became quiet, digesting everything he had just been told, collecting his thoughts. "Let me ask you a question then, Susan," he said. "You know a lot about non-Western medicine."

"Yes."

"You've always taken shit about this stuff. Especially from Nick."

"Nick's not the most enlightened guy," Susan said.

"Healers. Are there really people like that? People with powers? People who can touch? I'm not sure how to say it. We didn't get much exposure to that kind of…at least not in med school."

Kevin's heart began to race.

"No, Matthew," Susan told him. "We didn't hear much about the laying on of hands and yes, there are people who have special gifts. You've always been the scientist–not obnoxious like Nick–but not exactly open either. Why the sudden interest?"

Kevin fumbled for something to say but his vocal cords were frozen.

"Just curious," Matthew said. "You brought up Francie's story."

"Matthew, there's a world out there that standard medicine blindly denies, or worse, tries to destroy. We should explore it instead of trying to kill it."

"How?" asked Matthew.

"The same way as any new theory in medicine: apply the scientific method. Set up research protocols. See what's reproducible, what works, and what doesn't. It's already being done in some places. I can give you books to read if you're really interested."

"No thanks. I was just curious."

"Not like Kevin, who could care less about anything that he can't see or touch," Susan said.

She rose from the table. "I have some charts to finish at the hospital."

As she walked away, Kevin remembered once again the sensation of Matthew's hot hand on his and shivered. It was intense. He tucked it away with the bloody washcloth.

8

Eileen called Kevin on Saturday night to invite him to breakfast at five on Monday morning. He politely refused. She said that Matthew told her he and Kevin were becoming friends. Kevin said that when he did eat breakfast, it was most often day-old pizza, shoved into his mouth while running out of the front door. Eileen seduced him by offering a real home cooked meal, and then said, "It wouldn't hurt to let a first year suck up to the chief resident would it, Kevin?" He was hooked. Eileen not only understood the rules, but also was adorable enough to tell the truth and get away with it.

After rounds in the hospital, Kevin usually spent Sundays with his mother. She lived in a small brown brick classical Chicago bungalow in Harwood Heights, an ancient but stable neighborhood on the city's northwest side. During his father's terminal illness, Kevin had assumed responsibility for the lawn and the general maintenance of the house. An English teacher in a private school, Kevin's mother spent her days attempting to get the upper class children of Chicago to abandon their video games for great books. On weekends, however, the brilliant woman with a Masters degree from the University of Chicago reverted to her role as a mother, asking probing questions about Kevin's life while attempting to overfeed him, trying her best to make her only child feel guilty because she had no grandchildren to spoil. "As soon as you're ready," she would say in the familiar litany he endured each week, "this is yours." She was referring to her engagement ring, a three and a quarter carat Tiffany rock, the only remaining nugget of her parents' fortune that had disappeared in a series of bad real estate deals. Every Sunday morning, Kevin and his mother played the same game. She would take the ring off her finger and offer it to him to take home and save for his intended. Each week he would refuse. And every Sunday, they performed another ritual as Kevin handed her an envelope containing the proceeds from his moonlighting, added to whatever he could spare from his salary.

"I can't accept this," she would say as he gave her the envelope. When he first began to give her money, she ripped his checks in two, forcing him to resort to cash. "I can manage on what I make," she said.

He knew that was a lie. Her salary could support a modest lifestyle, but wasn't enough to make a dent in the medical bills that were owed after his father's death or to keep up the property taxes and home maintenance costs.

Kevin told her repeatedly to sell the ring, the only item of value she owned. She refused, claiming that it was for his wife. It wasn't the choice he would have made in the same situation.

Monday morning at five, Kevin knocked on Matthew's door as his twenty-dollar watch beeped the hour. The Taiwanese wonder was waterproof to two hundred feet, had a calendar, an alarm, a ten-year battery, and accurately measured his pulse. It was a gift from a pharmaceutical salesman to remind Kevin to prescribe his company's product over the generic equivalent. Kevin assured him that he would; he gave his competition the same guarantee. Were it not for the pharmaceutical industry, American doctors would be bereft of pens, Post-it notes, cheap canvas briefcases, coffee mugs, and thousands of other really useful things that the general public supplies to their physicians with each purchase of a prescription medication.

The smell of bacon hit Kevin square in the face as Matthew opened the door, dressed and ready for another day. Finishing the knot in his tie, Kevin followed his nose toward the kitchen–bigger than his but still hardly more than a large closet with no-frills appliances, complete with a light oak cafe table and two chrome and white vinyl upholstered chairs stained beyond the power of Clorox. Everything looked and smelled freshly scrubbed.

"This looks wonderful," Kevin said as his eyes surveyed the preparations. Eileen looked like she had rolled out of bed directly into baggy gray sweats. But where the same clothing would have made another woman appear frumpy and unattractive, the garments only increased her sensuality. Her sun-colored hair was softly pulled back and tied with a green ribbon, except for a few loose wisps that seductively played at the corners of her face. If she were his, Kevin thought, he would let breakfast burn on the stove while he dragged her off to the bedroom. He shook his head to dissolve the fantasy. Kevin had many gray areas in his life, but sleeping with a friend's wife was not one of them.

Eileen's smile couldn't hide her bloodshot eyes. "I thought it would be nice to send my two doctors off to work with a good breakfast."

Matthew stood near the stove, frowning at the eggs spluttering in a sea of butter at the bottom of the cast iron pan. "Cholesterol, Eileen," he said with a disapproving look. He picked up a knife and stabbed at the eggs in a mock duel. "Bad fat."

"Once in a while won't kill you," she said, taking the knife from his hand and placing it in the sink.

"If this breakfast is Eileen's attempt to get a cushy call schedule for me," Matthew said, laughing, "I wonder what she'll cook for Buckman?"

"A good bribe never hurt anyone," Eileen said. She moved like a beautiful automaton, going through the motions of an elaborate play. Grabbing two pieces of toast and over-buttering them, she dropped them on a plate, then filled the empty space with eggs and four strips of bacon. She studied the arrangement like an artist and added a fifth piece of bacon. She made an identical plate and set them on the table. "I hope you boys are hungry," she said. Matthew raised his eyebrows and shook his head in astonishment. Both men sat down.

"Tea or coffee, Kevin?" Eileen asked. "Matthew and I are tea drinkers, but I have instant coffee if you like." Kevin said he preferred tea, not wanting her to go to any more trouble than she already had. Eileen reached into one of the kitchen cabinets and retrieved two exquisite porcelain teacups, which she set in front of both men. Then she carefully arranged a matching teapot, creamer, and sugar bowl on the table. "English Breakfast or Earl Grey?" she asked. Kevin looked into the open cabinet; there was no third cup.

Kevin picked up the cup and looked at the bottom. "Whatever," he said, placing it back onto its saucer. "Limoges–pretty fancy stuff for a resident. You don't have to fuss for me."

"It's not a problem," Eileen said, pouring boiling water from a battered stainless kettle into the teapot. "The china was a wedding gift. Milk and sugar? You seem to know something about good dishes. That's unusual for a man."

"Both," Kevin said. "I've bought enough wedding gifts for my own friends to know something about china."

"How come a smart, good looking doctor like you hasn't been snagged by anyone?" she asked.

"Nobody's popped the question."

"You're quite a catch," she said.

Eileen did her best Jane Austen imitation of tea. She poured milk into Kevin's cup and then, taking the pot in her left hand and holding the cover down with the first two fingers of her right, she poured the tea through the bowl of a silver strainer that she had balanced on the rim of his cup. Kevin thought only presumptuous downtown hotels, Chanel-suited women, or genuine society matrons went through such formalities. He would have been happier with a clean mug and a teabag. As much as Eileen tried to make the routine seem natural, there was something inauthentic about her performance, as if she were acting for Kevin's benefit. But Kevin found Eileen's behavior extremely attractive. He liked women who fussed over him, whose attention and actions made him feel special.

Matthew seemed impatient. "Gee, Hon, this looks great, but I give. What's up?"

"I told you," she said. I wanted to give you a decent breakfast."

"Where I come from," Matthew said, "we call this comfort food. You left out the Twinkies, Ding Dongs, and M & M's."

"We don't have any Twinkies, Matthew, and I finished the M & M's two hours ago," Eileen said.

Matthew rose from his chair, walked over to an adjacent cabinet, opened it and grabbed a box of shredded wheat. He asked Kevin if he wanted some of the cereal, and for a brief moment Kevin felt torn between his two hosts. But, Kevin decided, anything cooked with large amounts of butter, even two-day old fish, tastes good. He concluded that Eileen was the more easily offended of the pair and declined the cereal. Matthew shrugged his shoulders at Kevin's response and dumped three large cakes of shredded wheat into a bowl. He completed his breakfast by opening the refrigerator and pouring 2% over the cereal. He returned to the table and pushed his plate away. Eileen reached over and used her fingers to pick up one of the straw-like cakes from his bowl.

"Truth is, I don't think I could eat the bacon and eggs myself," she said with a deep sigh. "I didn't sleep well last night."

"What's up?" Matthew asked.

"A lot of things. Mostly, my new job."

Matthew looked at her quizzically. "I thought you had that handled."
"Apparently not."

"Is that enough reason for a killer cholesterol fest?" Matthew asked.

"Some women cook in times of stress," Kevin said. "I, however, *eat* during periods of emotional turmoil."

Eileen said that Matthew also ate to relieve stress and expressed her delight that the two men were so much alike. Kevin's smile was a mask. No, he thought, Matthew and I are *very* different. He flashed back to Matthew's bathroom clinic, to the image of his blood on the sink belying the reality of his intact hand. But except for that mysterious part of Matthew that left him haunted and terrified, he wanted some of what he had, like a beautiful wife who would fuss for him.

"I forgot to tell you," Matthew said as he ate, "I had lunch with Susan." Eileen put the uneaten cereal back into Matthew's bowl. A tiny muscle in her jaw began to twitch. "I was upset about a patient. Kevin tried, but couldn't help me let go of my concerns. Susan was great. She's smart and knew exactly what I needed to lose some of my fear of Buckman and get back on course."

Eileen listened silently and then, as if a switch were flipped inside her, suddenly unraveled. "Couldn't *I* help you?" she asked bitterly. "I'm you're wife. Or would you prefer someone smarter and better than me? Maybe a *doctor* like Susan?"

Matthew stumbled over his words. "Stop this, Eileen. I'm sorry Kevin, this is not…Eileen, what's this about? This isn't like you—you've never been jealous."

Kevin watched in silence, not knowing what to think. His gut said that Matthew was as stunned as he was, completely clueless about his wife's behavior. But given his short history with Matthew, and now seeing this side of Eileen, it was apparent to Kevin that they were not Ken and Barbie. Eileen turned from Matthew to face the small window over the stainless steel sink. Tears spilled down her cheeks. "I'm worn out," she said. And she looked at Matthew and then at the dishes and with one swoop of her arm cleared most of the table, sending the expensive porcelain crashing to the floor. The teapot shattered, spilling hot liquid over the bottom of Matthew's pant legs.

Now it was his turn. "What's wrong with you? You'd think *you* killed someone. You've got no idea what upset is." He picked up a water glass that had survived Eileen's assault and dropped it on the floor. "Here. Let me help you finish the job."

Eileen seemed to wake from a trance. She grabbed Matthew's arm which was heading for the last remaining plate. Her voice was composed. "Matthew. Stop."

"Maybe we should go, Matthew," Kevin said. "It's getting late."

Matthew and Eileen stared at him as if they had both forgotten he was present. Matthew dropped his eyes and kicked at a shard of china. Matthew rose from his chair, pushed a segment of teapot aside with his shoe, and turned Eileen to face him. He lifted her chin, then held her while she sobbed.

"Would you like to tell me now?" he asked.

She pulled from his embrace. "It's difficult."

"Try me."

"Something isn't right."

Matthew kicked at the broken dishes. "I can see that, Eileen."

Kevin rose and began to move toward the door, desperately trying to construct a graceful exit line. Eileen took his arm. "Please, Kevin," she entreated. "It's this place. And the move from Peoria."

Kevin said that he understood, that it was normal for her to have experienced some depression considering the huge changes she and Matthew had gone through recently. But he was lying.

"Maybe I should call in sick today," Matthew said, looking to Kevin for a reaction, who gave none.

"Thanks, but I'm okay," Eileen said wiping the remaining tears from her face with her sleeve. "I'm just overwhelmed. You're going to be on call every third night. And then you tell me how wonderful Susan was to you. I felt a little jealous that she gets to see you and help you more than me."

"We'll clean up this mess together," Matthew said. "I don't care if I'm late. Kevin can make up an excuse."

"The last thing you need is Buckman chewing you out," Eileen said. "It's important for our future that you stay on his good side."

"You sure?"

"Well, if you're not sure, I am," Kevin said. "Eileen's right about Buckman. You don't miss rounds unless you've been admitted to the ICU and are a heartbeat away from death."

Matthew changed into a clean pair of pants. He and Kevin walked to the hospital in silence.

9

Rounds that morning were a stroll in the park. Buckman seemed to be preoccupied. He asked no questions and offered no abuse. The "vanilla rounds," as the housestaff called them, were becoming more common of late, a new and greatly appreciated aspect of the Buckman mystique. Before leaving the floor, Buckman cornered Kevin in the empty class-room and asked him to cover the dermatology clinic that afternoon. The resident previously scheduled would, he said, be "needed for a research project." Keeping to his unswerving policy of dumping diffi-cult or boring clinic assignments on first-year residents, Kevin sug-gested that he might be of greater use supervising the general medical clinic. He was surprised that Buckman hadn't considered that it was July and the new doctors needed more supervision. Buckman was par-ticularly careful about support for his residents, mostly to cover his own ass. In a university teaching hospital, the chief of the department is legally liable for the disasters of the housestaff.

Kevin had noticed that the Chief had begun to fray around the edges. Buckman made no major gaffes that the general population of residents might detect, but overlooked little things like countersigning verbal orders for patient medications, or forgetting small administrative details like requests for new equipment that became overdue. Of course, Kevin never let on when he recognized that Buckman had made a small error. If possible, he quietly and quickly fixed the problem in a way that Buckman wouldn't notice, or if that were not possible, made sure that he, himself was out of the loop of culpability when word got out.

Buckman saw the wisdom of Kevin's suggestion. "Send the resident with the yellow pen in his pocket: Matthew Harrison," he said.

"I'll send Matthew if you like, Dr. Buckman," Kevin said, "but I would rather choose someone else." Matthew was a wild card that he wanted to keep close to his side.

Buckman raised an eyebrow. "Is there anything about him that I should know?"

"No, sir," Kevin said.

"Good," Buckman responded. "Then send him."

Kevin told Matthew that he was the chief's choice.

"Is this a punishment?" he asked.

"Consider it an honor. It's a great clinic." Kevin was lying. The medical residents who rotated through derm had nicknamed the clinic "Siberia" for the isolation they felt there. Having little or no training in the look-alike world of skin rashes was frustrating enough, but to make matters even more difficult, the derm residents had a well-deserved reputation for rushing their patients through only the most cursory of exams. Medical residents assigned to the clinic were supposed to learn basic dermatology but they asked too many questions and slowed the pace. The senior derm residents hated when the afternoons ran overtime. It interfered with their moonlighting jobs.

Matthew had lunch with Phil and Kevin. He left early, despite their protests. Kevin managed never to be early to a clinic or anywhere in the hospital, as it increased his chance for extra work. All afternoon, Kevin was haunted by fearful images of Buckman storming into the clinic with

Matthew in tow, demanding to know how he had healed the procession of warts, psoriasis, and leprosy. After the sixth time Kevin failed to countersign an intern's chart and had left a medical student to do a procedure unsupervised, the head nurse pulled him into the supply room.

"Are you going to join us this afternoon?" she asked. "Or should I stop covering for you and alert the attending before you do some real damage?"

"Sorry," Kevin said.

"You've been staring at the door all afternoon. Are you expecting somebody?"

"Yes...no. It's just a bad day."

"Not allowed," she said. "These patients are real."

Except for his own screw-ups, which continued despite the nurse's warning, the afternoon was quiet until after derm clinic when Matthew paged Kevin. He asked Kevin to meet him in the residents' lounge. When he got there, Susan was waiting. Matthew had paged her too.

Susan and Kevin sat on one of the overstuffed couches, each of them wondering what this was about. After a few minutes, Matthew walked in and plopped down in the easy chair beside them. He stared at the ceiling, and then, with a huge sigh, said, "Tell me more about healers, Susan. Especially about touch."

"Yesterday and today," she said. "Why the sudden interest?"

Kevin began to squirm, sure that Matthew was going to admit Susan to the lodge. "I'm just interested," he said, sounding casual. "A question somebody asked me."

Susan, sensing Matthew's questions were more than idle curiosity, spoke cautiously. "In the Middle Ages, people believed the King's touch could cure scrofula. But it was a belief based on faith; no King really had the power."

"I thought you believed in all that stuff?" Matthew said. He looked perturbed.

"Before antibiotics, doctors prescribed placebos. And they worked. Did something happen?"

"Doctors are supposed to be curious."

"Then why are you so flushed?"

"It was just a question, Susan. And it's hot in here."

"I'm freezing," she said.

"Fuck off, Susan. I said nothing happened."

"Is that how you talk to me? I knew you before you knew what a white cell was."

"I asked you a simple question. If you don't want to give me an answer…"

"Okay," Susan said. "There *are* people who do have some kind of healing touch. Nobody can explain it." She paused. "Oh, my God. I'm so dense. Are you sick? Or Eileen?"

"Everybody's fine," Matthew responded. "Can't I just want to know?"

She reached over and took Matthew's hand. "Thank God. If you're really interested, I can help. All you need is an open mind. When do you want to start?"

"I don't."

She dropped his hand and sat back. "Am I going deaf? Kevin, didn't he ask about spiritual healing for the second time?" Kevin just shrugged.

"Yes," Matthew said with a charming smile. "I asked. You told me. It exists. Thanks."

Susan looked baffled. "You're welcome." She rolled her eyes and coolly informed Matthew that she had to leave.

"What was that about?" Kevin asked after Susan was out of earshot.

Matthew became anxious. "Derm clinic."

"I meant the attitude, the repeated questions about healers. Susan knows something's wrong."

"I'm looking for help. Everything's okay."

"Like hell it is."

"I've got the situation under control."

Before Kevin asked Matthew to elaborate, he hustled him out of the hospital. Matthew began his story during the short walk to Kevin's apartment.

When Matthew got to the dermatology clinic, a hassled resident assigned him to a woman desperate to see a doctor. Matthew was told that she was seven months pregnant, suffering from Pruritus of Pregnancy. "Uncomfortable but not serious," the resident said.

"I didn't know what that was," Matthew admitted.

"Don't worry," the resident had told him. "You won't kill her. Make sure she's okay. Give her an antihistamine. Check with OB if you're not sure which one."

The large waiting room of the dermatology clinic was cheerfully decorated with Marimekko fabric hung on the walls and draped from the ceiling. Royal blue couches served as resting places for the large numbers of patients who were shuffled through the clinic as fast as the residents could process them. The gray and tan carpet was rumored to have been selected to hide the dead skin shed by the psoriatic patients. Room six, the one Matthew was assigned, contained a desk, exam stool, and table. Seated on the exam table was a very pregnant redheaded woman wrapped in a paper gown worn backwards with the opening in front. She held it shut with great difficulty over her swollen abdomen.

Matthew closed the door behind him. "Good morning, Mrs. Young. I'm Doctor Harrison."

"Please call me Sheila."

"Okay." He sat down and looked directly into her eyes. "You seem uncomfortable."

Sheila forced her quivering lips into a smile. "It's awful."

"Why don't you tell me about it."

"I'm going crazy. I itch all over and can't sleep for more than an hour at a time. This is killing me."

Matthew stared at a particularly raw area on her right hand.

"I'm afraid for my baby." Tears welled in her eyes.

"What about the baby?"

"Well, I know measles can…my first baby was a miscarriage and…" She buried her face in her hands, using her elbows to keep her gown closed.

"Let's take these things one at a time, Sheila."

She nodded. Matthew took a moment to look through her chart. He explained to her that she couldn't have German measles because her blood studies showed that she had had the disease already.

Sheila's face came out from behind her hands.

"I'm not an obstetrician," Matthew said. "But I know that miscarriages most often occur in the first three months of pregnancy. Let me examine you so I can see how bad this is."

Kevin and Matthew arrived at their building. Matthew held the narrative until they climbed the stairs and were ensconced in Kevin's living room with two cold beers.

Matthew took a long swig and continued his story. Sheila had dropped her hands, permitting Matthew to examine her. "It's all over my body," she said.

Large red splotches covered every inch of her skin. The slightest touch seemed to make them redden further. Matthew put his stethoscope to her abdomen and searched until he picked up the baby's heartbeat.

"Sounds noisy in there. Are you hoping for a boy or girl?"

"I don't care so long as it's healthy. My husband wants a boy."

Matthew stood up and removed the earpieces. "Have you ever listened through one of these?"

"Not in a few months."

"Well, considering how frightened you've been, maybe you should hear this."

Matthew helped Sheila place the earpieces, brushing aside a strand of her hair. At first she had difficulty locating the sound, then a broad smile broke out on her face. Sheila removed the stethoscope. "Is that normal?"

"I'd be happy if that were my baby's heart," Matthew said. "Your skin is your only problem. Didn't your OB resident tell you that you already had German measles?"

"I don't get time to ask questions. Usually I have to wait a half-hour–undressed–for a few minutes with the doctor."

To Matthew's inquiry about why she was at the University Clinic, she answered that her husband had been out of work for three years and their insurance had terminated. Her own insurance didn't cover pregnancy.

Matthew didn't know what to say. He remembered that Osler, the father of American medicine, taught that, given enough time, a patient would eventually reveal the nature and cause of their problem.

"Between bathroom trips and scratching my skin, I don't sleep much," Sheila reiterated. "I've been making mistakes at work." She was again at the brink of tears.

"Is your boss angry with you?"

"He's single and has no idea how to handle a pregnant woman. My workload's up this month–even though he should see that I'm exhaust-ed."

"Have you told him how you feel?"

She dropped her gaze in shamed disappointment. "I didn't know what to say."

"What kind of work do you do?"

"Filing, mostly. Some computer work. For an insurance agency."

"Could you take some time off?"

"Not until my husband finds a job."

"Is he as excited as you are about the baby?"

A shadow fell over Sheila's face. "Jim's a great guy. He...we...we've never really talked about the miscarriage. He won't."

"Do you think the rash frightens him?"

"I think he's scared for the baby. He never cried when we lost the first one. I'm scared too."

"What are you afraid of?" Matthew asked.

"I'm worried...that this...this baby might die too." She began to sob.

Breaking all the rules of professional detachment, Matthew got up, put a sheet around her to cover the gaping gown and held her while she cried. When she was finished, Matthew let go and resumed sitting with her.

"You hugged her?" Kevin asked.

"It goes against what we've been taught about keeping a professional distance between patients and ourselves," Matthew said, relishing the warm feeling he was experiencing at the moment, "but it felt so natural to offer her comfort." Matthew took a swig of beer and continued his story.

"Sheila, your fear's real but unlikely. Both you and your baby are healthy."

She nodded assent.

"And if you look inside your heart–not your head–what do you feel is going to happen?

Sheila paused for a moment. "I think everything's going to be okay."

"I agree. What are you going to do about your boss?"

"He's giving me three weeks off with pay when the baby comes."

"If he's willing to do that, do you think he might understand your needs, maybe ease up on you a bit?"

Sheila smiled.

"I'm going to give you something for the rash. And I want you to tell your husband that your baby is alive and well. See if you can get him to talk about his feelings. First, tell him how *you* feel. It might make it easier for him."

Matthew rose from his chair and told Sheila that he had to check another patient. He was stalling, not sure which medication to prescribe or what dosage to use during pregnancy. He waited in the hallway until a resident appeared. Armed with the proper information, he returned to Sheila.

"Doctor Harrison, you're great." Sheila opened her gown to show him that in the area he had examined the rash was gone. Matthew took a deep breath. He began moving his hand unconsciously over her skin. Where he touched her, the redness vanished.

Matthew told Kevin that he tried to remove his hands, but they had a life of their own, erasing the rash in their wake. He said that Sheila was astonished–and grateful. "How do you do that, Doctor?" she asked.

Matthew scrambled to find a convincing explanation. "Hives can clear spontaneously," he said. She seemed to accept the logic, so he went on. "Under stress, your body releases histamine. It's what causes swelling and itching. When you relax, the effect goes away. You were afraid for your baby. Once you knew that it was okay, the hives got better."

"How did she respond?" Kevin asked.

"She bought it."

Kevin prayed for both their sakes that she did. "And how about you?" Kevin asked, a thousand red warning lights going off inside his head.

"There's nothing to get nervous about, Kevin. It *was* something from my hands, but she's convinced it was psychosomatic."

Even as Kevin told Matthew that he had done well, not only in his explanation to Sheila, but in the genuine and compassionate way in which he had treated her, he could not escape his dark and fearful thoughts. His hand and now Sheila's rash. He knew that even if Matthew and he could rationalize Sheila's spontaneous healing, his hand could not be explained away so easily.

What Kevin feared more than Sheila was his premonition that there would surely be a next time. Was Matthew's gift something new and spontaneous, or was his cool exterior hiding some dark secret? It was clear that Matthew wasn't one of the regular members of the fraternity and hell week might just be beginning. As Kevin sat there, his dim apartment suddenly alien to him, he realized Matthew had become a potential danger.

Listening to him talk so easily about Sheila and watching him repeatedly probe Susan for information, Kevin thought Matthew might be becoming too comfortable with his extraordinary and terrifying healing ability. He had assured Kevin that he could handle things, but Kevin wondered how long the lid could be kept on these mysterious occurrences and how devastating the fallout would be if the web of lies came crashing down on their heads. Kevin was in too deep to plead ignorance. He knew that Buckman would consider anybody with Matthew's talent to be a charlatan, and believed that, with Buckman's current level of stress, he was unreasonable enough to fire both of them without any investigation of the truth. And, then again, maybe they wouldn't be fired. Scientists would test Matthew and if he couldn't turn water into wine on their command, would conclude that he was crazy. And if Matthew tried to save himself by telling them about his hand, Kevin's fearful fugue concluded, would they declare him just as nuts as Matthew?

10

The next morning, Kevin walked to the hospital with Matthew. "I saw you leave a few hours ago," Matthew said.

"Two patients turned sour. And I had some research to do."

"Research? At two a.m.?"

"Yes, Mom," Kevin said.

"Sorry," Matthew said sheepishly. "I haven't been sleeping well."

"That makes two of us. It's easier to collect data at night when the floors are quiet." The half-truth came easy. The two patients were Sheila and Kevin himself. The research was about Matthew. As chief resident, he had access to Buckman's office and knew where Buckman hid the spare keys to his file cabinets. Like a B-movie detective, Kevin pored over Matthew's records, looking for anything that would help him understand Matthew. But neither the neatly hand-written applications for the residency program or the state medical license, the exemplary high school and college transcripts, nor the glowing letters of recommendation offered anything but the picture of a perfect person. Almost too perfect, Kevin thought as he walked home in the rain.

Arriving at the sixth floor, Matthew gathered his patients' charts and checked for overnight changes and laboratory data. While Kevin quizzed the residents who had been on call, Matthew made a quick visit to each of his own patients so as not to be blindsided by Buckman on rounds.

A sudden rush into the classroom signaled Buckman's approach at 6:28. He started immediately at half past the hour. "Good morning, doctors. A young woman is admitted with a drug overdose complicated by rhabdomyolysis. Would one of the medical students please define the term for us? You there, what's your name?" Buckman asked pointing to a student sitting in the front row.

"Homler, sir."

"Do you know the answer?"

"Deterioration of the heart muscle, sir?"

"Very good, Dr. Homler."

"And now for the residents. What are the causes of rhabdomyolysis?"

All eyes avoided Buckman's in the fear-filled silence.

"Nobody?"

Matthew raised his hand.

"Harrison. Why the raised hand?"

"I think I know, Doctor Buckman."

"Well, what is it?"

"Crush injury…cocaine toxicity…"

"Go on." All eyes in the room were now on Matthew—mostly rooting for him.

"Status epilepticus…a muscle enzyme deficiency."

"A less common cause?"

"Um…the…uh. Oh yeah, the bite of the Samoan sea snake."

"Not quite, Doctor Harrison. It's the Malaysian sea snake."

A few residents moaned. "Maybe Bucky can leave for two years to study it first hand," Phil whispered.

Buckman continued. "Nevertheless, an excellent answer, Doctor Harrison. An impressive example for your colleagues to follow. Just one thing, though. You're not in second grade. You don't have to raise your hand."

Matthew smiled. "Yes, sir."

"So much for the morning question," Buckman continued. "Let's assemble in five minutes outside of room 603. I'm going to demonstrate a proper patient interview for a group of sophomore medical students. It wouldn't hurt the residents to attend."

Buckman had barely cleared the doorway when Nick shouted, "Way to go, Mattman."

Matthew smiled. He and Nick left the classroom for the nurses' station where Nick unsuccessfully attempted to bribe a nurse for the diagnosis of the patient in room 603.

"Sorry, Doctor Shulman," the nurse said. "I don't know what she has for *any* amount of chocolate. She's been here an hour but nobody's seen her yet. If you want to impress Dr. Buckman, you're going to have to do it honestly."

Kevin joined them.

"How did you pull off the snake answer?" Kevin asked Matthew. "Did you sneak a look at Buckman's notes?"

"Just lucky. I read an article about it last week. And anyway, I've decided that Buckman's not so bad."

"You're sick, Mattman," Nick said.

"You might do a bit more reading yourself, Nick," Kevin said.

"Maybe." Nick shrugged and walked away.

Kevin was puzzled and asked Matthew to explain his positive change in attitude regarding Buckman.

"I had a great dream last night," Matthew said.

Kevin swallowed hard. "I'm almost afraid to ask."

"I dreamed I graduated and Buckman was smiling as he gave me my diploma. It's an omen. I'm going to finish the program here."

"Bucky was smiling?" Kevin asked.

"Yes," Matthew said, "Why?"

"Buckman only smiles when he's thoroughly humiliated an intellectual foe, gets something that he knows in his heart he doesn't really deserve, or watches a rival chief's career go down in flames."

The residents and students waited outside the door to 603 for Buckman's return. Five minutes became forty. When he arrived, it was without apology or explanation.

"Students. This morning's patient is a fifty-one year old social worker whose name is Rachel Fremont. That's all I'm going to tell you. The key to this exercise is for you to pay attention and observe carefully. This is one time I won't ask you questions. Do not say anything unless I specifically call on you. Understood?"

A series of murmurs answered his question. Buckman opened the door, leading the parade.

"Good morning, Miss Fremont. I'm Sanford Buckman, chief of medicine. These are my students and residents."

"So many?" Rachel asked. "Is this necessary? I'm a private patient. When the other doctor asked if I would do this, she didn't tell me there would be this many students."

Rachel's graying hair was thick, and her face showed a strong character and compassionate nature. Kevin disliked her attitude. The residents and students had work to do, training to get.

Buckman was gentle but professional. "I'm only going to interview you, Miss Fremont. As a social worker, I thought you might be willing to contribute to the education of these future doctors. You, of all people, understand the importance of learning good communication skills. But if you have an objection, we'll leave."

Rachel responded with resolve. "I may be a social worker, Dr. Buckman, but in this bed I'm a person. I'm sick and wouldn't have tolerated a hundred hands prodding and poking me today. But you may ask all the questions you wish."

"Thank you. Now what brought you to the hospital?"

"I guess I would have to say it's a lack of energy. For quite a while–maybe four, maybe six months–I haven't had all the strength I used to have. I know doctors sometimes blame low energy on depression, but that's not the case with me."

"I'll take your word for that, Miss Fremont. Have you lost any weight?"

"Yes."

"How much?

"I'm still what you might call hefty, but I've lost over twenty pounds. That's two dress sizes. And don't ask for my actual weight," she added with a twinkle in her eye. "Teach your students not to ask a lady that question."

Buckman did not return her smile. "Have you been on a diet?"

"Not a chance. I've never believed in dieting. But I'm not as hungry as I used to be."

Buckman scribbled a note on Rachel's chart. He turned to the class and explained that she was an ideal patient to interview–her answers were concise, but that would not be the case with all patients. Some ramble on for what seems like forever. "The average doctor interrupts his patient after only seventeen seconds. Don't make that mistake."

Buckman continued to question Rachel and lecture the students. Matthew stood next to Kevin at the outer edge of the crowd.

"Kevin..." Matthew tapped his shoulder.

"Not now."

"Kevin. She's got a gastrointestinal lymphoma."

"Shut up, Matthew," Kevin said. But it was too late.

"Excuse me, doctors," Buckman said, noticeably irritated. "Do either of you have something to say about this case?"

Kevin attempted to douse the fire. "Nothing, Doctor Buckman."

Matthew's attention was riveted on Rachel. Kevin went cold as Matthew said it again. "She has a gastrointestinal lymphoma." Kevin wanted to choke him.

Buckman heard the words. Unfortunately, Rachel heard them too. "Lymphoma? That's cancer." The red lights and sirens began to flash and roar in Kevin's head. Rachel turned to Buckman in panic. "How does he know that, Doctor Buckman?" she asked. "Who is he?"

"A new resident." He turned to Matthew. "Please explain to Miss Freemont that the 'she' you were referring to is a different patient you were discussing with Dr. Hargrove."

Matthew went ashen. "I can't, Doctor Buckman."

Buckman turned red. Kevin thought he might rupture a blood vessel; it would have been the best thing for Matthew if he had. "Harrison. Out of the room. Kevin, go with him."

Matthew was clearly shaken, but less than Kevin thought was appropriate given his present circumstances.

"What was that?" Kevin asked.

"I don't know. I couldn't help myself. But I couldn't lie."

"Then you'd better construct a good defense before Buckman flays you alive."

Buckman dismissed the class, who exited the room, every face turned to Matthew, universally puzzled but thankful not to be him. They scattered quickly, not wanting to catch the shrapnel when Buckman exploded. Susan stopped a respectable distance away, pretending to examine a chart.

Fifteen agonizing minutes later, Buckman stepped from the room, as composed as a cobra.

"I'm waiting, Harrison," Buckman said. "I've spent the last quarter hour with an understandably emotional Miss Fremont."

Matthew trembled as he spoke. "You're correct to be angry with me, sir. I'm sorry. I shouldn't have spoken in front of her." He paused and took a breath. "But I'm sure about the diagnosis."

Buckman fumed. "Do you have some special knowledge about this case? Have you spoken to or examined this patient?"

"No."

"Would you explain how you arrived at your diagnosis? Considering the extreme rarity of that particular tumor, do you understand how outrageous it would be for you to make that diagnosis–or for that matter to diagnose *any* lymphoma–with nothing but a history of weight loss? Do realize that it's virtually impossible to make the diagnosis you're proposing without a gastric biopsy?"

Each question was louder than the one before it. None were intended to be answered.

"I'm sorry, Doctor Buckman, but all of a sudden I just knew that Miss Fremont has a lymphoma. I understand the remote possibility of that diagnosis but I *know* I'm right. I saw it."

Kevin could not believe what he had heard, the sound of Matthew putting the noose around his own neck and throwing it over a tree branch–all by himself.

Ten seconds went by. It felt like hours.

"You saw it? You saw it? What the hell's going on here, Harrison? Are you trying to play some hero-bum game with me? An off-the-wall stab at a rare diagnosis makes you famous overnight while an error is forgotten tomorrow? Maybe in Peoria, but not here, doctor."

Buckman was literally hissing at Matthew. Kevin stood frozen to the floor. "Now tell me again. Explain it so I understand. How did you make the diagnosis."

"It was an intuition, sir."

Buckman whispered, "A what?"

"An intuition. I don't know how to explain it to you, Dr. Buckman. I don't understand it myself. I just knew it."

"You just knew?" Buckman shouted. "You used the word *lymphoma* in front of her. She's an intelligent woman. Now she's terrified by your *intuition*."

Buckman stopped, anticipating a response. None came. "We're doctors here, Harrison, not clairvoyants."

"Yes, sir. I'm sorry, sir."

"I suggest you be sorry to Miss Fremont. You're her doctor now. And if you don't want to get your ass thrown out of here and bounced back into surgery–and I mean that quite seriously–you'd better do an impeccable work-up. Impeccable, Harrison. Do you understand?"

"Yes, sir, Dr. Buckman."

"And as long as we're getting things straight, I trust you'll stop harassing our patients with your hot hands."

Matthew looked genuinely puzzled. "I'm sorry, sir. You've lost me."

"It seems that a young woman has been singing your praises for 'laying on of hands.' You're on the edge, Harrison. And you too, Kevin, if you can't keep my service free of problems like these. If you don't already know about the woman in the derm clinic, Kevin, you should."

"Sheila?" Matthew asked.

Buckman's eyes narrowed. "On a first-name basis with her, are you?"

"I don't know what she said, Doctor Buckman." Matthew said, "She had hives that resolved spontaneously."

"She claims you touched her."

"I *examined* her," Matthew said, unable to restrain his anger. "Aren't we supposed to do that, Doctor Buckman? Is it wrong for a patient to get better and believe that her doctor helped her?"

Now Matthew was kicking the chair out from under his own legs. Buckman roared. "Mind your tone, Harrison. I don't want any fucking new-age bullshit in my hospital!"

Matthew trembled visibly. So did Kevin, fearing he was next in line. "New-age what?" Matthew asked.

Buckman glared at Matthew, stunned that a resident would stand up to him. "Apologize to Miss Fremont. And make it damn good. Tell her what an ass you were. And don't let me hear anything negative about you again–ever. Trust me, Dr. Harrison, I hear about it all."

Buckman turned and walked away.

Matthew calmed down enough to apologize to Rachel and start her work-up. To give him the best shot at redeeming himself, and to protect his own hide, Kevin divided Matthew's patients among the rest of the residents, allowing him to give his full attention to Rachel. Buckman never made an idle threat.

Matthew, making an appearance as Dr. Jekyll, earned Rachel's confidence. The medical workup was masterful. A thorough physical exam revealed no masses or abnormalities. All the lab tests–blood studies and an upper and lower GI series–were normal. Kevin reviewed it with Matthew, buffing it as though their lives depended on it, making sure Buckman would find even the nursing notes in perfect order. All Rachel needed was a gastroscopic examination of her stomach before she was declared well.

After they were done, Kevin and Matthew walked home together, discussing the day and working on the explanation Matthew would give Buckman when he presented Rachel's case on rounds the next morning.

Every healing event that Buckman was aware of was filled with ambiguity. Sheila Young was easy for Matthew to explain. "She doesn't understand that her body healed *itself*, Kevin. She wants to give me the credit. Buckman should understand that."

"He should," Kevin said, "but he's going to be suspicious anyway. With time, and *if nothing else happens*, Buckman will find better things to think about, or fresher victims."

Rachel Fremont, however, was a problem. Matthew stuck to his "intuition" story. He put his hand on Kevin's shoulder and stopped walking. Matthew asked for his complete confidence and told him about the six-inch band of greenish-white luminescence he saw hugging the contours

of her body. Kevin listened as carefully as he could. He tried to understand but, like the healing of his hand, auras had no place in his reality.
Matthew seemed disappointed with his resistance.

"Why did you become a doctor?" Matthew asked. The question
caught Kevin off guard. "Why aren't you a teacher, or a lawyer, or a
social worker like Rachel?"

"I wanted to teach," Kevin said, "but that was in another lifetime. I
wanted to write too, mostly poetry. Why did you quit surgery?
Especially after two years?"

Matthew picked up a twig from the sidewalk. He began to snap it
into smaller pieces. "I told you. I touched people and they healed. Like
your hand. You fainted. I panicked and ran. It was insane, but, at the
time, in a manner of speaking, so was I. If I could have figured out what
part of me was doing this, I would have grabbed a scalpel and excised
it. I still would if I could."

"What did you tell Eileen?"

"Everything but the truth. I told her I had chosen the wrong special-
ty. It sounds crazy when I think about it now, but I rationalized that as
an internist I could limit my physical contact with patients. Surgeons
have to touch people."

"Why didn't you do something else?" Kevin asked.

"You're kidding?"

"No. If it weren't for the low salary, I would have been happy as a
teacher."

"I never thought about the money," Matthew said. "The only thing
I've ever wanted was to practice medicine. I love taking care of people.
I was *born* to be a doctor."

"No youthful dreams of being a star first baseman? Or a fireman?"

Matthew grinned. "I triple-lettered in high school and college, but
my heart was always set on medicine. You know those see-through
models you could buy in hobby stores?"

"The visible man?"

"Man, woman, heart, brain, ear, and eye. I had the entire series, my very own plastic patients. And I spent every Saturday in the medical section of the Museum of Science and Industry."

"Do you still want to be a doctor, Matthew?"

"Of course I do. I'm through running."

"Then you'd better learn how to stop this shit now. Or you won't *have* to run. Buckman'll see to that."

Kevin reflexively swept his hand across a spider's web on a tree branch at eye level and destroyed it. Then aware of what he had done, he wiped his hand forcefully against the coarse trunk of the tree several times to rid himself of the web and its mangled contents, abrading the skin of his hand in the process. He began to bleed, not much, but enough to be seen in the fading light.

"Shit."

"Let me see," Matthew offered, attempting to grab Kevin's hand.

"Not again," Kevin said, laughing. "I'd rather bleed."

"Your blood, your call," Matthew said, laughing with him.

11

Matthew climbed the stairs, three at time. "Want to come in?" he asked.

"Where's Eileen?

"She's at a school meeting. Are you hungry?"

"No, but I could use something to drink."

As Matthew sat picking at some cold food Eileen had left for him, Kevin toyed with a large glass of scotch and examined his hand. The second round of cuts, a series of shallow abrasions, were still there, the blood having clotted into a series of burgundy lines that were real, something he could touch. "Maybe we should see if this thing actually works," he said.

"Sure," Matthew said, feeling validated.

Kevin extended his injured hand and placed it flat on the table. Matthew rubbed his hands together like a pitcher preparing to throw a fastball. He breathed deeply, slowly advancing his own hand until it touched Kevin's. "Do you feel anything?" Matthew asked.

"No. Do you?"

"No."

"Good," Kevin said, withdrawing his hand from Matthew's. "Maybe it's over."

Kevin joined him in his dinner of scraps and leftovers. "Would you like to get out of here?" Kevin asked after they had eaten and cleaned up the kitchen. "I have to check a few patients at the hospital." Matthew agreed to tag along.

"When we pass by the morgue," Kevin said, "keep your hands in your pockets."

Matthew laughed.

Kevin visited a dozen problem patients, paging the residents on call and discussing the cases with them. Matthew agreed on a time and place to rendezvous and left to make social calls on his own patients, who were delighted to have the personable young doctor stop by to chat.

After Kevin and Matthew reconnected, they stopped at the Emergency Room, to be sure no trouble was brewing that would have Kevin back there as soon as he got home. The E. R. was a zoo. Two drunken street people, having done battle with broken bottles, loudly cursed each other as their lacerations were being repaired by residents barely able to tolerate the stench. A fearful young child, a victim of random gunfire, was screaming as she was prepared for surgery. Despite Kevin's trepidation, Matthew held her hand until she fell asleep from the preoperative sedation, but nothing supernatural occurred. Unable to delay for even the brief elevator ride to the third floor, a young mother had delivered her baby on a cart in the hallway. The scent of birth, all trauma and promise, lay everywhere.

A few of the patients were regulars. "Nice to see you again, Don," Kevin said to a man arguing vociferously with Steve Rhinelander, a first-year resident. "What's the disease of the week?"

"I'm in pain, doc–a kidney stone." He winced like an Oscar nominee and doubled over. Don Severn was fifty, the nondescript middle class guy in a polyester shirt and tie that populates crowd scenes in crummy movies. His characterlessness was his greatest asset when it came to his tenure in the E.R.

"He's got blood in his urine," Rhinelander said. "He's insisting on pain medication before his x-rays."

Kevin grabbed Don's wrist firmly. Don attempted to twist out of his grip. "Did you watch him give the urine specimen?" Kevin asked.

"Are you kidding?" Rhinelander asked.

"Check out his bloody cuticles. One quick dip in the specimen cup and he gets his fix. It's an old trick."

"You're hurting my hand," Severn moaned. Kevin released his grip; Severn's dash for the exit was stopped by two security guards. Kevin asked them to escort him into a room and remain with him until Rhinelander could examine him properly.

"How did you know that?" Matthew asked, amazed.

"Don's a scumbag who does this for drugs–sometimes for money. He has a dozen malpractice and worker's compensation suits pending. He's also been caught attempting to steal drugs from our medicine closet. Every big city has its share of Dons. After a few years they become part of your family."

"Can't I just boot his ass out of here?" Rhinelander asked, clearly annoyed.

"Finish your workup. One of these days he actually will be sick. We wouldn't want to miss anything–even on him." Rhinelander left, shaking his head in disbelief.

Matthew said he was ready to go home. "Jamison has a problem with a patient who swallowed a foreign body," Kevin said. "Hang out for a few minutes more and we'll walk together." Matthew acquiesced, and Kevin went to help the second year resident.

"Carlos! What are you doing here?" Susan asked, entering the procedure room of the E. R. two minutes after Kevin.

"Then you *do* know him," Kevin said. "Jamison said this guy refused to cooperate until you arrived."

The young Hispanic man on the gurney lunged toward Susan, almost pulling the IV out of his arm, but the handcuffs attached to the chrome side rails kept him from moving to more than a sitting position. The guard who had accompanied him from Cook County Jail dropped the sports section he was reading and rose from his chair. "Try that again, Olivera, and I'll smash your face."

"Olivera?" Kevin asked.

"My ex-husband," Susan said grimly. She turned to Carlos, furious. "What are you doing here, you piece of scum?"

Carlos was the last man in the world Kevin would have pegged as Susan's type. He was tall, dark, and scary, his face characterized by numerous small scars and a scraggly growth of beard. His arms were covered with crudely drawn blue-black tattoos.

"Susan," Carlos said. "You don't answer my calls or letters. I had to see you. You're mine no matter what you did."

Kevin looked at an x-ray film on the viewing box. A child could have identified the opaque shadow in the middle of his chest. "He must have wanted to see you pretty bad if he swallowed a teaspoon. Someone from GI is on the way to remove it. Do you want to watch?"

"If she's not here, my mouth stays shut," Carlos said.

"A spoon?" Susan asked him. "Is that how much you love me?" He smiled at her. "Next time try a straight razor."

Kevin asked Susan to step outside into the corridor. "You were married to *that*?"

"I was young," she said. "Each time I think about that part of my life, I want to change the channel."

"You don't have to tell me about it."

"It's not a long story," Susan said. "But it's an ugly one." She was sur-prisingly forthright. "Carlos and I were married for six months. I was seventeen, a kid, but apparently not young enough for him. I discovered *my husband* forcing himself on my six-year-old sister. My testimony sent him to jail for twenty years."

Kevin felt Susan's body tense as he put his arm around her shoulder. "I can't even begin to understand or know what to say," he said softly.

She pulled out from under his embrace. "I'm okay. But I can't say the same for my sister."

"What have you got for me tonight, Kevin?" Dave Kauffman asked as he poked his head around the corner. "Another Darth Vader?" The sen-ior fellow in gastroenterology was referring to a case he'd presented to the medical residents in which a six-year-old child was rushed to the hospital after ingesting a foreign body. When asked by Dave what he had swallowed, the child had proudly said that it was an Imperial Storm Trooper. And it was—a two-inch high metal action figure complete with a tiny laser blaster. Dave had removed it and placed it in a showcase in the GI department which displayed objects that had been retrieved from various body cavities: toothbrushes, wedding rings, coins, keys, and the Storm Trooper, the star of the collection.

"This should be easy," Dave said. The three of them returned to the room. Dave explained the procedure to Carlos who signed the consent form with his handcuffed hand. "Good night, Mr. Olivera," Dave said as the nurse injected the IV line with Demerol and Versed, a potent chem-ical cocktail that induced an effective but safe level of anesthesia.

Susan and Kevin watched on a nineteen inch Sony color monitor while Dave passed a half-inch scope down Carlos's esophagus just to the edge of the spoon. Taking a thin snare, Dave passed it through the scope and, like a child hooking a toy in a twenty-five cent amusement park machine, grabbed the edge of the spoon with the snare and pulled both the snare and the scope from Carlos's mouth. "Not quite Tiffany," he said examining his prize.

"I don't want to be here when he wakes up," Susan said.

"Me either," Kevin said. "I'm going home."

Kevin thanked Dave, said goodnight to Susan, and went off in search of Matthew. He found him his with his hands on the head of a filthy sixty-three year old derelict, an alcoholic in restraints. "What are you doing?" Kevin asked.

"He was seizing," Matthew said, removing his hands. "Nobody else was here."

"How much Valium did you give him?"

"None."

"Why didn't you push the arrest button, or call for a nurse?"

"I didn't need to. It was like a dream, as if I was watching myself from somewhere outside my body."

Kevin struggled to remain calm. "And then what happened?"

"I put my hands on his head. It seemed like the most natural thing in the world." Matthew took a deep breath. "The seizure stopped."

"Did anybody else see what happened?"

"I don't think so."

"Let's go home," Kevin said.

"I'm not leaving him alone." Matthew smiled, "I rarely make the same mistake twice."

"I'll get an orderly to stay with him," Kevin said.

They returned to Matthew's apartment and sat at the kitchen table. "Have you got any more scotch?" Kevin asked.

"You finished it. We have a couple bottles of pretty decent red that we've been saving for a special occasion. Eileen doesn't like to keep too much in the house."

"Get a bottle," Kevin said.

Eileen came home two bottles later. "What's going on?" she asked.

They had drunk without any but basic conversation, swallowing the wine like medication.

"Is this what doctors do on nights when their wives are out?"

"You're home pretty late," Matthew said, checking his watch. She ignored the comment.

"This is my fault," Kevin said. "I asked Matthew if you had anything to drink and he volunteered the wine."

"One bottle for each of you?"

"Let me explain," Matthew said.

"I'm sure you will." Her eyes blazed. Kevin rose from his seat and offered it to her.

"I'll stand."

Matthew spoke slowly, carefully choosing each word so as not to lie to Eileen, creating a sanitized, palatable version of the truth. "Buckman's upset with me. He was interviewing a patient and I spoke inappropriately. I had a hunch about the woman's diagnosis. I shouldn't have said anything in front of her."

"What did you say?"

"That I thought she has cancer."

"You know better than that," she said, concerned.

"I do. I apologized. The patient and I are cool. There's more."

"Maybe I'd better sit down," she said, taking the chair.

"I treated a woman in the derm clinic with a psychosomatic problem. She believes her rash disappeared because I touched her as part of the exam."

"Touched her?"

"Now you sound like Buckman," Matthew said. "You can't examine a rash properly without touching it. Her problem was a stressful pregnancy. She miscarried her first baby. I'm the only doctor who's really listened to her and cared. Is that such a bad thing?"

Eileen was silent for a long moment as if she were composing her response. "Is Matthew in trouble?" she asked Kevin.

"Buckman has a short fuse," Kevin said. "Matthew shouldn't have said anything during the interview, but he did outstanding damage control. That'll count for something with Bucky."

"It won't happen again," Matthew said.

Eileen raised her eyebrows. "I'll bet not. But I don't understand why Buckman would be upset by a neurotic woman who gives the credit to her doctor."

"Buckman is an ass," Kevin said. "He misinterprets events and stubbornly believes his own distorted reality."

"Can you talk to Buckman about this, Kevin?" she asked. "Is there any way you can straighten out the misunderstanding?"

"Not really," Kevin said.

"I'm confused," Eileen said. "Isn't it part of your job to support the residents?"

"With Buckman, sometimes it's best to just let things drop."

"This isn't Kevin's fault," Matthew said. "Or his responsibility. You don't understand."

"No, I don't understand," she said, barely containing her emotions.

"Everyone makes mistakes, Eileen. I'm just trying to be happy, to be the kind of doctor I always dreamed about. And I will. Don't worry."

12

The next morning, when Kevin stopped by Matthew's apartment to walk with him to the hospital, there were no smells of coffee and bacon. A pillow and blanket were loosely piled in the corner of the couch.

"Don't ask," Matthew said when he opened the door.

"I don't have to," Kevin responded, pointing to the floor register.

Although they had arrived with time to spare, Matthew became involved in a lengthy discussion with a nurse about a medication order he had given and was late for Buckman's classroom rounds. He slipped into the first available seat. He had missed the beginning of Buckman's spiel.

Buckman froze in mid-sentence and stared at Matthew with a haunted and apprehensive look that unnerved him. "I think I've said enough about yesterday's patients," he said, his eyes finally releasing their hold on Matthew's. "We've had eight new overnight admissions. We'll start our rounds outside of room 634 in twenty minutes." As Buckman slipped from the room, loud buzzing whispers broke out everywhere.

"Nice going," Nick said. Matthew looked bewildered.

Susan pushed her way toward Matthew. "I hope you have a good explanation."

"I was on the fifth floor–a misinterpreted order."

"I'm not talking about your being late. You were right."

"Thanks," Matthew said smiling. "About what?"

"About Rachel Fremont," Kevin said. "She does have a lymphoma–a million to one shot. Her gastric biopsy confirmed it."

The blood drained from Matthew's face. "I got sidetracked by the nurse and didn't have a chance to check her this morning," he said.

"How did you know, Matthew?" Susan asked, bursting with curiosity.

Matthew shut the door to the classroom. He described the strange light he had seen around Rachel Fremont. Susan listened calmly. Kevin began to feel queasy when she admitted that she too, on occasion, had the same experience. She told Matthew he was not unique, but doctors were afraid to speak openly about their intuitive experiences.

"Oh, Jesus," Kevin said. This was not what he wanted Susan to say.

"We're not talking religion, Kevin." Susan said. "Spirituality and medicine are not mutually exclusive."

"Tell that to Bucky." Kevin said. "Ask him if God's answered any of his prayers about Francie."

Matthew grimaced. "This is why I've been asking you about healers. And why I shut you down. You were getting too close. The question is, Susan, what do I do?"

"These experiences are more common than we would like to admit," Susan continued, ignoring the question. Her voice rose excitedly. "My mother was very spiritual. It comes with being Hispanic, like the *curanderos.*"

"I've seen the candle shops," Kevin said.

"The day my father died of a cerebral hemorrhage," Susan said, "my mother had a vision. She knew where his car was parked and called the police. The squad car must have cruised the block twenty times. The police told her she was loco. But finally she and my uncle went to the exact spot in her vision. The car was there. My father was dead behind the steering wheel. Why can't doctors have gifts like my mother? To have a healer in the hospital, one with an M.D., is a rare opportunity. You're not the first, Matthew."

"Maybe I should become a televangelist," Kevin muttered. "Let me tell you about my hand!" He exaggerated, waving both arms in the air to an imaginary crowd.

Matthew shot him an angry look.

"We need allies, and fast," Kevin said. "We've got to tell her."

"You're probably right," Matthew said.

Kevin told Susan about his hand. Then Matthew told her about the seizing drunk in the emergency room.

Susan's mouth dropped open. "*Madre de Dios*," she whispered.

"Yeah, I'm ready for a bit of God myself," Kevin said nervously. He feared that once the story about his hand broke, if Buckman didn't fire him, he would turn Kevin into a lab rat for every researcher investigating paranormal healing. His freedom to moonlight would be sharply curtailed. And his mother really needed the money.

They sat in silence for what felt like an eternity.

Susan spoke first. "You're here for some higher purpose."

Matthew frowned. "I'm here to finish my medical education."

"Of course you are," she said. "Spontaneous healing is real. University medical centers study it."

"They'll find a way to license it so only doctors can use it," Kevin said

"Always the cynic," Susan laughed, then added more seriously, "Maybe he should tell Buckman."

"If Buckman knew I could heal by touch, I'd be toast, like Sandra Herrington. He would can me for being a psycho—and he'd be as correct as the police were about your mother."

"My mother wasn't crazy."

"Neither am I," Matthew said. "That's why I've been so scared of Buckman and what he can do to me—and to anyone like Kevin who gets 'healed' or like you who just gets involved. I didn't ask God to give me this thing–this special ability. I don't understand it. I have no say about when it happens. And even though part of me is amazed and awed each time it happens, I'd destroy it before I'd let it ruin my career or hurt my friends. I want to be a doctor, an ordinary run-of-the-mill guy who goes to an office each day for forty years, makes a decent living doing what he loves, comes home each night to his wife and children, and then dies at the age of ninety having made the world a healthier place. I'm in deep shit, guys, and I'm asking for help."

13

Matthew and Buckman made an obvious effort to avoid each other during rounds. Whenever Matthew's face was turned from him, Buckman looked at him with a mixture of anger and confusion. When rounds were done, Buckman asked Kevin to join him in the classroom. He shut the door behind them. "What do you think of Harrison?" Buckman asked. "His work. His character. Do you think he's material we want here at the Research?"

Kevin's father had taught him to play chess, and with the game, the value of studying each of his words as if they were moves on the board. Buckman was a master player. Each time he asked a question, Kevin searched between his words for checkmate.

"I'm just the chief resident, sir."

"Meaning?"

"I'm not sure that I'm the one to make that kind of judgment."

"Stop equivocating, Kevin. You've given your opinion of residents' work in the past. You've volunteered a great deal of information when you thought one of the housestaff was a potential problem. It's been of great help to me." Buckman leaned forward, his eyes at once hooded and piercing.

"That's true, sir. But it's only the first week. It's too soon to form an opinion of the new residents. Perhaps in a month or so."

"It's not too soon for me, Kevin. I can't quite put my finger on it, but something isn't right with Harrison. What do you think of his lucky guess about Rachel Fremont's diagnosis?"

"It was highly probable that she had cancer, Dr. Buckman."

"Did a gastric lymphoma cross *your* mind, Kevin?"

"Lymphoma would have been on my list of differential diagnoses."

Buckman raised his voice. "I asked you if you considered specifically *gastric* lymphoma as the mostly likely diagnosis. Did *you* think about it at that point in her history?"

Kevin winced. "No, sir." The man had already missed the most important diagnosis of his life with Francie. He wondered if Matthew's intuition had rubbed salt in the wound. "Maybe Matthew had a deja-vu, a flashback to a former patient. I've done that on occasion."

"I considered that and called his former chief. Matthew didn't come within a mile of a gastric lymphoma during his surgery training. Are you aware of the exceptional rarity of that particular tumor?"

Kevin swallowed hard. "Yes, sir."

"I want you to pay special attention to Dr. Harrison. Become friends with him. Learn what you can about him and let me know anything I should."

"Yes, sir. You can count on me."

"I'm sure I can. By the way, have you any plans for practice next year?"

"Not yet, sir."

"You're a good man, a promising internist. Keep performing as well as you have been and I have no doubt you'll end up where you belong."

Kevin knew what he was saying. He just couldn't figure out if it was checkmate.

Matthew refused Kevin's invitation for lunch, choosing to wander the streets around the hospital rather than eat. Kevin didn't blame him. Matthew was on the edge. And Kevin wasn't exactly back home in his Barcalounger, himself.

The medical clinic shared the identical physical layout as the derm clinic, but all similarity ended there. To spend more than a day there, you had to like gray: gray walls, dirty gray vinyl-covered chairs, gray patients. The place even smelled gray. Arriving for the afternoon clinic, Matthew encountered a ruckus raised by a patient attempting to register. The clerk was having a difficult time keeping the patient calm. Senior residents learned from experience to let the clerks untangle the patients' administrative problems themselves but Matthew jumped right in.

"I'm Doctor Harrison. Can I help?"

The man was in his young thirties, with thick wavy brown hair shot through with gray. His brown eyes were softened by the crepe-like skin of a person with chronic illness. His head seemed too big and weighty for his frail body.

"My name is Larry Trenton. This asshole keeps telling me I need a ticket before I can see a doctor." He sat down in a chair, weak, breathing hard.

"I'll take care of you right now," Matthew said gently.

"You can't do that," the clerk said. "Every patient has to have a stamped receipt before they're seen by a doctor. It's hospital regulations. He should be back in ten minutes–or as soon as he learns to follow instructions."

"I'll make sure he does the paperwork," Matthew said, directing Trenton to one of the examination rooms. "Have a seat. I'll join you in a moment." Matthew waited until he heard Trenton close the door behind him. "I didn't mean to override your authority," he said with a smile. "He seems pretty sick."

The clerk shrugged his shoulders, relieved to have one less hassle. "Make sure he gets a pink receipt. Or get it yourself."

Kevin arrived on the scene. "I'm going to see patients with you this afternoon," he told Matthew.

"Why?"

"For your protection."

"I don't need any *protection*." Matthew's fine blue eyes narrowed.

"I just had a chat with Buckman. You do." He also had a phone call from the insurance company assigning him two physical examinations that needed to be done by five that afternoon. Cursing under his breath, he politely asked the clerk to give them to somebody else.

Matthew told Kevin about Trenton. They entered the exam room where Larry sat waiting for them on the exam table.

"Mr. Trenton, I'll be examining you," Matthew said. "This is Dr. Hargrove, the chief resident."

"Why the supervisor?" Trenton asked Matthew. "Are you really a doctor? You barely look old enough to jerk off."

Matthew laughed. "My medical license is on file in the administration office."

Kevin cleared his throat. "It's Dr. Harrison's first week at this hospital. He's not familiar with protocol. I'm a kind of mentor until he learns the ropes."

"Show him how to cut through the red tape," Trenton said. "I need to get into the AIDS program."

Medical records that Larry had brought from his own physician had confirmed his diagnosis. Kevin's preference would have been to transfer Larry to the hospital's AIDS clinic–the area's first and last line of treatment for HIV patients whose care is underwritten by the government. But Buckman demanded that all patients get a thorough examination before any referral was written. Sloppy practice allowed too many things to be missed and mistakes to be made that hurt the patients and sometimes returned to haunt the residents. For the rest of his life, Kent Johnson, a resident who graduated five years ago and currently practiced in Evanston, a northern suburb, would have his reputation tainted by a huge malpractice judgment. In failing to perform a complete physical exam on a young woman, he missed a breast cancer that could have been successfully cured.

Trenton volunteered more than medical information as Matthew examined him. "I look like dog shit now, but I used to be well off. I made an excellent living doing real estate appraisals and had a great apartment in boystown. You're not gay, are you, Doctor?"

"No," Matthew said.

"A breeder. No offense, but you're cute."

Matthew smiled. "None taken."

Matthew began to examine Larry's abdomen, pressing firmly, watching for a reaction. "It must be tough to lose your health and your income," he said. "Tell me if this hurts."

"Do we have to go through this? I didn't come here with a stomach ache. We both know you're going to send me to the AIDS clinic. Ouch. That hurt."

"There?"

"Yes. Don't do it again."

Playing the teacher, Kevin asked Matthew for a differential diagnosis of Trenton's pain.

"It could be his gall bladder, or his pancreas," Matthew answered. "There's something there."

"Look, Doc, I'm at the end of my rope. I don't want another workup. I just want to get started on a protease inhibitor."

Kevin spoke up. "Dr. Harrison has to finish his exam before he can send you anywhere. When was the last time you saw your doctor?"

Larry looked sheepish. "A few months ago."

"A lot can happen with AIDS in a few months, even a few days," Matthew said.

"Come on, Doc. Have a heart."

"I do," Matthew said. "If you want a referral, lie still and answer my questions. I'm here to help you, but you have to help me too."

Trenton drew his eyes downward. "Do whatever you want," he said.

"Thank you, Mr. Trenton. Now tell me if this hurts."

"Hey," Trenton cried, "what the hell are you doing?" He flinched away from Matthew's hand.

"What are you talking about?" Matthew asked.

"Your hands. They're hot, man, really hot."

Kevin froze in terror and watched Matthew move his hands over Trenton's abdomen.

"Whatever you're doing, Doc, it feels weird."

Matthew's hands dropped to his sides. He looked gray, the favorite color of the medical service.

Trenton sat up. "What *was* that?"

"Are you okay?" Kevin asked Larry. His momentary paralysis was gone, his protective reflexes on full-scale alert.

"I don't know," Trenton said. "Dr. Harrison looks like shit. I, on the other hand, am buzzing like a good hash high."

"What did you feel when Dr. Harrison examined your abdomen?"

"Electricity. What do you think it was?"

Kevin did his own examination of Trenton's abdomen. "Nothing here but the painful area that Dr. Harrison found. He must have pressed on one of your major nerve trunks. It's the same stunning sensation as hitting the ulnar nerve in your elbow, the thing we call the 'funny bone.'" The words came naturally and sounded persuasive. They might even have been true.

"It did kind of feel like that. But I'd be a whole lot happier if you'd ship me to the HIV clinic. I'd like to get started on their protocol." He turned to Matthew. "I'm sorry about the crude crack. I feel much better now."

Kevin reached over to the desk, found the appropriate form, and handed it to Matthew, who carefully filled in each space and gave it to Trenton. "Be sure you get a receipt or the clerk will have my hide nailed to the wall," Matthew said.

"Such a handsome hide that is," Trenton said with a laugh. "Thanks."

Matthew got up and left the room with Kevin. As the door to the exam room closed behind them, Matthew's knees buckled. He stopped to lean against a wall. Two residents saw him and moved in their direction to help, but Kevin waved them away.

"Take a breath and stay calm," Kevin said. "We have a clinic to finish. Maybe it *was* a nerve trunk you hit."

"We both know that's not true. Something happened in that room. I'm scared of this."

"So am I, Matthew, but right now, all we have is a patient who felt something."

Kevin felt boxed into a corner by Matthew, Buckman, Trenton and a thousand others. The rest of the afternoon clinic was grueling. Fortunately, no one threw away his crutches and walked.

14

From the depths of sleep, Kevin heard pounding on his door. The two-inch high orange numbers on his nightstand clock read 12:37.

"Kevin, open up. It's me." Kevin stumbled out of bed and into the living room. He unlocked the deadbolt and removed the chain. What now? His fears were intensified when he opened the door to Matthew.

"You have to come with me," Matthew said.

"Come in while I get dressed," Kevin said, his pulse racing. "You look like you slept in your clothes."

"I did."

"Where's Eileen?"

"Asleep. I hope."

They walked into Kevin's bedroom. Matthew told him he had just gotten a call from Nick in the emergency room.

"I told Nick that I wasn't on call, but he kept whispering for me to get dressed and get to the E.R. ASAP."

"Whispering?"

"Larry Trenton's had multiple episodes of vomiting and diarrhea. He's upset and he's insisting on seeing me." Beads of sweat formed on Matthew's forehead. "Nick said that someone from administration had been called and was there."

Matthew and Kevin ran to the Research. They headed directly to the central desk, where, amid a frenzy of gunshot wounds, drug overdosed teens, and screaming children with ear infections, nobody noticed Kevin check the log-in sheet for Larry Trenton's location.

They found Trenton moaning on a gurney, and Nick talking to a man in a Brooks Brothers' suit and yellow silk tie, perfectly knotted even at one in the morning.

"So, it's the Bobbsey twins again," Larry said, weakly.

Nick looked up and greeted them.

Kevin recognized the man talking to Nick. "Doctor Harrison," he said, "This is Dan Stevenson from hospital administration." Stevenson was Buckman's hatchet man.

"What the hell did you do to me?" Larry asked.

Matthew was trying hard to keep calm. "Just a second, Mr. Trenton." He turned to Stevenson. "Why are you here?"

"Not from my love of adventure, I assure you, Doctor. This patient's been causing quite an uproar, saying lots of interesting things. But let me ask *you* the same question. Why are *you* here? And *you*, Dr. Hargrove?" He looked at Nick, who busied himself with a pale and haggard Larry.

A nurse entered the cubicle and handed Stevenson a pocket-sized tape recorder. Nick stood behind Stevenson and pointed first to Matthew and then to his middle finger. Dan pushed the red record button. "Something the legal department likes us to do for everyone's protection."

"Mr. Trenton," Matthew said, turning to Larry. "How are you feeling? I understand you're having a problem."

Trenton laughed. "That's an understatement. What the hell did you do to me? The hot hands or whatever shit you pulled today. I felt great and then, all of a sudden I started puking my guts out. Shitting them out too." Matthew listened as Trenton elucidated the details of his present situation. "Anyway, fix me." The words were barely out of his mouth when he leaned over a basin and dry heaved.

When Trenton had regained his composure, Matthew responded. "Mr. Trenton, I didn't do anything but examine you."

"How can you stand here and lie about it, Dr. Harrison? Three of us in this room know something weird happened."

"Mr. Trenton," Kevin said. "AIDS can produce many problems that would cause nausea and diarrhea, including a number of opportunistic infections. Symptoms can start suddenly. You might just have the flu."

"You know it's not the flu. Your buddy looks like hell. You're worried, aren't you? I'm gonna die."

Kevin had to take control of the situation. "Mr. Stevenson, this patient was assigned to me in the clinic. His condition has changed and I need to examine him. Would you please leave?"

"I don't think so, Doctor Hargrove."

"Has Mr. Trenton filed a complaint with the hospital?"

Stevenson hesitated. "No."

"Then what's your problem? Mr. Trenton, if you want Dr. Harrison and me to help you, you can ask Mr. Stevenson to leave."

Trenton paused for a moment, then said, "Get lost, Stevenson, before I sue the whole fucking hospital."

As Dan and Nick left, Kevin pointed to the recorder that Stevenson had placed on the table next to the gurney. Matthew shut it off.

"Mr. Trenton," Matthew said, "I have no idea what happened in that exam room."

"Then you admit something *did* happen?"

Matthew clicked on his pocket flashlight and asked Trenton to open his mouth to check for signs of dehydration.

"Why am I sick?"

"Most likely it's a virus," Kevin said.

"I don't think so. I feel like shit and I know it had something to do with Dr. Harrison touching me. I'll forgive you both if he gives me a second treatment with those hands of his. Before I got sicker, I had a few hours when I actually felt well."

Kevin explained that their first priority was to get Trenton something for the nausea and diarrhea. He ordered an injection of Compazine while Matthew drew three tubes of blood, carefully placing them in a special plastic bag used to transport HIV infected specimens.

Trenton appreciated their concern. "Thanks for coming to see me tonight." He shifted feebly in the bed, as if his very bones hurt. "But I did feel something today. I got zapped. Once I'm in the AIDS program and on protease inhibitors, I'll be out of your hair."

Matthew smiled. "I hate to see anyone as uncomfortable as you were."

"Dr. Hargrove, can you explain what's going on?" The only voice that could shatter Kevin's composure at that moment came from behind his back. "Why did I get called in the middle of the night?"

Buckman wore a paint-stained plaid shirt and baggy cotton pants. It was a shock to see him this way, looking like a harmless old man. Buckman addressed Trenton, "Are you the patient causing the commotion?"

Trenton looked confused. "Doctor Harrison, who is this asshole?"

"This is Dr. Buckman, the *Chief of Medicine*," Matthew said.

"Why is he here?"

"Mr. Stevenson called me," Buckman answered. "Is everything under control here?"

Trenton winked at Matthew. "Well, since you asked, I sure could use your help getting priority at the AIDS clinic, sir."

Buckman frowned. "Has Doctor Harrison caused a problem?"

"Him?" Trenton asked. "He's a fucking prince. You should take lessons from him." Buckman was silent as Trenton continued. "I'm sorry if you had to get out of bed, Dr. Buckman, but there's been a mistake. The good doctor here saw me today, well, actually it was yesterday. I'm sick and wanted him to see me again. He has me feeling much better now. Go home and get some sleep."

Buckman was clearly upset. "Mr. Trenton, what did Doctor Harrison say that made you change your story?"

Matthew protested, but Buckman silenced him with a hand.

"You're out of line," Trenton said, angry. "If you're suggesting I'm lying, you best stop before I complain to the state board of medical examiners about *your* unprofessional conduct. I have friends in Springfield. If you want to do something while you're here, get to work and cut the bullshit in your hospital."

Buckman collected himself and withdrew without another word to Trenton. On his way out of the room, he said, "Let me know what happens to this patient, Kevin."

When he was out of earshot, Matthew smiled down at Trenton. "Thanks."

"No problem. I get off saving handsome men. And I meant what I said about a second shot at those hands of yours."

Matthew was silent as if considering his next move. "If I admit that something did happen and if I try again, do I have your promise that you won't tell anyone?"

Trenton looked puzzled. "Sure, but why hide something like this if its real?"

"It scares the shit out of me. It doesn't always work when I want it to," Matthew said.

"Would you try again?"

"What have we got to lose?" Matthew reached down, unbuttoned Trenton's shirt and put his hands on his abdomen.

"I'm sorry if I caused either of you a problem," Trenton said after a minute. "Your hands are *really* hot–not quite the same jolt as earlier, but I do feel something. And I feel better. Thanks for trying."

"Maybe we can use this to your advantage," Kevin said. "We can order a STAT consult from the resident on call for the AIDS service. He'll have to see you tonight. I'm sorry if you had a rough time today."

Trenton smiled. "Thanks. My lips are sealed."

Kevin and Matthew stood in the hallway and gathered their wits. "What am I going to do?" Matthew asked.

"Get real, Matthew. After tonight's guest appearance, it's *we*."

Nick joined them. "Do you boys want to let me in on what's happening? I don't understand, but I want to help."

Matthew told Nick about Larry Trenton, including the part about his "hot hands."

"You're joking?" Nick asked, pale.

"I wish we were," Kevin said. "Matthew's dealing with something uncontrollable and bizarre. We're being careful and covering ourselves. Susan is helping and now so are you. Hell, even Trenton's helping."

Nick's mouth felt dry. He swallowed before the words could escape. "Jesus Christ, Mattman, I'll do anything I can for you. I'm on your side."

Matthew smiled. "Thanks."

Suddenly, bright red lights bounced off the walls of the corridor. The doors to the ambulance dock opened and eight blood-soaked youths were wheeled in. "Gangbangers," shouted one of the paramedics.

The E. R. erupted in activity. Residents and nurses moved in the unchoreographed dance of triage. Nick rushed to help. Kevin, sensing Matthew's emotional condition and fearing the possibility of a healing occurring in the presence of witnesses, told him to stay out of the way and help only as a last resort.

"Can't I just go home?" Matthew asked.

"Not yet."

It took about five minutes for the staff to move the victims into rooms as the paramedics chanted their mantra of vital signs and details of each youth's injuries to the nurses and doctors.

Another ambulance pulled up to the dock. The nurse at the desk yelled for Kevin, "Dr. Hargrove, we have an M. I. She's stable, but needs a resident. Can you take her until somebody on duty gets free?"

"Sure," Kevin said.

Kevin turned to Matthew. "I know you want to leave," he said. "Stick with me while I take care of this patient."

A nurse wheeled the elderly lady into the cast room, the only free space available in the E. R., a quiet area isolated from the main trauma section. The nurse left for a moment and then returned with a portable cardiac monitor and defibrillator, which Kevin helped attach to the patient. Before she left, the nurse slipped an oxygen catheter around the patient's head.

Rosie Summerfield was a recent widow who admitted to seventy-three. She looked like the grandmother Kevin had always wanted, the kind with warm cookies waiting in her kitchen. Rosie had spent an uncomfortable night, unable to sleep. She had called for an ambulance, complaining that something was about to happen to her. The dispatcher was in the process of explaining that she should call back if something actually *did* happen, when she collapsed. The paramedics arrived four minutes later to find her lying on the floor of her bedroom.

"Mrs. Summerfield, I'm Doctor Hargrove. This is Doctor Harrison. You've had a heart attack, but you're in the hospital now. Just relax. I'm going to examine you."

Rosie mumbled something unintelligible, and then she contracted in pain.

Matthew stepped to the side of the cart. Rosie took a long look at his face, and then shifted her gaze to the ceiling, apparently searching for something somewhere in the air. She began to whisper. "Sweetheart? You're here."

Kevin looked to the ceiling where Rosie was staring. There was nothing but the stained acoustical tile. Matthew took Rosie's hand in one of
his and lifted his other in the air.

"Matthew, what's happening?" Kevin asked, but Matthew didn't
answer. He glanced at the EKG strip. It showed a minute of flat line, followed by a normal heart rhythm.

"Did you see him, Kevin?" Matthew asked, letting go of Rosie's hand.
His speech seemed distant, flat, like a space alien's.

"See who?"

Rosie's eyes met Kevin's. "My husband," she said feebly.

"See him?"

"Well, not really see him," Matthew said. "More like feel him, his
presence."

"I don't want to go," Rosie said. "Not before my next grandchild." She
sighed, closed her eyes, and appeared to fall asleep.

"Are you both crazy?" Kevin whispered to Matthew.

"No," Matthew continued as if he was reporting the nightly news.
"Her husband said that whatever she chose would be correct. They were
unable to touch each other, so I took their hands and closed the gap. It
was a strange feeling–as if I were bridging time and infinity, the present
moment and eternity."

Kevin shook Matthew by the shoulders as one would awaken a sleep-
walker. "Get your head out of the ozone," he said.

"I'm spaced," Matthew said. "What happened?"

15

Eileen was up when Matthew got home. She was wearing a blue chenille robe, smoking a cigarette that she dropped into a half-empty can of diet cola as Matthew locked the door behind him.

"Hi," he said.

"You're not on call tonight."

"You were asleep. Nick called about a patient of mine."

"He couldn't handle it without you?"

"Buckman was there too." He saw the fear in her eyes. "Everything's okay."

"Just tell me what happened."

Matthew took a deep breath. "A patient I saw earlier in the day was causing a huge commotion. He insisted I come to the hospital. Buckman showed up after a hospital administrator called him. It was a huge misunderstanding."

"I've got a bad feeling about this, Matthew."

"The guy has AIDS. He likes me, thinks I'm cute." Matthew smiled, hoping to mitigate the facts.

"Stop it," Eileen said, upset.

"The patient probably has a virus. He's in bad shape from his disease and dehydrated from a few hours of vomiting. He thinks that my examination triggered his symptoms."

"Did it?"

He cleared his throat. "Kevin was there. He thinks I traumatized a nerve trunk in the guy's abdomen."

She thought about his answer. "Too many strange things are happening to you, Matthew. After what Kevin said about Buckman, I'm scared he's going to think something's wrong with you and cut you from the program."

"We'll be okay," he said, taking her in his arms.

Kevin woke to the sound of the telephone and the memories of the previous evening. A female voice he didn't recognize asked for Matthew. The clock read 3:58. To Kevin's protest that she had the wrong number, she responded that Matthew's phone was off the hook. "Tell him to come to the hospital as soon as he can," the voice said. "Rosie Summerfield wants to see him." Kevin mumbled something, hung up the phone, and pulled off the blue and white comforter as a cold chill swept his body.

"Get up," Kevin said, pounding on Matthew's door.

Matthew was wearing yesterday's clothes. Eileen stood nervously in the living room.

"You got a phone call," Kevin said. "Rosie wants to see you."

Matthew gave Eileen a quick kiss and a forced smile. "Relax. Nothing's going to happen." He wondered if she believed him.

At the hospital, the nurse in the Cardiac Care Unit gave them disapproving looks. "Mrs. Summerfield's been asking for Dr. Harrison. She says it's important, that he saved her life. She's in bed ten. Residents aren't supposed to disconnect their phones."

Kevin said that Matthew, who wasn't on call, had had a rough night helping in the emergency room.

Kevin and Matthew walked into Rosie's cubicle, expecting to see a typical post-arrest patient, gray and weak, but Rosie looked as though she had spent two weeks in the south of France. She smiled broadly at Matthew. The multicolored lines on the screen of her cardiac monitor could have been that of a woman of twenty, the regular beeping from the unit confirming the visual display.

"How nice of you to come. I'm sorry, but I don't remember your names."

Matthew told her who they were. "How are you feeling?" he asked meekly.

"I'm feeling wonderful. I don't know what came over me. But you two look terrible."

"We've had a very hard night, Mrs. Summerfield," Kevin said.

"Well, of course. We all did. You were so good to both of us last night."

Matthew wondered what besides their names Rosie had forgotten. "Could you do something for me?" he asked.

"Of course."

"I'm a little fuzzy about last night. Dr. Hargrove took care of you in the Emergency Room. You had a cardiac arrest. You say *I* saved your life. What do you think happened?"

"You don't remember my husband being there? You helped us. We couldn't touch each other without you." She began to get upset, as if Matthew did not believe her.

Matthew took her hand. "It's okay. I wanted to hear it from you so I would know that I hadn't been dreaming. But you can't tell anybody else what happened. Some doctors and nurses might not understand."

Rosie brightened. "It was wonderful, Dr. Harrison–a miracle."

Kevin was alarmed at hearing Matthew openly admit to Rosie that something unearthly had occurred. He wondered who Matthew would tell next. "I'm sorry to disappoint you both," he interjected, "But people see things when their brains are deprived of oxygen."

"Doctor Hargrove, I'm not a crazy old lady looking for attention. And Dr. Harrison's lungs seem to be working just fine."

Matthew smiled gently at her. "Sam was there; so was I."

"There," Rosie said triumphantly to Kevin, "I never told Dr. Harrison my husband's name."

Kevin stopped at the nurses' station, poring over Rosie's chart. "Damn it. There's no mention of her husband's name," he said, slamming the chart shut.

Matthew laughed. "How would I know Sam's name if it didn't happen? Let's talk. We have an hour before rounds."

They ended up sitting in a park two blocks from the hospital. Except for a dozen cooing pigeons, they were alone on the concrete bench.

"What if Rosie tells someone?" Kevin asked.

"Sooner or later *somebody's* going to talk about it," Matthew said.

Kevin exploded. "*I'm* in this almost as deep as you."

"I'm the one who's going to get nailed for this, Kevin."

"You're so fucking naive. Buckman's watching you."

"That's not exactly news."

"Your little 'gift' is beginning to cost me."

"I don't understand, Kevin."

"Moonlighting, Matthew. Phil and I do insurance physicals. We pop downtown to an office for an hour and get a hundred bucks. Sometimes two a day."

"You can do what you like with your own time."

"Do I have to spell everything out for you? Successful business executives don't work the night shift. We make appointments during clinic hours."

"What you're doing is risky, Kevin."

"My father died two years ago. I have financial obligations."

"I didn't know. I'm sorry."

"He'd been out of work for two years when his cancer was discovered. My mother had less than adequate insurance. We spent thousands to get dad the best care available. I'm glad we did it and I'd do it again. But Mom can't possibly pay back the loans with her salary and live a decent life. It's up to me to do whatever I can. Why do you think I don't own a car?"

"It never crossed my mind."

"I love my mother. I loved my father. Love involves risk and sacrifice. The job is a legacy, handed down among senior housestaff. Since you became our resident fucking saint, Buckman's been on my case. He told me to stick with you all the time. That doesn't leave space for extra work. Do you understand?"

"It's clearly against the rules."

"Welcome to the big city. Rules are meant to be broken. The problem with you is you keep getting caught. And you break the wrong rules–bucking for beatitude like a Christian Martyr."

"What do you want me to do about it?" Matthew asked, upset.

"Make this go away. Or conjure up my lost income, Houdini."

Matthew exhaled hard. "This thing I've been given is something wonderful that heals and helps people. That's what I've wished for my entire life. I should be excited and happy but I hate it."

"Probably not as much as I hate the moment you walked into the bathroom and saw my cut hand. Don't get me wrong, Matthew. I've been the beneficiary of whatever this is. I hate to sound ungrateful, but I can't afford to give up my moonlighting to baby-sit you. You're going to have to help me even if you have to lie a little. I've been lying for you every day. Quid pro quo."

"I can't, Kevin. Any lies you tell on my behalf are your own."

Kevin saw the resolve in Matthew's eyes and knew his lies were about to come crashing down on his head. He had forgotten the advice a college roommate gave to him the night he was sent home for breaching the honor system: Don't ever trust anyone with your secrets, particularly a guy who wants to do the right thing.

16

Kevin's prayer was answered. The next two days were completely normal. He had asked his mother if he could change their usual routine and join her for breakfast at seven on Sunday morning since he had planned to spend the day with Matthew. He expected the sullen response he got when he told her he'd have to skip cutting the grass that week. Whenever he had sought an excuse from yard work in the past, she had shamed him by saying that his father always insisted that a trim lawn was the mark of a good neighbor.

His mother's dark mood had not lifted by the time he arrived. She picked at her breakfast without her usual banter. "Why don't you tell me what's wrong?" Kevin asked. "Are you upset because I cut my visit short today?"

She promptly burst into tears. "I can't burden you with this, Kevin. You do so much for me already."

"What's going on?" he asked.

She sighed, her noble face exhausted. "I'm not going back for the fall term."

"What happened? Your students love you."

"The school has been forced to make cutbacks–even in English."

"But you have tenure."

"No, Kevin. You must have assumed that I did. Private schools run by a different set of rules."

"You're wonderful. And smart. You can get a job."

"You've been so sequestered in school, Kevin, that you're out of touch with the real world. I'm sixty. Most school systems won't consider me because of my years of experience. I'm competing against younger teachers who are on the entry level pay scale." She was grim and matter of fact and Kevin hated it.

"That's terrible," he said. "Schools should want your experience and wisdom. What about your pension?"

"At least I have that," she said. "But because of the early retirement, it's going to be less than I expected. I'm not eligible for social security for two more years."

"I'll help you," Kevin said.

"You already do, but it's still going to be close," she said. His mother held up her left hand. Her fourth finger was bare. "I'm sorry."

He rose from his seat and hugged her, missing the familiar feeling of her ring pressing into his shoulder muscles. Worrying about the probable loss of his moonlighting, now more important than ever, caused him to blow a stop sign in the car he had borrowed, almost hitting a young girl on a bicycle.

Kevin brought a late Sunday lunch to Matthew's apartment: bagels, cream cheese, and black coffee from Starbuck's–enough for five. Matthew had asked Nick and Susan to join them. They began with small talk. Kevin asked about Eileen. "She's at the Art Institute with a cousin," Matthew said. "She won't be home until five."

"What does she say about this?" Susan asked.

Matthew began furiously slicing bagels. "Could we forget about Eileen and get to the matter at hand?"

"You didn't tell her, did you?" Susan asked.

Matthew put down the knife. "I didn't lie to her." He shot a hard look at Kevin. "But I didn't tell her the gory details either."

"Don't you think you should?" Susan asked.

"I will. As soon as I can get enough of a handle on what's happening so she won't go unglued. She has her own problems. Between the move, the job, and what she knows about me, she's pretty stressed." Matthew didn't tell them that, as much as Eileen loved him, she needed a sense of ordered control. He feared she would never understand or accept this thing and might abandon him if she knew the whole truth.

The phone rang. Matthew grabbed the receiver. "Hi, honey," he said.

His face went white. He put his index finger to his lips and punched the button for the speakerphone. "Harrison, I want you in my office immediately." Without another word, Buckman hung up.

Kevin's pager began to vibrate. He removed it from his belt and looked at the display. "I'm going with you," he said. "The page was from Buckman's office." Kevin dialed the number. The chief's personal line rang only once before he answered it. In as angry a voice as he had ever heard from him, Buckman ordered Kevin to his office at once. Kevin hung up the phone without answering.

"He's going to fire me," Matthew said.

"He can't do that without a hearing," Susan said. "Am I right Kevin?"

Kevin nodded. "You can't be discharged without being brought before the administrative board, unless it's a morals charge. Buckman knows the rules."

"The last thing Buckman wants is a lawsuit," Susan added. "He hates negative publicity."

"Something isn't kosher," Nick said. "It's Sunday morning. I don't think you should go, Mattman. Tell him that you'll see him tomorrow."

"And what happens tomorrow?" Kevin asked.

"He gets a lawyer," Nick said.

Matthew thought for a moment. "No, it's better to go and get this over with, Nick. I think Kevin and Susan are right. The worst that Buckman can do is present charges to the resident board. And the best thing would be to tell him the truth. At least some of the truth."

The outer office was empty. Buckman opened his office door and asked Kevin to join him. He instructed Matthew to take a chair and wait.

"Thank you for joining us, Kevin," Buckman said. "You know Dan Stevenson."

"I've had the pleasure," Stevenson said, extending his hand. Dan wore the same suit, this time with a dark green tie.

"What's this about?" Kevin asked.

"We have a problem, Kevin." Buckman always moved his pawn first. "Actually, Kevin, we have two problems. As chief resident I thought it best to bring you into the matter as soon as possible." The match had begun.

"Me, sir?"

"You are the housestaff representative to the administrative hearing committee, are you not?"

"Yes, sir."

"I have two cases that merit punitive action; two residents who have breached hospital regulations." Buckman leaned back, ostentatiously comfortable.

"Sir?"

"The first, and I won't use names at this point, is a resident who's suspected of touching patients improperly. There's no *solid* evidence, but you know the old adage, Kevin, about smoke and fire."

Was that his entire attack on Matthew? The chief could never make it stick. Kevin wondered where this gambit was going.

"The second case is a resident who we believe is moonlighting during clinic hours. The evidence isn't *prima facia* but would be easy to obtain."

Kevin's stomach twisted. He began to stammer. "Why…why are you telling me this, sir?"

"I intend to see that justice is carried out. It's my responsibility as Chief of Medicine. Which one do you think is the greater offense?"

"What about due process, sir?" Kevin asked.

"Due process? Well, of course. But I could obtain records from the insurance company clearly proving the second resident's guilt."

"And in the other case?"

"That's a bit more complicated," he said. "But I think that with your support and help, the matter could be discreetly handled." He paused before continuing. "You and I are much too busy to worry about the second case if we choose to concern ourselves with the first."

A sudden rush of adrenaline sharpened Kevin's well-developed reflexes for self-preservation. "I believe the choice is clear," he said.

"A wise decision, Kevin. I'm sure you understand that this issue isn't personal. I have a responsibility to our profession. I don't know what Dr. Harrison is doing, but something is definitely wrong with him." A look of exquisite disgust crossed his face, and Kevin understood how profoundly Buckman despised Matthew's challenge to his sovereignty. "I cannot permit a doctor like him to stay in my program. I also don't wish to create a messy situation. With your support, I think we can convince him to leave quietly. Do you understand?"

Kevin swallowed hard. "I do, sir. I'm on your side."

"You see, Stevenson?" Buckman said to the administrator who had sat silent during the exchange. "I told you that Kevin would do the right thing. I have great plans for this young man, Dan. I see him in a lucrative North Shore practice. He'll be a wonderful assistant professor in my department."

"Just one thing, sir," Kevin said.

"Yes?"

"The resident that you said was moonlighting?"

"You have my word that the matter will disappear forever. Mr. Stevenson is my witness."

Kevin understood that he had just been bought and paid for.

Kevin walked numbly out to the waiting room, knowing that what he was about to say to Matthew would change both of their lives forever. He searched for the right words, understanding that he was at risk and that what he said and how he said it would mean the difference between winning and losing in the treacherous game he was playing with Buckman. But his worry was in vain. A slight spin on the story triggered Matthew's natural nobility. "You don't have to tell me what happened," Matthew said. "It's written all over your face."

"Buckman's got enough to nail us both," Kevin said. "He's threatening to take us to the hearing committee."

"I won't let that happen," Matthew said. "Not to you, at least."

"You can't stop him."

"Watch me."

They walked into Buckman's office. Although Kevin felt defiled by Buckman's tactics, he refused to acknowledge in his own heart that he had compromised himself. He convinced himself that with time the stain would fade and that eventually he would come to see that he had done the right thing. He knew he had taken a great risk in not telling Matthew the entire truth, yet he justified his actions by deciding that if one of them had to be sacrificed, at least Matthew would still have his extraordinary power.

Buckman over-graciously gestured to the chairs in front of his desk and asked them to sit. He pointed to the figure on the couch behind them. "This is Mr. Stevenson, from administration."

"I know who he is," Matthew said.

Stevenson mumbled a greeting.

"Doctor Buckman," Matthew began as he sat down, "I can explain a lot to you..."

Buckman raised his hands. "Save it. I'll be blunt. I'm going to give you a choice between spending the rest of your life as a doctor or leaving the profession."

Stevenson spoke up, "That's a bit rough, don't you think, Sanford?"

"Be quiet, Dan," Buckman said.

Buckman rose from his chair and began to stalk the room, moving behind them so they had to turn to see him. "I no longer want you in my training program. Whatever you've been doing–the 'healing' in the dermatology clinic, your roll of the dice diagnosis of Rachel Fremont, the AIDS patient who thinks you're God, and now the old lady who claims you traveled with her to heaven and back–I won't allow this to continue in my department."

"But, Doctor Buckman, these things have clear explanations," Matthew said.

"Stop, Matthew," Buckman said. "Make this easy on yourself. The choice is yours. You can leave quietly or cause a fuss. If you cooperate, your record will show you left for personal reasons–make up your own excuse, whatever you want. Mr. Stevenson is my witness. You can find another training program. Go back to surgery. I won't sabotage your future. With the Freedom of Information Act you can read my letter of recommendation. But that's it. You're out. You decide on what terms."

"What about a hearing?" Matthew asked. "Maybe I should call a lawyer. Mr. Stevenson?" Stevenson was mute.

Buckman continued. "Call the Supreme Court, Harrison. If you cause a problem for me, I'll make sure everyone knows that you're a plague on the profession, a snake oil salesman trying to deny proper medical care to hospital patients. I can make your life infinitely more miserable than you can make mine. Don't challenge me to a pissing contest. You'll have to take boards someday."

Matthew went white. "You're kidding?"

"Not in the least."

Matthew paused, suppressing his anger, carefully considering his next words. "If I agree to go quietly, there's one stipulation."

"And that is?" Buckman asked.

"Kevin had nothing to do with any of this. You have to promise that you'll take no action against him for what you assert I did."

Kevin's heart, or what was left of it, sank into his shoes.

Buckman smiled. "I'm glad you understand, Matthew. I'll take you at your word." He turned to Kevin. "You may remain in the program and keep your position as chief resident."

"Thank you," was all Kevin could manage to say.

Buckman broke in. "Ahem. Yes, well, Mr. Stevenson will arrange for pay until the end of the month. You must clear out your locker immediately but you can keep using your apartment until then. I wouldn't want you and your wife on the street."

"Thanks a hell of a lot," Matthew said.

"One last point," Buckman continued. "You may not discuss this arrangement with anyone. I would deny this meeting occurred and it would be your word against mine."

Matthew slammed the door behind him as he left the room.

"Good work, Kevin," Buckman said, his eyes burning with anger. "However you got him to defend you was a stroke of genius–or luck."

"Thank you sir. May I go?"

"Yes, that's all."

Fuck you, Kevin thought to himself as he left the office.

He found Matthew cramming the contents of his locker into two plastic bags used for patients' personal belongings.

"I'm sorry," Kevin said.

"I almost dragged you down with me," Matthew said, sadly.

"What are you going to do?"

Matthew's mind reeled. "I just hope to hell I figure out how to explain this to Eileen."

For a moment, Kevin felt so guilty that he thought of telling him the truth, but the damage had been done. Why twist the dagger that fate had stuck into Matthew's heart? Matthew left the hospital. Kevin, saying that he had work to do, remained behind.

Matthew saw their Volkswagen parked in the street. Eileen was home early. He took a deep breath and slowly climbed the stairs.

Eileen looked harried. She pointed toward the remains of breakfast in the kitchen. "Where were you? Who was here and what's all this mess?"

"How was the museum?"

She looked at the bags he had dropped in the front hall. "What's that?"

Matthew, anger replacing the numbness he had been feeling, was in no mood to whitewash the truth. "Buckman fired me."

She turned pale and sank into one of the living room chairs. "He can't do that without a committee or official procedure. You're getting back in that program. We'll get a lawyer."

"No. He can still hurt me. He was gracious enough to let me quit," Matthew said sarcastically. "I left with a spotless record."

"How could you let him do this to you? Unless there's something you didn't tell me." She fixed him with a quizzical look.

His throat tightened, but he managed the words. "I'm a healer, Eileen."

"Of course you are, Matthew. You're one of the finest doctors I know."

"Eileen," Matthew said quietly, "I touch people and they get well. My 'hunch' diagnosis turned out to be right. The rash in the derm clinic disappeared."

She looked at him as if he were a ghost.

He told her the truth. She heard his words, but what he said was so foreign to her reality that there was no fertile soil in her mind upon which anything he told her could take root.

"All I know, Matthew, is that I love you."

He allowed himself to breathe. "Would you just hold me? Please?" He moved toward her, about as vulnerable as a man can be.

She rose from her chair and put her arms around him, not knowing what to feel. "What are we going to do?" she asked.

"Find a new apartment close enough so you can keep your job. Then I'll get back to work."

She breathed a sigh of relief. "Do you think you can find another training program in Chicago?"

"No," he said, stiffening with anger. "I quit more than Buckman's program today. I'm getting as far away from medicine as possible."

17

Kevin spent the next few days in hell. Although his well-constructed life had been saved from disaster, he did not now and would never feel completely safe. Buckman's promises were only words, the same words that Kevin himself had twisted to make Matthew believe his own problems were of Matthew's making. Kevin was desperately afraid his spiritual loan would be called in while he was so deep in debt.

Matthew and Eileen, hurt, angry, and embarrassed, tried to leave their hell behind them. Although Buckman had offered the use of the apartment until the end of the month, they decided to lose no time in distancing themselves from the medical center. Offers of help and requests by friends to visit were politely refused. Rather than stay and lick their wounds in an environment that reminded them of what they had lost, they took only one day to find a small, furnished apartment convenient to public transportation and shopping. Eileen, hopeful that Matthew would reconsider his decision and find a new training program, insisted on a month-to month lease. They loaded their clothes and personal items into their car and left for their new life.

As the whirlwind of activity diminished, the reality of what had happened to them settled hard in their hearts. Eileen burst into tears as the last box of dishes was emptied and stored in the cheap metal kitchen cabinets. "I hate this place," she sobbed. "It's ugly."

Matthew held her, felt the emptiness within himself. "It's not forever."

"I'm so scared," she said. "What are we going to tell our parents?"

"The truth," he answered, firmly.

The knock on the door startled them. "Who knows we're here?" Eileen asked, drying her eyes on a kitchen towel.

Matthew opened the door to find Susan.

"I followed you," she said. "I want to help."

Matthew looked at his watch. "Shouldn't you be working?"

"Kevin gave me the afternoon off."

The three of them sat in the living room. The inexpensive furnishings were clean, but soulless. The bare windows and the walls gave the room the appearance of a prison.

"This is all I can offer you to eat," Eileen said, embarrassed, opening a box of pretzels. "I was about to go out and buy some food."

"I know you didn't quit," Susan said.

"So much for polite social banter," Matthew laughed. He told her what had happened, including Buckman's gag order and warning that he would deny the truth if confronted.

"This makes no sense," Susan said.

"Is there a reason for anything?" Matthew asked, angry. "Sometimes I think we're just pods wandering around this planet by accident."

"Will you come to my place for dinner tonight?"

Eileen, frightened, lonely, wanting to be anywhere but this place that represented failure and disgrace looked at Matthew.

"Thanks. We need friends. I'm starving," Matthew said, putting a smile on his face.

Susan's apartment was in a non-university building in a Hispanic neighborhood, northwest of the Loop. Groups of people, segregated by age, congregated on stoops or stood in the street, speaking in loud animated Spanish. The rich smells of chilies and corn meal flowed from open windows and doorways. Susan's door, with three deadbolts and retractable steel grate, could have stopped a SWAT team.

Susan received Matthew and Eileen with warm hugs. "The food's almost ready and I have some interesting news to share. Nick and Kevin are here too."

Susan's apartment was filled with a haphazard proliferation of shelves crammed with esoteric books and statues of both eastern and western deities. The odor of jasmine incense mingled with kitchen aromas.

They sat down to eat. The music that drifted up from the street competed with Barber's "Adagio for Strings" on Susan's stereo. Matthew shivered, remembering the movie that used that music as its main theme: *Platoon*. Ever since he'd first seen the film, he'd been haunted by the scene in which Sergeant Elias had run into a jungle clearing, helpless, while enemy bullets had cut him to his knees. Elias had been betrayed by his Master Sergeant for telling the truth. Matthew had seen it at least ten times and had cried each time the innocent Elias died with his arms extended to the sky.

"Did you hear about Larry Trenton?" Susan asked.

"No," Matthew responded. "He might have tried to reach me but my number's been erased from the medical center directory." His feeble laugh died in the air, alone.

"He got to the AIDS clinic," Nick said.

"That's great," Matthew said.

"That's not the news," Susan said. "He's HIV negative."

"When did this happen?" Matthew asked. He turned to Eileen. "I told you about him." She shook her head in acknowledgment.

"We heard today," Susan said. The word from the clinic is that Trenton claims you caused it."

The knife Eileen was using slipped from her hand and clattered on her dish, splitting it into two neat pieces. Susan, frowning, got up to replace the plate.

Matthew smiled. "I'm really happy for him, but does it matter what he thinks?"

"It matters a great deal to him," she said. "He's grateful to you for what you did."

Matthew stared at his plate. "What did Buckman say about Trenton's amazing recovery?"

"He called it an unexplainable phenomenon, but not an impossibility," Kevin said.

"Did he suggest I had anything to do with it?" Matthew asked.

"Buckman hasn't mentioned your name in the past few days," Susan said.

"Of course." Matthew rose and started to circle the table, his fists alternately clenching and opening. Eileen stood up and put her hand on his shoulder.

"Calm down, sweetheart. These are our friends."

"Let's talk in the den," Susan said. "I'll do the dishes later." They moved to a small room, furnished with a couch and two chairs, vintage Salvation Army, draped with colorful serapes.

At Susan's request, Matthew reviewed his short history as Buckman's resident. She and Nick listened carefully. Eileen, continuing to protect herself from truths she didn't want to hear, did not. Kevin paced the room as Matthew spoke, his jaw taut, finally sinking into a chair when Susan shifted the conversation to the number of compliments Matthew had received from patients.

"I made people feel better," Matthew said. "Isn't that what I was supposed to do?"

"They didn't just feel better," Susan said, "they *were* better. The people you touched knew something special had happened to them, something beyond the norm."

Matthew frowned, absentmindedly rolling his yellow pen in his fingers. "This whole thing has been a crazy nightmare."

"God sends opportunities for us to learn about ourselves," Susan said.

"I wish God would keep his lessons to himself," Matthew said, jamming the pen back into his pocket.

"What are you telling Matthew to do?" Eileen asked, refocusing on the conversation at hand, hoping Susan could convince him to get his career back on track.

"He shouldn't hide what he can do," Susan said.

"What if I want to hide?" Matthew said, rising from the couch and pacing the room. "There has to be a rational explanation. Or at least some way to control what's happening."

"Control?" Susan asked. "You don't need control, Matthew, you need to learn balance—the same way you learned to ride a bicycle. Be patient with yourself. Have you made any plans?"

The question floated leaden in the air.

Matthew answered flatly. "No."

"How about working in a clinic? You're still a doctor, you've got your license, and I have a good friend who needs your skills." She told Matthew about Hector Gutierrez's charity clinic located close to downtown in one of the of the city's bleakest neighborhoods. There was not much money in the job, she explained, but he would be helping many poor people while he did some good for himself. Nick supported the idea, saying that Matthew could work in the clinic until he found a new training program and that charity work might look good on his application.

Eileen brightened for the first time in two days. She wanted Matthew to fulfill his dream of being a doctor; it dovetailed nicely with her vision of the lifestyle that went with the degree.

"I've already called Hector. He can meet you tomorrow night around eight."

Matthew frowned. "At night? Won't the clinic be closed?"

"If you were working at a menial job, scraping every penny to make ends meet, could you take time off to see a doctor?"

"I never thought about it that way," Matthew said.

"Start to think differently," she said. "About everything."

"I am," Matthew said. "That's why I won't do it."

18

Matthew Harrison, B.A, M.D. discovered that having too much education was a handicap. He scoured the newspapers for jobs, called employment agencies, and applied for positions at local businesses. Each potential employer wanted to know why Matthew wasn't treating patients.

"High school dropouts get the jobs that I don't," Matthew said, over dinner in the sparsely furnished apartment. Eileen had assembled their bookcases, hung their photos, and scattered their personal effects in an attempt to add warmth to their home. She hung Matthew's medical diploma where she knew he would see it. He acted as if it were invisible.

"Doctors don't normally bag groceries," Eileen responded.

He smiled. "They think something's wrong with me. Maybe I should tell them the truth."

She moved her chair closer to him, put her arm around him. "We can't make it on my salary and your last paycheck won't stretch more than a few weeks. Why don't you call Susan."

"No," he said firmly.

Three days later, he found a job with a small construction company that didn't ask too many questions or require a written application with past job history or references.

"Union?" Peter Gregoriou, the owner, asked. A short, powerful man who chronically chewed on a cheap, unlit cigar, he appraised Matthew with eyes that could pierce steel.

"No."

"Can ya hang drywall?"

"My dad taught me," Matthew said.

"Ya look strong, but not like a guy in the trade. Where've ya worked?"

"A hospital job. I fixed things."

Peter said, "Ya look okay and ya speak English. We're non-union and pay cash–fifteen bucks an hour. I'll give ya a shot. Be here tomorrow at six."

Matthew smiled and thanked him. He didn't know or care if the salary was fair. He was grateful to have the job and knew that hard physical labor wouldn't leave him much energy to think about his past–or anything else.

Matthew loved the work. He befriended some of the younger men in the crew and tried to interest Eileen in socializing with them and their wives. Eileen reluctantly agreed to, her Neiman Marcus expectations fading into a J.C. Penny reality.

"Pizza and bowling aren't my thing," she said as they undressed from the evening with Matthew's co-workers.

Matthew tried to make light of it. "Having a high score of thirty-five won't get you in the hall of fame."

She fought back tears. "I hated tonight. Those people…"

"They don't drive Mercedes, but they're real–the kind of people I used to dream about having as patients."

"You could still have that dream."

He felt her sadness, understood that he had unilaterally renounced the life she wanted. She had grown up with food and shelter, but no extra money for nice clothes or the little luxuries that soften the hard edges of reality.

"This is who I am now, Eileen," he said gently, taking her chin in his hand. "I like it."

Matthew worked hard to make his life as a doctor become a distant memory. In just a few weeks, it was as if that part of him had never existed. Susan visited every few days, each time attempting to get Matthew to work at Hector's clinic–or anywhere in medicine. Kevin visited weekly, avoiding anything but superficial conversation.

Matthew quickly put on muscle from the physical labor; Eileen lost weight. They fought frequently, the subject always the same, his position immovable, her tears filled with sadness and anger. He was determined never to return to his former existence as a physician. She was waiting for him to come to his senses.

Peter took a liking to Matthew, who was the hardest worker in his crew. Seeing how intelligent and trustworthy Matthew was, Peter gave him a raise two weeks after he started and made him an unofficial assistant foreman.

"Ya work hard," Peter told him repeatedly, "but ya belong somewhere else. There's something special about ya."

"I'm just an ordinary guy," was Matthew's response.

A month into his construction job, Matthew was outside a townhouse in Lincoln Park unloading materials for a remodeling project when he heard shouting inside the building. He dropped the carton of nails he was holding and ran inside. John Hendrickson, a carpenter in his late fifties, lay on the floor ashen, damp with sweat, not breathing.

Another carpenter, Tad Nowicki, almost as pale at Hendrickson, was pushing on his chest.

"I used my cell phone," Tad said anxiously. "911 is on the way."

Matthew dropped to his knees and loosened Hendrickson's shirt. "What happened?" he asked.

"He's had two heart attacks," Tad said. "He's been bitching about his left arm hurting for the past three days. He just grabbed his chest and dropped."

"Stop what you're doing," Matthew said. "Let me do it."

Matthew put his head on Hendrickson's chest, listening for a heartbeat. He grabbed a flashlight and checked John's eyes. "His pupils are sluggish, but okay. He's most probably had another heart attack. You've got to clear his airway before you start chest compressions."

Tad moved aside. "Where's 911. We need a doctor."

"I am a doctor," Matthew said, between breaths.

Peter asked Matthew to join him for a beer after the paramedics had stabilized Henderson and loaded him in the ambulance. One of them had asked Matthew if he wanted to ride with them to the Research. He laughed and told them he wouldn't be caught dead there.

"Why didn't ya tell me the truth?" Gregoriou asked, gulping his beer. "Why were ya' hiding?"

"I'm sorry," Matthew said. "I really needed the money."

"I don't get it, ya should be taking care of people, not hauling sheet rock. Ya saved Hendrickson's life but I can't let ya stay. For your own good. There's something wrong with a guy who runs away from who he is."

"I know," Matthew said, smiling.

19

"If Matthew takes the job, I think it would be in your best interest to volunteer at the clinic," Buckman told Kevin who had been summoned to Buckman's office. Kevin withheld as much as he could, but figured that if he didn't tell Buckman what Susan had told him about the clinic, someone else would. Considering that Buckman had the power to snuff his career at will, it would have been suicidal for him to play any role except that of supplicant.

"What about my duties as chief resident?" Kevin asked.

"Another senior resident can handle your responsibilities on the days that you're away from here. I'll arrange for everything." Buckman smiled and shifted in his chair. "I've spoken to some doctors in Highland Park. They're eager to meet with you regarding an associate position after you graduate." He paused for a moment and stirred himself into a pale imitation of a smile. "We also discussed the possibility of your working in their office on weekends for the remainder of this year. It would be a good way for them to get to know you. It pays much better than insurance physicals."

Kevin ignored the reference to his moonlighting which he now limited to evenings, sharply reducing his extra income. "How much time would you suggest I spend there?"

"Whatever it takes, Kevin. Let me be blunt. I'm not sending you there to care for the poor. We have enough of them here at the Research." Buckman's face darkened. "Your job is to stick with Harrison. Find out what he's up to."

"But, sir, he's out of the Research. Isn't that enough?"

"Kevin, there's something not right about him and I want to know what it is. He's practicing medicine at a construction site. One of his 'patients' was admitted to the CICU today." Buckman made no attempt to hide his animosity. "I want you to find out whatever you can, and then I want you to bring it to me so I can have the state department of professional regulation solve the problem. He doesn't belong in our profession and he's a danger to patients—including the poor, who can be so terribly gullible around charlatans. Am I making myself perfectly clear?"

"Yes, sir. I understand." Kevin also understood that he had to find a way to appease Buckman and to protect Matthew. Susan's comments about balance rang true for him. Because of the detestable way in which Buckman had cornered him, he believed he had no other choice but to save himself, even at Matthew's expense. He also felt responsible for what he had done and wanted to make amends for the harm that he had caused Matthew. But Buckman was a morally bankrupt bastard who, without a moment's hesitation, would destroy Kevin's future if he did not play his game.

Hector Gutierrez's clinic was an ancient warehouse in the barrio, not the medical building Matthew had imagined. A simple hand-painted sign hung over the door: Medical Clinic. It looked like a prop from a cheap old movie.

Susan parked in front and left the keys in the ignition. "Are you sure you want to do that?" Eileen asked.

"Everyone knows it's mine. It won't be touched."

Susan, Matthew, and Eileen had to weave their way into the building through a sea of patients waiting on the sidewalk. They were mostly Hispanic, but there were also blacks, Asians, and a few Native Americans who turned to smile at them and offer greetings in a variety of languages.

The place smelled clean—not an antiseptic smell, more like a field after a rainstorm. Every surface of the high-ceilinged room was painted white. The walls were covered with a crazy quilt of children's art, the floors, Pirelli tile, a gift from a wealthy patron. The lighting consisted of huge industrial halogen fixtures that gave a blue-white cast to everything. Exposed pipes and heat ducts ran in all directions. Serendipity reigned, with no two pieces of furniture or people matched. Everything, including the patients, appeared to have been rescued from the city dump.

Susan took Matthew's arm and led him behind the well-worn, ink-stained counter that served as command headquarters. A nurse greeted them. She was in her early thirties, Hispanic, attractive, sporting too much makeup. A three-inch scar distorted her right cheek. She and Susan hugged and spoke in Spanish, then Susan introduced her as Carmen.

Carmen's smile could have melted even Buckman's concrete heart. "It's so wonderful to have you here. Let me know if you need anything. Anything at all." She left to find Dr. Gutierrez.

Eileen appeared shocked and avoided touching anything. Susan could not suppress a smile. "Not what you expected?"

Eileen smiled weakly. "It's a move in the right direction."

Hector Gutierrez looked more American Indian than Hispanic—a burly, middle aged barrel of a man, with beautiful black shiny shoulder length hair, unruffled by the heat. Hector extended his hand to

Matthew. "Doctor Matthew, you're hired. Would you like to start right away?" His smile burst forth as a laugh. "We're rather busy and need you badly. Could I show you the place? You come too, Mrs. Harrison." His accent was as thick as homemade salsa but his syntax was definitely not from the streets.

Hector, five inches shorter than Matthew, clasped his new recruit around the shoulder and led him down the hallway. "Look, my friend, I can tell you're overwhelmed. I'd better offer you an inducement. Free living quarters. That's our best perk. A nice clean room with a cozy bed and a radiator. We'll feed you our famous buffalo stew. We have three crockpots, always full. Peter Eaglefeather, our Indian, takes care of them."

"Indian?" Matthew asked.

"We leave politically correct bullshit at the door. Peter's one of our healers."

"Is he a doctor?" Matthew asked.

"No," Hector said. "He's a shaman."

Eileen tensed. "A what?"

"There's a fairly large Native American population that uses the clinic, and the Chicanos also have strong ties to Indian culture. Peter helps to bridge the gap between old beliefs and modern medicine."

Eileen glanced at Matthew. "Does Mr. Eaglefeather see patients on his own?"

Hector laughed. "Yes. There are enough patients to go around. Maybe we shouldn't tell you about Brian, Mrs. Harrison. He's an acupuncturist."

"Is there any real medicine practiced here?" she asked.

Matthew shot Eileen a disapproving look. "I could be happy here, Dr. Gutierrez."

"Your friend, Kevin asked for a volunteer position," Hector said.

Matthew was stunned.

"I thought it would be a nice surprise," Susan said.

"He started a few days ago." Hector smiled broadly. "He's in one of the treatment rooms, suturing a laceration. You can talk to him later."

Matthew asked questions about the facility, the availability of interpreters for non-English speaking patients, and finally about malpractice coverage. Hector laughed and said that the clinic couldn't afford such an expensive luxury as liability insurance and that if someone sued them and won, they could have the clinic's ancient equipment. "Susan tells me you have natural abilities as a healer," Hector asked. "Is that true?"

"Yes," Matthew said, taking Eileen's hand.

Hector winked at Susan. "I haven't had a full weekend off for six months. My children don't know who I am anymore. The job is yours for the asking."

"What about salary?" Eileen asked.

"We pay what we can when we can and sometimes have to borrow it back. Patients pay only what they can afford and that's not much if anything at all. We turn no one away."

"That's the kind of practice I always wanted," Matthew said.

Hector saw the panic in Eileen's eyes. "Don't decide until the two of you discuss it. Go upstairs with Susan. Let her show you the living quarters. Think it over. I can tell already that I like you."

"Thank you," Matthew said. He didn't care about the heavy workload or the near nonexistent pay. He also knew he was going to have to be the best salesman in the world to convince Eileen to accept his decision.

"Whatever you decide, I thank you for coming. Both of you." Hector disappeared down the hall.

The free room was about the size of a walk-in freezer and smelled of chlorine bleach. An inexpensive dresser held a selection of toothbrushes, toothpaste, and shaving equipment, marked with the names of different hospitals.

"What about the bathroom?" Matthew asked, testing the bed with his fist.

"There are two down the hall," Susan said. "You share them with Peter and Brian."

"Brian's an acupuncturist?" Matthew asked as he opened the drawers of the dresser.

"Medicine's been practiced that way for thousands of years," Susan said. "Some patients feel more comfortable with it."

Matthew picked up the items on the dresser one by one. "Don't you think some alternative medical care is bullshit?"

"In the wrong hands it is," Susan said, "Doctors who take three day courses and practice only for profit."

"Are the two guys here the real thing?" Matthew asked.

"Like you," Susan said.

Eileen sat on the bed. The metal frame had been repainted recently enough that the odor of the white enamel had not yet dissipated. The room faced a back alley. "It's good they spiffed this up for us," she said, trying not to cry. "With what you're going to make, we can't afford our own place anymore."

"Hector really wants you," Susan said.

"This isn't the Mayo clinic," Matthew said.

Eileen brightened. "Does that mean we're leaving?"

"No. I might learn something here," Matthew said.

Eileen, no longer able to restrain her tears, dabbed at her eyes with a tissue. "Give this place a chance," Susan said, gently. "Matthew's one of the few who has a heart big enough to do this job. It'll be hard at first–for both of you. The conditions are poor, the equipment and sup-plies outdated."

"I'm happy for the first time in weeks," Matthew said, taking Eileen's hands. "You wanted me to be a doctor. But if you don't want to stay, I can find another construction job."

Eileen smiled thinly. "We'll try it."

Susan clapped her hands in delight. "Hector will love it. There's so much to learn here. Eileen, did you see the paintings downstairs?"

"Yes," she said.

"The children love Hector. That's how they pay their bills. I expect Matthew to have his own collection. You can help with the children too." Susan kissed each of them on the cheek.

20

Eileen stood by the heavily barred window in the upstairs bedroom listening to the distant city. The geometric pattern of the privacy glass scattered the moonlight into thousands of diamonds. A sparrow's nest was wedged into the corner of the gray stone sill. An ambulance siren headed toward the Research.

"Welcome," Kevin said, walking in the room.

Matthew smiled. "Volunteer?"

"Susan's bleeding heart. Senior residents are entitled to two months of elective service. I thought this place would look good on a résumé."

"I'm glad to see you, Kevin," Eileen said. She hoped that Kevin's two-month tenure would set an example for Matthew to follow. Some charity work was commendable, but not as a career. "You three better get downstairs," she said, turning to Matthew. "There's a million people who need you."

"Make that two," Susan said. "I'm on call."

"Thank you," Matthew said, smiling, taking Eileen in his arms. They left Eileen alone to explore her new home.

Flipping the light switch on in the bathroom, Eileen was blinded by the glare of polished porcelain. True to form, none of the fixtures matched: pink toilet, almond sink, avocado fiberglass shower with a large crack that was neatly repaired with silicone rubber. The floor and the walls were white plastic tile. It smelled of pine air freshener, the plastic box type that lasted for weeks. She checked carefully but could not find even one body hair on any surface and wondered what kind of compulsive person kept a bathroom this clean. "It could be worse," she said aloud before breaking into sobs.

The waiting room was still filled with patients, looking at Matthew and Kevin with the eagerness of those long neglected. Carmen was not at her desk.

Hector emerged from an exam room with an obese older woman whose musty scent could kill tulips at ten paces. She carried her worldly goods in two Marshall Field's shopping bags. She hugged Hector, who, to Kevin's surprise, hugged her back.

"So, my friend, have you made a decision?"

"*Su casa est mi casa*," Matthew said.

"Wonderful!" Hector exclaimed. "Could you start now? I'll have Carmen get Truman Holiday. Kevin will see the first two or three patients with you, Matthew, to show you the ropes. Truman's a regular—an easy case. Use room four."

Truman Holiday, an ancient black man, reeked of alcohol and had probably gotten close to soap the last time he walked past a drugstore. A week's growth of gray beard covered his chin. Kevin envisioned legions of lice frolicking in the ragged folds of his clothing.

"Since I have seniority here," Kevin said to Matthew, "I'll assist you." Matthew shot Kevin a look and sat at the small desk while Kevin made himself comfortable in a far corner.

"Two docs. You're both new here, aren't you?"

"What seems to be your problem?" Matthew asked.

"Something wrong with your eyes?"

"Why did you come to the clinic tonight?"

"I'm here for a bowl of the chief's stew."

"Peter?" Matthew asked.

"Yeah, him. I talk to Carmen when I'm down. And get some stew."

"Is there anything I can do for you?" Matthew asked.

"No. Just don't get mean and turn me away." Matthew was speechless. "What did you say your name was?" Holiday asked.

"Matthew Harrison."

"Yeah, well good to meet you, Doc Matthew. You're okay. Good bye to you hiding over there, too." He rose and left the room.

"Are you sure you want to spend your life taking care of Hector's drunks?" Kevin asked.

Matthew flashed his brilliant smile. "Absolutely. They're *my* drunks now."

Carmen brought in a five-year old boy with a severe cough. His mother was Hispanic, a slight woman, poorly but immaculately dressed. Her deep brown eyes were filled with fear.

Matthew sat the boy on the exam table, listened to his chest, checked his ears and throat. His mother wiped a glob of green mucus from his nostril with a tissue. The diagnosis was easy: bronchitis complicated by malnutrition.

"Your son has a bad cold that has settled in his lungs."

"I understand."

"I'm going to give him an antibiotic. It'll take a few days to work. You must finish all the medicine."

"Yes, Doctor." She paused, and then looked hard at Matthew. "But we cannot get the medicine."

"He needs it. He could become very ill."

"We have no money."

The woman blanched when Matthew inquired if she had a welfare card. "What's wrong?" he asked.

"We are illegal."

"I understand," Matthew said.

"What can I do, Doctor?"

"Come with me," Matthew said. The child's dull eyes worried him. He picked the boy up in his arms and carried him out into the hall. Kevin and the boy's mother followed. Hector and Carmen were discussing a patient.

"So you've gotten your feet wet," Hector smiled.

Matthew asked Hector if they could talk in private. Hector laughed and told Matthew that there were no secrets in his clinic. As discreetly as he could, he informed Hector of the patient's immigration status.

Hector laughed again. "That's not a problem."

"You're kidding?"

"No, Matthew. It's a way of life here. What were you thinking of using?"

Matthew suggested ampicillin for both its broad-spectrum antibacterial coverage and its low cost. Hector agreed and explained that a local pharmacist supplied the clinic with outdated medications slated for destruction.

Kevin bridled at the idea. "Outdated medicine?" he asked.

"Not *that* outdated. It's better than nothing," Hector responded.

"Can't you get closed down for that?" Kevin asked.

Hector grunted a laugh. "The establishment doesn't care about us. We do them a favor by keeping some of the non-paying 'customers' away from the big hospitals like yours, Kevin."

Hector gave orders to Carmen for ampicillin and Tylenol. She led the mother and child away. Hector turned to Matthew. "That's it for the night. Why don't you two come and talk."

They sat in a treatment room. Hector rubbed the back of his neck. "This place is a circus," Kevin said to Matthew.

"Three rings," Hector said, smiling.

Matthew frowned. "My first patient was a hopeless alcoholic, Dr. Gutierrez. I didn't treat him. I'm not sure what I did for him."

"We would do something for him at the Research," Kevin said.

"You already did, Kevin," Hector said. "You put him though your alcohol rehabilitation program four times, then tossed him in the street when his money ran out. Truman comes here to know that he's not alone."

Hector smiled. "Five years ago I started this clinic with six thousand dollars. It was all the money I had. A local businessman needed a tax loss, so he rented the place to me for a dollar a year. The building was a rathole. I got local unions and neighborhood organizations to donate help. It was chaos until Truman showed up. He organized everyone and stayed sober until the renovations were finished. Imagine that."

"I think I have a lot to learn," Matthew said.

Hector reached into his pocket and removed a battered wallet. The phone rang at the front desk.

"Here's a signing bonus, Matthew–fifty dollars."

"For what?"

"Tonight's work. Don't spend it on fast booze and cheap women. I'm afraid that all I can offer you, Kevin, is two days per week with no signing bonus or pay."

"I need something else," Matthew said. "My shoulder hurts. Probably tendinitis."

"Let me examine it," Hector said. "Kevin, you can help if you like."

Kevin checked his watch. "I've got other fish to fry," he said with a smile. He rose and left, saying goodnight and thanking Hector for allowing him to work at the clinic.

Hector carefully moved Matthew's arm in several directions as he asked a series of questions.

"Ouch! Stop." Matthew said.

"How about when I press there?"

"It's worse."

He gently lowered Matthew's arm. "Your diagnosis is correct. What do you think is the cause?" Hector asked.

"Maybe my last job," Matthew said. "I don't really know for sure."

"Me either," Hector laughed. He was the Anti-Buckman–openly admitting his non-omniscience. "Would you like an injection of cortisone?"

"If it's not too outdated," Matthew said, smiling.

Hector collected the necessary medications and supplies. He swabbed the area with alcohol, then worked a two-inch long needle into the joint and slowly injected the medication. When Matthew yelped with pain, Hector said that was a sign that the cortisone had hit its mark. He handed Matthew a Tylenol with codeine tablet and suggested that he get as much sleep as possible. As Matthew was putting his shirt on, Hector again pulled out his wallet and handed Carmen, who had by now returned, a fifty-dollar bill. "Sorry it took me so long to get this to you. I appreciate your help."

"Hector, you know I love you," she said.

He handed her a stack of bills and instructed her to deposit the rest into their account at a local bank. "There's four hundred here. How much more did we take in today?" he asked.

"One hundred seventy-five dollars and thirty-five cents," Carmen said.

"Who paid the thirty-five cents?" Matthew asked.

"Truman," Carmen said.

Matthew reached into his pocket and offered the fifty dollar bill back to Hector. "For my treatment," he said.

"No, no, my friend. It's professional courtesy."

"I feel I owe you something."

Hector raised his hands in protest. "Believe me, you'll earn that."

"Where did all that money come from?" Carmen asked, changing the subject.

"Peter phoned me at five-thirty this morning. A well-dressed man with a knife wound was at the door. I came over and sewed him up.

When he was done he asked how much he owed. I told him five would do nicely. He opened his wallet and gave me ten fifty-dollar bills." They all laughed. "Turn's out he's a local pimp."

21

Matthew slept soundly the first night under Hector's roof. Eileen did not. The next morning, she left for work, arranging to meet Matthew that evening to collect their belongings and advise their landlord to look for new tenants.

At seven a.m., the waiting room was already half filled. An old man lay on the floor, rocking back and forth in agony. Two children waited in their mother's arms, a little girl sobbing softly, a boy screaming.

"We'll have to see the little girl first," Carmen ordered.

"The boy seems worse; she's just crying," Matthew said.

"He's afraid. The little girl is hurting."

"How can you tell the difference?"

"You learn to listen and look. I taught Hector. I'll teach you. Go to room three, Dr. Matthew. I'll bring you some patients."

Matthew smiled thinly. "Start me off with easy ones!"

"Hector already told me that," she said with a wink.

Before Matthew got to the exam room, Hector appeared, excited. He and Matthew exchanged warm greetings. He grabbed Matthew's arm and rushed down the hall to the heavily barred back door. Every examination room was filled. As they passed an open door, a man retched. Hector stuck his head into the room. "The sink, George. Not the floor." Then he turned to Matthew. "I've got a little boy with a hot appendix that may have already ruptured. Peter has the van outside. He's sick enough that I want you to go with him."

"What hospital do we use?" Matthew asked.

"The Research. What else?"

Matthew turned red. "Can't we call an ambulance?"

"Not unless you want to pay two hundred dollars for a fifteen minute trip. You work here now. They won't bite you." He smiled and put his hand on Matthew's shoulder before realizing what he had done.

"It's okay," Matthew said. "The cortisone worked."

Matthew opened the back door and walked into the alley behind the clinic where the smell of month-old garbage cooking in the July sun assaulted his nose. Three dogs circled the carcass of a dead rat. A brown Ford van, scratched and dented, stood idling. Matthew climbed in the back seat where a young boy lay waiting.

Peter Eaglefeather drove at breakneck speed, absorbed in the music pouring from a small portable stereo on the dashboard. He was six feet two inches of powerful but lean muscle. His large hands were all sinew and vein. His eyes, however, were too blue and he had too much body hair to be Native American.

"Who's singing?" Matthew asked.

"Johnny Clegg. Do you like it? He's South African. A white guy." Eaglefeather's voice was deep but delicate, a dance of words.

Matthew did not answer the question. He looked down at the silent young boy he held on his lap. "Where's his mother?"

"Mexico."

"His father?"

"Temp job. A different place each day. No way to reach him until tonight. Sister brought him. Then split."

"How are we going to obtain a signed consent for him if he needs surgery?" Matthew asked.

"Hector called ahead. Fixed it with a friend. Guess there's one good guy at the Research." Peter ground the pedal to the floor, cornering hard enough to force Matthew against the door. The young boy tensed and cried out. Matthew held him, gently stroking his forehead, feeling the familiar heat in his own hands.

Peter pulled into the emergency entrance of the Research and opened the back door of the van. They took the boy inside and handled the paperwork. One of the residents recognized Matthew. "Multiply any loaves and fishes lately, Harrison?" he asked with a sarcastic smirk. Matthew hid his pain, smiled, and ignored him.

They left the child in the hands of Bob Cohen, a surgical resident who promised that he would give the boy his full attention. Returning to the car, Peter grabbed a leather bag from under the front sea and removed a six by two-inch bundle of dried grass tied with blue and white string. He lit a match and ignited it, waited for a good flame, and then blew it out. Acrid smoke poured from the smoldering weeds. Peter climbed into the back of the van and moved the smoke around until the van was filled. He got out and stubbed the end onto the concrete, snuffing it.

Peter motioned to Matthew. "You can get in now."

"What was that?" Matthew asked.

"Smudge. Sage."

"For what?"

"Clears the energy field."

"The what?"

"The negative energy field. From the boy."

"They didn't teach me about that in med school," Matthew laughed.

Peter drove back almost as recklessly as he had on the outbound run. "How do you like the clinic?"

"I just got here," Matthew responded.

"Heard you got fired from the Research. What did you do? Kill somebody?"

"I cured them. It pissed off the administration."

Peter slapped the dashboard and laughed. "We'll let you dry your feathers and learn to fly."

"Slow down and explain," Matthew asked.

"The eagle," Peter said. "It's your totem animal."

After a prolonged period of silence, Matthew asked, "Tell me more."

"Ever see *Field of Dreams*?"

"Sure," Matthew said. "It's about baseball."　·

"Maybe. Maybe not. The voice doesn't come out of the cornfield. It comes from your heart. You soar above the ordinary, even when everyone else thinks you're crazy. You're a powerful shaman."

"Maybe so, Peter."

They arrived back at the clinic. Before Matthew exited the van, Peter added in a soft, calm voice, "Your pain will teach you. Help you on your journey. Fly with it."

The rest of that day continued like Peter's wild morning ride. Matthew worked non-stop until two in the afternoon when Hector called a thirty-minute lunch break. Carmen met him in the hallway and gave him a piece of paper with a scrawled picture of a smiling boy on it.

"What's this?" he asked.

"Raoul, the boy you took in the ambulance this morning. His sister brought it over from the hospital." Her long finger pointed to some letters on the bottom of the page. "She wrote that for you."

It said: *gracias.*

"Oh, and there's something else," Carmen added. She handed him a piece of paper with a phone number and a name that he did not recognize: "Please call me. I can help you. Todd Lawrence." He stuffed the note in his shirt pocket.

The break took place in the "war room" at the end of the hall. Unlike the rest of the clinic, this area was in total disarray. Scattered over a mismatched couch, a scarred wooden table with four chairs, and three bookcases, were medical journals, multi-language instruction sheets for patients, and opened boxes of drug samples. A large cork bulletin board hung over a sink, its layers of papers looking as if they would fall off from sheer weight. An oscillating fan sat on a table by the barred open window. A strong herbal odor from the three crockpots filled the room: curry, sage, and fennel.

Brian Anthony introduced himself to Matthew. He was around thirty years old. A permanent five o'clock shadow covered a handsome face set with intense green eyes. Carmen said that Brian had earned three black belts in martial arts. She handed Matthew a bowl of hot stew, brown, thick with chunks of meat and bits of herbs. Matthew put the bowl down on the table next to his chair.

"It won't kill you," Peter said.

Matthew looked at the stew. "I should skip lunch and keep working. The waiting room is still full."

"Sit down," Hector said. "We have a few house rules. The first is that you have to take care of yourself so you can take care of others."

Carmen looked at Matthew. "You'd better eat it before the spoon dissolves." Everyone but Matthew laughed.

22

Highland Park Medical Specialists, Inc. was located in a three story stone and glass office building within walking distance of the commuter train station and upscale shopping area that form the heart of the wealthy northern suburb. The interior of the building, a rich combination of honey maple and royal blue wool upholstery, was the work of one of the nation's leading medical office designers. The staff uniforms coordinated with the color scheme and general design.

While Matthew spent his first day at Hector's, Kevin met with Dr. Ben Listman, one of six partners in the practice. Listman, a short man in his sixties, impeccably groomed except for gray eyebrows that desperately needed to be raked into place, said that Buckman suggested Kevin was a perfect match for them. "We have other applicants for the position," Listman said, "but Buckman's recommendation carries weight." Listman discussed arrangements for Kevin's "off campus research," a euphemism that Buckman had created to allow Kevin one day a week away from the medical center—Kevin's 'reward' for his cooperation in helping rid the Research of Matthew.

"You'll be paid half the patient fees that you generate, with a minimum guarantee of five hundred dollars per day," Listman said. "You can
also work on Saturdays if you're available." Kevin was stunned by
Listman's offer. It was vastly more than he earned doing insurance physicals and he would be practicing real medicine while securing a future.
Best of all, he was doing both with Buckman's blessing. The only problem was that in order to keep his coach from changing back into a
pumpkin at midnight, he had to give the fairy godfather his asking
price. Kevin shook hands with Listman and was handed over to
Barbara, a redheaded nurse who led him upstairs to "his" office and
exam suite.

In sharp contrast to Hector's clinic, the exam rooms in Highland
Park were equipped with the latest medical equipment and furniture.
Before Kevin saw his first patient, Barbara had him read a prepared
script into a desktop microphone. After twenty minutes of hearing
Kevin's voice, the building's central computer was able to transcribe the
patient notes he dictated directly onto their charts. Barbara explained
that he would only need a pen to sign prescriptions. "It's the latest medical miracle," she said.

"Oh, I know a few others," he said.

"I just can't lose weight, Doctor," said Kevin's first patient that day.
Brad Simon was twenty-five years old, half as wide as he was tall. Brad
could afford the best food, graceful living conditions, and a health club
membership.

"Can't?" Kevin asked.

"I work out, and try to eat right. Something must be wrong with my
thyroid."

"Have you had it tested?"

"Oh, yes."

"Was it abnormal?"

"No, but I still think it's the problem, or possibly my brain chemistry."

Kevin envisioned Brad's home, a treadmill gathering dust in the den, his kitchen stuffed with high-fat snacks. With only a few questions, Kevin determined that Brad ate three times as many calories per day as he should. His daily exercise consisted of watching television.

"I want a diet pill," he said. "I've tried everything else."

Buckman had lectured the residents ad nauseum on the futility and dangers of using pharmaceutical solutions for lifestyle problems. Kevin spent ten minutes explaining the side effects of the medication Brad had requested, and offered a referral to a therapist skilled in eating disorders. "I need the pill to get over the first hurdle," Brad said, petulantly. Barbara told Kevin later that he requested a transfer to another physician in the group.

Throughout the afternoon, Kevin found himself becoming angry in a way he hadn't at the Research. A significant percentage of these affluent patients wanted every tiny pain in their bodies eradicated with a prescription medication. One particularly obnoxious woman demanded to see a senior physician when Kevin suggested that the ridges in her fingernails were normal. "They bother me and I want them fixed," she said. "I pay a great deal of money for my health insurance." Kevin mollified her as best he could.

After the last patient had left, Barbara gave Kevin a computer printout of the fees he had generated. Scanning the numbers, he felt much better about the frustrating patients he had treated. He'd made as much in one day as in an entire month of insurance physicals and not a single one of the patients smelled bad. Quite an improvement over the blood and guts of the Research or Hector's little charity effort.

As Kevin was about to leave, Barbara knocked on his office door and said that he had a visitor.

"Dr. Hargrove, I'm Todd Lawrence." He was five eleven, dressed in casual clothes, a poster boy for the all-American-squeaky-clean look.

"How can I help you? I don't need life insurance and I have no money to invest."

"I understand," Todd laughed. "Dr. Buckman referred me to you. Larry Trenton did too." Kevin jolted upright.

"Who are you?"

"I manage a spiritual wellness center in the city. You can phone Dr. Buckman and ask about me." An arctic frost swept through Kevin's bones. Buckman? Spiritual?

Todd smiled through his perfect teeth. "My center provides emotional and spiritual help for many of the patients you see. We work in harmony with physicians."

"Can you be more specific?" Kevin asked, distrustful of Todd and the entire conversation.

"Of course," Todd grinned. "Doctors have enough to do handling the medical needs of their patients, some of whom believe that you should be available for hours to discuss their emotional issues. Our center offers workshops for the chronically ill, including an AIDS outreach program and other seminars that address the needs of the community. One of our participants, Larry Trenton, told me about your friend, Dr. Harrison. That's why I'm here."

"What does this have to do with me?" Kevin asked.

"When Larry first told me that Dr. Harrison had extraordinary healing powers, I didn't believe him. I called Dr. Buckman and told him that I wanted to meet Dr. Harrison and perhaps have him lead workshops at my center. He hung up on me."

"That's typical of him."

"But then he called me in response to the literature I sent him about the center. He asked me to see you first, as he wasn't sure how Dr. Harrison would receive me. Dr. Buckman also said that it would be wise for me not to mention to Dr. Harrison that I had talked to him."

"What else do you do in this center of yours?" Kevin asked.

"We sell nutritional supplements and support a small clinic for alternative practitioners. But before you get upset, Dr. Hargrove, let me assure you that we don't allow rip-off artists to work at our center. Can you introduce me to Dr. Harrison?"

Kevin glanced at the printout of his daily charges. "I don't think I have a choice."

23

"I want to stop at the Research," Matthew said to Eileen after they had collected their things from the apartment. "I have to check on one of my patients."

Eileen was delighted that Matthew was willing to return to the Research and that he referred to the child as "his patient." She fantasized Matthew's reinstatement into the program after a series of successfully treated patients that were, perhaps with Kevin's help, brought to Buckman's attention.

Juan Gomez, Raoul's father, was overjoyed to meet Matthew. He and his wife treated both Matthew and Eileen with great deference. "You did a miracle today," he said.

Matthew smiled. "The doctors in this hospital are very good. I just brought him here."

"No," Juan said. "My son said he felt something wonderful when you touched him. And now he's better."

"Let me speak with his doctors," Matthew said. He asked Eileen to wait with Juan while he left to find the resident in charge of Raoul.

"Really interesting case," Billy Hogan, third-year resident in surgery told Matthew. "The kid was septic: sky-high white count, classic rebound pain in the right lower belly. An hour later he's better than new. He thinks you're a witchdoctor."

"How do you explain it?" Matthew asked, feigning sincerity.

"I checked the labs twice and did his admission physical myself," Hogan said, screwing his face in a gesture of confusion. "Maybe I was wrong."

"Check the staff directory under Alternative Care," Matthew said with a straight face. "Maybe the kid's right."

Matthew returned to Juan, waiting for him outside Raoul's room. "He'll probably go home tomorrow morning," Matthew said smiling broadly.

"No operation?" Juan asked.

Matthew grinned. "No. I'm going to say goodnight to him. Would you like to come with me, Eileen?"

Matthew and Eileen walked into the room. The young boy, seeing Matthew, bounded out of bed and jumped into his arms.

"Whoa, cowboy. This can't be the same sick little boy I brought here today."

"You are the best doctor," Raoul said, hugging Matthew tightly around the neck.

"I think so too," Eileen said, smiling.

"Dr. Matthew don't hurt like other doctors," Raoul said. "He has *las manos de Dios*."

Matthew's power, awakened from hibernation, resurfaced. What started as an occasional drop in Hector's clinic became a trickle: patients were cured miraculously–not everybody and not at Matthew's will.

Three months passed. The clinic's patient load increased as word of Matthew's ability spread through the community. Even as Matthew loved his work, his feelings about his healing gift were mixed. He loved when it produced an unexplainable cure and he hated that he could not offer it to everybody. He also disliked the notoriety that was an inevitable part of the package.

"Another reporter called today," Matthew said unhappily. "Todd Lawrence too. I refused to speak with either of them."

"Something special *is* happening here," Hector said to Matthew in the war room, the cool night air of autumn mixing with the vapors from the crockpots.

"I'm as baffled by it as I ever was," Matthew said. "Many of my diabetic patients are requiring less insulin. Some have given it up completely. A number of the cardiac patients have abandoned their medications, claiming they never felt better in their lives. But I want the world to leave me alone and let me practice medicine. I'm a doctor–the last thing I want is to become a public freak."

Sanford Buckman and Todd Lawrence did not want Matthew to remain anonymous. "Stick with him," Buckman said to Kevin during what had become a series of regular meetings. "I hope your lack of information doesn't mean that you've decided to protect him." Buckman's attitude toward Matthew had become increasingly irrational, as though Matthew was a personal demon to be exorcised at any cost.

"I'm not sure what you're looking for," Kevin said, "I can't fabricate something that isn't happening."

"Of course you can't. That would be stupid. I know that you understand that this matter requires discretion. That's why I recommended you to Ben Listman. You're a winner, Kevin."

Kevin swallowed hard. "Thank you, sir," he said.

Buckman smiled. "Now what about this Lawrence character?"

Kevin had been waiting for the opportunity to ask Buckman about Todd. "I don't understand why you sent him to me." he said.

"Lawrence is a fraud. He's an opportunist, a streetcorner hustler with no scientific training or background. If I can connect Matthew to him, I might be able to expose both of them at the same time."

Despite the stress of having to cope with Buckman's covert activities, Kevin's money problems were solved by the legal moonlighting job. His Sunday visits to his mother were more like the enjoyable experiences they once had been. His mother had tried in vain to find a teaching job and had settled for a minimum wage position selling women's clothing. Sneaking a look into her desk drawer to examine one of her recent paycheck stubs, it had become clear that she needed his extra income from the Highland Park job more than ever.

On one particularly busy day, Matthew appeared more tired and irritable than normal. By the time evening rolled around, his mood had changed from difficult to impossible. When Hector inquired about the reason for his negative attitude, Matthew said that his shoulder had begun to hurt again.

"Do you want me to look at it?" Hector asked.

"I'm too busy," Matthew said.

"Maybe you should see Brian," Hector said.

"I'll live with it," Matthew said.

Hector suggested that Matthew quit for the day and get some rest. Matthew said goodnight and walked upstairs.

The next morning Matthew told Hector that he could no longer stand the pain. Hector told Matthew that until he saw Brian, he couldn't treat patients. "It's not fair to them," Hector said. "If you're in pain, you can't give them your full attention."

Brian's room was pure Zen, with white walls, a full-body exam table, a desk, and a chair. His supplies were neatly arranged on a white laminate bookcase: tiny glass bottles with Chinese labels, boxes of individually wrapped whisper-thin needles, and three small plastic statues of laughing Buddhas. A calligraphic scroll hung on the wall. New-age piano music played softly from a portable tape player. It was an advertisement for mellowness.

"What's the smell in here?" Matthew asked.

"Moxa," Brian said. "It's a combination of herbs that we burn either on the skin or attached to the needles. The scent lingers."

"Like smudge?"

Brian smiled. "You've been in the van with Peter. What can I do for you?"

"I have tendinitis," Matthew said. "Hector won't inject cortisone twice."

"Hector's a wise doctor," Brian said.

"Can you help me?"

"I don't know. Let me examine it."

Matthew removed his shirt. As Brian examined his shoulder, the gentlest touch brought cries of pain.

"I don't really understand what you do," Matthew said. "But I'm willing to learn."

Brian smiled. "Do you know what it is that *you* do?"

"Not really," Matthew laughed.

Brian took his wrist. "I'm going to take your pulses."

Matthew surrendered his arm. Brian felt his wrist at the base of his thumb.

"You have a great deal of anger," Brian said. "Your liver is congested."

"I think I'm just exhausted."

Matthew lay on the table while Brian swabbed his skin with alcohol and inserted needles into his shoulder, chest, and earlobes. Explaining to Matthew that the needles required time to alter his energy system, Brian left the room to treat another patient.

Brian returned after twenty minutes and removed the needles. "How's your shoulder?" he asked.

Matthew was pale and sweating profusely. "I don't feel so good."

"I can see that," Brian said. "May I make a suggestion?"

"Yes."

"I'll get Peter to do some body work."

"I'm not sure. I really don't feel well."

"He's quite gifted. I'll get him."

"No," Matthew said. He began to retch. "Get Hector."

"Hector would be lost here," Brian said. "Peter knows what to do with blocked negative energy."

At Brian's request, Peter entered the room, somber, his brows tense. "Can I help?" he asked.

Matthew opened his eyes.

Peter's voice was gentle. "Turn over. On your stomach." Peter placed one of his massive hands on Matthew's neck, the other just above his waist. He slowly moved his hands over Matthew's back muscles, working deeper with each pass.

"Shit!" Matthew yelped.

"Hurt there?"

With each "yes," Peter pressed deeper.

Suddenly Matthew grabbed his shoulder and began to cry, rocking back and forth like a child, retching and dry-heaving. Sweat poured from his body. Peter kept his hand in the center area of his back. "Why are you holding your shoulder?"

"You hurt it, God damn it. You were pressing directly on the sore area."

"I never touched your shoulder," Peter said. "I was pressing the middle of your back, on your rhomboids."

"Whatever you touched," Matthew said between dry heaves, "the pain was in my shoulder."

"What does it feel like?" Peter asked.

"Like…like a God damn stiletto."

Peter listened.

Matthew took a deep breath. "A pointed knife, a fucking six inch carpenter's nail sticking in my shoulder." He rocked back and forth.

Peter frowned. "When were you stabbed in the back?"

Matthew stopped rocking. He spoke slowly. "When I got thrown out of the Research."

Peter gently stroked Matthew's back, covering him with a white flannel sheet until the storm abated. "Lie here for a few minutes," Peter said. "We'll talk." He and Brian left the room, turning off the light. Matthew lay limp and empty on the table.

Fifteen silent minutes later, Peter returned. "How's the shoulder?"

Matthew sat up and rotated his arm. He smiled. "It feels much better," he said. "I'm sorry, Peter."

"For what?"

"I lost control."

"You should do that more often. It's good for you."

24

Matthew heard Eileen's sobs halfway up to the second floor. He tore up the remaining stairs and burst into their room to discover her on the floor next to the bed, shaking in terror, holding her right arm. Dresser drawers were half-opened, their contents scattered. Picking up an over-turned chair covering Eileen's body, Matthew helped her onto the bed.

"I'll call the police," he said, trying to remain calm.

"God damn you," she said through her tears.

Matthew was bewildered by her response. "Who did this?"

"One of your fucking patients–probably looking for drug money."

Matthew swallowed hard. "We can call the police later. Let's get that checked first." He carefully examined her injured arm. "It's bruised, but nothing's broken."

"We're in this place because of you," she said, crying.

He held her tightly until the two of them were calm. The closeness became an invitation for greater intimacy. He slowly undressed her, then himself. They made love, not joyously and spontaneously, but des-perately and needy from their shared fear and isolation.

Matthew, holding Eileen in his arms, sensed it happening before she did. Where his hand was touching her arm, the bruise was visibly vanishing.

"*Oh my God,*" she whispered, watching the last of the dark purple stain disappear. She pulled away from him and began to tremble. "*Who are you?*"

"I'm the guy who loves you, Eileen," he said gently. "And until this moment, I've never been so completely happy to have the power I've been given."

Images she had carefully tucked away in corners of her mind suddenly reappeared: Matthew's shaving cut the night of the reception, the conversation in which he used the word "healer." Unable to grasp what had just happened, she forced them back into their hiding places. She began to cry, "Can't somebody else treat the winos and junkies?"

"These are my patients," he said. "You can't condemn them all for the actions of one pathetic addict."

"Then at least get a second job so we can move out of here."

"I'm already working twelve hours a day. It won't happen again," he said. "There'll be a deadbolt on the downstairs door by tomorrow evening and I'll walk you to and from the car."

The next morning, Matthew had barely begun to examine a young woman with mild asthma when a series of loud blasts reverberated around him. Totally rattled by the noise, he calmed his patient then left the room to find Hector and Carmen in the hallway. "There's been a shooting," Carmen said. "Three people are involved."

"Where?" Matthew asked.

"Outside our door," Hector answered. "Let's move." They ran through the waiting room and pushed their way into the crowd that had already formed.

Twenty feet from the clinic, three bodies lay on the sidewalk, their pooled blood glistening in the late morning sunshine. "Let us through, please," Hector and Matthew said in unison.

"I'll check her," Carmen said, dropping to the side of a twenty-something Hispanic woman floating in her own plasma. Two infants clung to her, screaming.

Matthew kneeled to examine a young black man, poorly dressed but clean. Hector took the third, another black man in his mid-twenties with russet-dyed dreadlocks. His white silk shirt was stained bright red.

"This one's gone," Matthew said. "Half of his head is missing. Who needs help?"

"Dr. Matthew, over here," Carmen yelled. Two women had taken the children off to the side. Carmen prepared an IV while Matthew opened the woman's floral print cotton dress to show three gaping bullet wounds. The victim's breathing came in shallow gasps. Matthew turned toward Hector, "This woman's in trouble. What have you got?"

"A flesh wound, no penetration. Lots of blood but it doesn't need sutures."

"Let's switch," Matthew said. "You have more experience with serious trauma."

They traded positions. Carmen started an IV in the woman's arm.

"She needs blood," Hector grunted. "Can you get a second IV started, Carmen?" Hector worked frantically to stop the bleeding while Carmen searched for a second vein. Matthew cleaned and bandaged the wound in his patient's shoulder and joined them, asking what he could do to help. "Squeeze the IV bag," Hector said. "We need to get the fluid in fast. We're losing her."

Two ambulances and three police cruisers arrived simultaneously, just in time for the young mother's heart to stop, her life draining through her shattered left ventricle, her blood trickling down the cracks in the sidewalk. Matthew wanted to start CPR but Hector told him she had lost too much blood and was gone. Matthew stared at her lovely young face, strangely peaceful in contrast to the flurry of activity around her still warm body. By now, Peter had joined them. He put his hand on Matthew's shoulder. "You tried hard. All of you." He bent down to look at her. "Even death has a certain beauty," he said.

While the ambulance crews removed the victims, detectives interviewed Hector, Matthew, and Carmen, as well as witnesses to the shooting. "I think we've told you everything we know," Hector said, asking the police if they could return to work.

One of the detectives said they might be needed for further questions. The paramedics thanked them.

A policeman who had been questioning the wounded man with dreadlocks pointed to Matthew. "Hey, doc, what did you do to Jackson?"

"You know him?" Matthew asked.

"Your patient, Doctor, is the number two drug dealer in the neighborhood. He says that he was shot but you healed him. He's freaking out."

"Let him," Peter said. "He probably got bloodied when the young man's head exploded."

"Jackson insists that a bullet creased his shoulder. He says the Doc did something—hot hands was how he put it."

"Who are you gonna believe?" Hector interrupted, aware of the consequences for Matthew if the truth appeared in a police report. "A drug dealer or a doctor?"

"Tell him it's a sign from God to stop his evil ways," Peter said. "Anything else, officer?"

"I guess not. Thanks."

"Who were the others?" Matthew asked in a shaky voice.

The policeman shook his head, disgusted. "Innocent bystanders. We assume it was an attempted hit on Jackson. The woman was a young widow. The children are hers. The boy worked next door at the bodega. He was a high school student; his boss says he was a pretty decent kid who had gone outside for a smoke."

While they were talking, a Channel Seven van pulled up to the curb. A man stepped from the van, straightening his tie and jacket, fixing his long dark hair in the driver's side view mirror. The minicam crew readied themselves, checking their electrical connections and sound levels. As the man turned from the mirror and began to speak into the camera, Matthew recognized him as Eric Espinoza, an investigative reporter. Espinoza did a voice-over to a shot of the bloodstained sidewalk and then interviewed local residents. Jackson managed to get the reporter's attention.

"It was a miracle," Jackson shouted to the television crew. "That doctor over there," he said, pointing in Matthew's direction, "He touched me. He healed me."

Hector put his arm around Matthew and hustled him toward the clinic. Peter stopped them just short of the front door. "I think that would be a mistake," he said quietly. "If you bolt, that reporter's going to be on you like mold on yesterday's bread."

"Maybe it's time to let the public in on Matthew's secret," a voice from behind them said. Todd Lawrence looked so composed it was hard to believe he had ever seen his own blood, much less anyone else's.

"Who are you?" Matthew asked.

"Todd Lawrence. This could be a wonderful opportunity for you. And for the world."

"This is none of your business," Matthew said.

Eric and the minicam headed in their direction. "You have to say something, Matthew," Hector said.

"We'll cover for you," Peter said.

"I can do this by myself," Matthew said.

Espinoza stuck the microphone in Matthew's face. "Doctor, do you have any comment about Mr. Jackson's statement that you healed him with a miracle?"

Matthew smiled, the even-tempered public man. "The real miracle here is that more people weren't hurt."

"But," Eric pressed, "Mr. Jackson is adamant that something happened."

"Something did happen," Matthew said. "Two innocent victims died because of his drug dealing."

"Why did you bandage him if he wasn't shot?"

"Anybody looking for attention can pick up a bloody bandage," Matthew said, looking directly into the camera's lens.

"Take a walk with me, Dr. Harrison," Todd said during a short break in the war room a few hours later.

"I have patients to see," Matthew said. "What do *you* want from me?"

"Come on. Let's get some fresh air."

The two of them walked to a small park a block away, a tiny oasis of concrete benches set among grass and trees. Hector said that it had been donated by a neighborhood business as a goodwill gesture when they departed for the suburbs, taking two hundred jobs with them.

Matthew was sullen.

"Perhaps you could use your healing power to benefit others and help yourself at the same time," Todd said.

"I should have helped that mother," Matthew said, "instead of the drug dealer."

"That was pure chance," Todd said. "Bad luck. You have a gift from God. It could be different if you shared it instead of hiding it from the world."

"I don't want my gift to be turned into a circus act."

"You don't know what's possible until you try," Todd said, picking up a discarded newspaper from a bench and sitting down. "There's something I'd like you to do."

"That depends," Matthew said.

"There are workshops–some in my center–led by other doctors like you. I'd like to invite you to attend some of them. You might discover that you want to lead your own."

Matthew laughed. "I work from eight until midnight and hardly have time to read the sports pages."

"At the risk of making you angry, Dr. Harrison, that's another way of hiding," Todd said.

Matthew rose abruptly. "Thanks for the offer."

"I'm only telling you the truth as I see it," Todd continued. "The only way you'll learn about your gift is to meet and talk to others like yourself."

"I'll consider it," Matthew said.

Just before quitting time that evening, Hector handed Matthew an envelope. "What's this?" Matthew asked.

"Take it. I can finally pay you something." Inside the plain white envelope was six hundred dollars cash. "Word about you is spreading. We've gotten some paying patients. I got a big surprise yesterday."

"How big?"

"A woman claims you performed a miracle for her. She offered a miracle in return. I can't say more about it yet."

Matthew thought this was the answer to his prayers. He couldn't wait to share this news with Eileen. If the money continued at this rate, they would be able to afford an apartment in a decent neighborhood. He excused himself and ran upstairs.

The envelope was on his pillow. The note was short: I'm sorry but I need some space. Please don't call or follow me. I'll be in touch when I'm ready. I still love you. E.

25

"I'm very proud of you," Kevin's mother said while they were having breakfast.

"Thanks, Mom. Why?"

"I received the nicest phone call the other day from Dr. Buckman."

Kevin's scrambled eggs suddenly tasted like paste. "Buckman?"

"Yes, dear. He was very sweet. He called to tell me what a wonderful job you were doing as chief resident. He said that it's his custom to call the parents of his senior residents and let them know how well their children are doing."

"*That's* news. Did he say anything else?"

"Well he did, but…"

"But what?" Kevin said.

"I don't want you to be upset with him."

"Mother, *please. What did he say to you?*"

"Don't raise your voice, Kevin. Dr. Buckman told me about the position he found for you for next year. He said how pleased the doctors in Highland Park were with your work and how happy he was to have placed you in a successful practice. He felt terrible that he had spoiled your surprise by telling me first."

Kevin pushed his plate away. "The job's not as secure as Buckman told you."

"Really, dear? He seemed so positive."

Hector and Kevin sat in Susan's dining room after a simple dinner of salad with seared tuna, French bread, and a good Merlot. Soft piano music drifted through the apartment from a radio somewhere in another room. Susan pulled no punches in sharing her concerns about Matthew.

"If your wife left you, would either of you make a few phone calls and leave it at that?" she asked.

"I understand what you're saying," Hector said. "If it was my Rita, I would break down her door and carry her home. But it's more than just Eileen. Considering what he's been through, I feel he's doing fine."

"He's beginning to open up," Kevin said. "Todd Lawrence has convinced him to attend a seminar at his center, and I'm going to call Eileen and see if she'll talk to me."

"What do either of you know about Todd?" Susan asked.

"I think he's okay," Kevin said, his gut contracting with the lie. "Smooth, but harmless,"

"He's a salesman peddling his next workshop," Hector said. "All image and very little substance."

Susan handed each of them a portion of chocolate mousse in a small blue bowl.

"Despite what I think of him, Todd's made a donation to the clinic," Hector said.

"Why would he do that?" Susan asked. "When did he first show up? Don't you think he wants something? And I don't understand *your* conversion, Kevin, Todd's the kind of alternative therapist you've always considered a fraud."

"Anyone can change their opinion," Kevin said, his eyes glued to the table. The last thing he wanted was Susan's probing honesty.

Hector smiled broadly. "Do you want to hear the good news?"

"Sure, why not?" Susan said.

Hector made them promise not to reveal what he was about to tell them. He said that one of Matthew's patients had come to him and pledged some securities to the clinic. "Nothing's final," Hector said, "but it represents a hefty down payment on the building. I wanted her to give the money to Matthew but she refused."

Susan smiled. "She can't be one of your regulars."

"You can't keep Matthew a secret. Rich people have diseases too," said Hector.

"What does Matthew think of the gift?" she asked.

"I hinted at it, but haven't told him the details," Hector said.

"Why not?" Her eyes fixed his.

"You and I understand each other when it comes to non-traditional medicine," Hector said.

"We've attended seminars together on cutting edge and 'new-age' medicine," Susan said.

"A few of these healers are really gifted," Hector said. "It's too easy to get trapped in an ego game. Especially someone genuine like Matthew who's been through as much personal anguish as he has."

Susan frowned. "You're going to take it upon yourself to keep this wonderful news from Matthew just so he doesn't get a swelled head? What does that say about *your* ego?"

"Hear me out, Susan," Hector pleaded. "Matthew could be an important link between traditional and non-traditional medicine, a genuine healer accepted by mainstream medicine. I want to protect him, to give him a chance to mature before people like Todd have a chance to use him. No matter how pure one's motives are, fame and money are seductive, especially to somebody who's emotionally vulnerable."

"I hope you're right," Susan said. "I see the healer, but also the hurting insecure kid behind the mask–the one who believes that God screwed him."

"I'm not naive," Hector said softly.

"I never thought you were," Susan said.

The conversation reached an uncomfortable lull. Kevin looked at his watch. "I have to go, Susan. The dinner was wonderful."

"The same goes for me," Hector said. "I appreciate your concern."

Susan walked them to the door. "You two are Matthew's best friends. Please don't let him down."

26

"Eileen, how are you?" Kevin asked, picking up the phone at midnight and recognizing her voice.

"I'm fine," she said, sounding disturbed. "I need a favor."

"Of course."

"It's about my father," she said. "He has cancer." Eileen explained that she was uncomfortable with the quality of care her father was receiving in Peoria. "I can't ask Matthew for help."

"I understand," Kevin said and asked her a few questions regarding her father's illness and treatment. Because she was upset and not a reliable source of accurate clinical information, Kevin offered to call her father's physician and speak with him.

He could feel her relief. "That would mean so much to me and my mother. You're a sweetheart, and thank you for not probing me about Matthew."

He didn't have to probe. He knew that Matthew was devastated when Eileen left, calling her parent's home three or four times a day. After a week of her refusing to speak with him, Matthew decided to give her the space she had requested. Work became the balm for his pain, and now, Kevin thought, heading for sleep, her father's terrible illness might be the key to their reconciliation.

Matthew, looking exhausted, dragged himself into the war room at seven a.m. The smell of an early morning rain wafted through the open windows.

"Morning, Matthew," Peter said, dumping a plate of sliced carrots into one of the crockpots.

"Where's Hector?" Matthew asked.

"In an exam room," Kevin said. "We need to talk."

Hector entered the room and greeted them.

"I need an evening off," Matthew said.

"Of course," Hector replied. "What's up?"

"I'm going to church. With Todd."

Peter's eyebrows raised. "Church?"

"Todd wants me to meet other people with powers like mine."

Hector sat on one of the chairs. "I'm not sure I trust him."

"Personally," Matthew said, "I think he's a snake. But he's said that he can connect me with other healers." Matthew explained that Todd had told him about Camille Drake, a woman purported to be a healer who was to lead a service at a church in Chicago. "Todd says she's genuine. The local diocese endorses her."

"Who can argue with the house of God?" Peter asked with mocking sincerity.

"I'm going to her service," Matthew said. "Todd's going to introduce us. Would any of you like to come with me?"

"When is it?" Hector asked.

"Tomorrow night." Hector and Peter refused; the clinic could not spare everyone at the same time. Normally, Kevin would not be caught dead at a healing service, even one sanctioned by the Church. But needing fresh material to feed Buckman, he told Matthew that he would be delighted to go with him.

"I hope you're right about Todd," Peter said. "He seems as authentic as an Orthodox Rabbi dancing at his only son's church wedding."

Kevin asked Matthew if he could speak with him alone. Hector and Peter excused themselves. "Eileen called me."

Matthew's face lit up. "Is she okay?"

"She is, but her father has end-stage lung cancer. I spoke with his doctor this morning."

"Jesus Christ, Kevin, what do I do? She's not answering *my* calls and she phones *you* for help."

"Do you want her back, Matthew?"

"Of course."

"Then go see her father. Heal him."

"Look what happened when I fixed the bruise on her arm. She freaked."

"You don't know for sure that's the reason she left."

Matthew grimaced. "It didn't help. But no matter how angry or scared I am that I might lose her forever, her father didn't do anything to me. I'll go Sunday."

Later that day, after a department meeting at the Research, Buckman was delighted when Kevin told him that Matthew was going to see Camille Drake. "That's wonderful news. I told you that Todd Lawrence would connect Harrison to other imposters. Sooner or later Harrison will hurt someone and you'll be there to witness it. By the way, Kevin, give my regards to your Mother."

Todd picked them up in his ancient Mercedes for the trip to Bensenville, a suburb a few miles west of O'Hare. "You two are in for a treat," he said. Kevin sat in the back seat and enjoyed the view along the Eisenhower expressway. He thought about Susan's concerns and concluded that if the events of Matthew's life had happened to *him*, he would not be on his way to church, but to a courtroom, and Buckman would be suffocating under the mountain of lawsuits filed by his attorneys *and* the ACLU.

"I'm looking forward to this," Matthew said.

"Have you given any thought to next year?" Kevin asked, disturbed by Matthew equating himself as a physician to someone Kevin considered, sight unseen, to be a quack. If she were real, Kevin thought to himself, she would be at Holy Name Cathedral or the Vatican, not St. Bumble of the Briarpatch.

"You mean another residency?" Matthew asked, his arm slung over the leather seatback. "I've written letters and made calls, mostly to university hospitals. They want to know why I left the Research. When I say 'personal problems,' they aren't thrilled."

"Have you considered going directly into general practice?" Todd asked. "With your healing gift, you might not need a formal residency." He sounded, as always, like the genial late-night news anchor he could have been. Kevin had to admire his unflappability, his perfectly set social thermostat.

"Forget it, Todd," Matthew said. "I don't mind working with Hector for as long it takes to put my life in order. If I stay in Chicago, I'll continue to volunteer for his clinic, but I want to finish my training in a university program where they accept me for who I am."

"I think you're on the right track," Kevin said. "I don't give a shit what Buckman did to you. You can get past it, start over and become more than a simple G.P. hacking out a living from snotty nosed kids and old ladies with vague arthritic pains. You were born to be a Michigan Avenue internist–like me. You're a BMW, not a Camry."

"I don't need a Gold Coast practice, Kevin. All I want is Eileen and patients who need my help."

"Whatever your heart tells you to do is the way," Todd said, looking smoothly ahead into the parting traffic. "But you should always keep yourself open to the unexpected. *I* do."

They arrived at St. James, a huge crumbling yellow brick Catholic Church in Bensenville, one of Chicago's working class western suburbs. The parking lot was full but Todd drove into an empty space reserved for clergy. "My center is helping to sponsor this event," he said.

The large crowd inside the parish hall reflected the number of cars outside. The buzzing of the hopeful blended with the piercing scrunch of wheelchair tires on the stone floor. Colorful banners with doves and crosses hung on the walls. The three of them sat near the middle of the room, adrift in a sea of people of mixed economic classes and nationalities. Next to Kevin sat a family of four–badly in need of soap and water–with a child in leg braces. Next to them, a young black couple held a baby with hydrocephalus, its head too large for its tiny body. A white couple who appeared to patronize the same clothing stores as Todd sat silently in front of them, the woman wiping tears behind Porsche sunglasses. Behind them, a middle-aged woman spoke loudly and slowly in Spanish to a tiny old woman dressed in black.

"It's an upscale Hector's," Matthew said, feeling unsettled. He had seen worse cases at the Research, poorer people at Hector's. But nowhere had he ever experienced such a deluge of naked hope, such a vast collection of people willing to bypass science for God's lottery, each one believing that he would be heaven's choice to leave his wheelchair in the dumpster and thumb his nose at the medical establishment.

"Illness has no respect for financial status," Todd said. He was right, Kevin thought. He had seen the polar opposites–Hector's barrio clinic and the practice in Highland Park. Now he was seeing the mid-point between the two extremes. It rankled him to relate himself to these masses; to know that no matter where you fall on the scale, no matter what your bank balances are or the labels in your clothing, all of us–physician gods included–share fears of pain and illness and a terror of death. Kevin's father had faced death bravely, accepting his lot with calm resolve from the moment of his diagnosis until he slipped away. He was the one, Kevin remembered with a painful shudder, who had taught him about honor and honesty–the shamed parent who stood next to his eight year old son in the manager's office in Walgreen's as he returned the comic book he had slipped under his shirt, the man who gave him extra household chores each time a dime or quarter was missing from the top of his dresser.

But this wasn't the place to dwell on his father's probity or to summon up his possible opinions of his adult son. Kevin swept him from his mind and focused on the present moment. It was no wonder, he thought, that so many people crowded into this room. These were the ones for whom medicine no longer held any hope, the nameless patients who reminded doctors of their own mortality, the ones doctors kept at an emotional distance because it was easier for them not to face their own vulnerability.

The man next to Matthew, a bricklayer from Rockford, was quadriplegic–an accident at work. He said his name was Ralph Hurden. "You drove an hour for this?" Matthew asked.

"I've heard about Camille from people in my church," Ralph said. "They told me that she performs miracles."

"What does your priest say?" Matthew asked.

"He didn't try to stop me from attending, just warned me not to expect too much."

"Good advice," Kevin muttered.

In the aisles were people on gurneys, some appearing close to their last breath. "How many other physicians, besides us, do you think are in the audience?" Matthew asked.

"Probably none," Kevin said, almost wishing that a medical emergency would happen and that he could come to someone's aid in the old-fashioned, black bag and prescription medical way.

Matthew was jolted to attention by a trumpet fanfare as a man in a tan suit, introducing himself as Jonathan Langley, one of Drake's assistants, began an oration. Between comments about Camille's special relationship to God, Langley loudly exclaimed, "Praise the Lord–Praise Jesus." The audience echoed Langley each time. Matthew squirmed; Kevin joined in, not at all serious.

"Are you okay, Matthew?" Todd asked.

"This isn't what I expected," he said.

"I'm not too tickled with the holy-roller stuff, myself," Kevin whispered.

"I'm not sure I belong here," Matthew said, as the people around them jumped to their feet, loudly shouting their adoration for Camille as if she were a movie star. "Maybe I should call a cab."

"This is the warm-up," Todd said with a sidelong smile. "It's for the rubes. Wait a while."

Rubes? Matthew thought. He and Kevin felt more uncomfortable with each passing "Hosanna" and "Praise Jesus," which had by now swelled into a chant. It seemed that a lot of people had been here with Camille before; the chants seemed practiced. Some jumped in even before Langley reached the studied pauses in his discourse.

Then came the star of the show. Camille Drake, a short, plump woman with a seventies bouffant hairstyle, swept onto the stage in a white gown. She looked more like a woman who chased blue light specials at K-Mart than a celebrated healer. But the air crackled with electricity as the crowd, primed by the warm-up man, roared for ten minutes. Camille accepted the accolade with a smile as wide as the Chicago River.

Act two was a personal replay of Camille's story. With her passionate praise for God and Jesus, Camille went on for twenty minutes about how she had heard the word, how it told her to go into the world and heal. "She looks like a member of the woman's Altar Guild who's seen Jesus in a tortilla," Kevin whispered to Matthew, who laughed.

Next, Camille herself called for the parade of supplicants and groupies, who passed in front of her. "Come to me, those of you who suffer, you lambs who thirst for Jesus." She spoke personally with a number of them, knowing some by name, her words general, her demeanor well rehearsed. She placed her hands on their heads, asking them to "Receive the Lord and be healed." Kevin compared her to Matthew. Matthew was a real person; Camille was the *Agnus Dei* as interpreted by the Marx Brothers. His gut told him that the only genuine article in the room was sitting at his left.

Because the crowd was standing, rocking on its heels, Kevin and Matthew had difficulty seeing the stage. They listened as a man in leg braces and crutches was carried to the front of the room by Drake's assistants. A small army of young, well-dressed youths, Camille's people judging by their well-organized behavior, positioned themselves in the aisles, each with a woven wicker collection basket. The murmuring energy had by now increased to a fever pitch. "Throw off your braces and walk to God," Camille told the man. The man cried, shouting that he was ready. Matthew and Kevin stepped onto the seats of their chairs, just as Camille's assistants removed the man's braces. Three young men helped him to stand.

"Not him!" Matthew growled.

"Excuse me?" Todd asked.

"I know that guy," Matthew said. "His name is Don Severn. There's nothing wrong with his legs. He steals drugs from hospitals." Matthew continued, his voice hostile. "Severn's an actor, Todd, a no-good crook."

"I would have used a less kind word," Kevin said, disgusted.

"I had no idea. That's terrible," Todd said, clicking his tongue.

"Let's split, Kevin. I've had enough of this ersatz Elmer Gantry," Matthew said.

Apparently so had Ralph, their fellow pilgrim from Rockford, who had overheard their comments. His face was florid, his eyes wet with tears of betrayal. "Would you guys mind helping me out of here? This is nothing but a show."

Matthew got down from his chair. "Sure."

"If you'll get me back to the vestibule, I have an attendant waiting for me. He'd rather smoke a cigarette than hear this bullshit. You have to tighten the belt on my wheelchair first."

Matthew pulled on the strap. Ralph's face contorted in pain. His body jerked in an involuntary spasm. "What are you doing?" he asked. "It feels like my insides are on fire."

"You'll be okay if you just relax," Matthew said, calmly.

"I *felt*. I *moved*. It was like a spark," Ralph said. "I'm not supposed to feel anything," he said, his voice all awe.

"I know," Matthew said.

While Matthew and Kevin stood rooted to the ground, the crowd around them throbbed in their Camille-delusion and Ralph's limbs jerked in uncoordinated spasms. Finally the tremors diminished. Matthew wiped Ralph's face. "Are you okay?" he asked him.

From behind them, a man noisily pushed his way through the crowd until he stood next to them. "Dr. Harrison, we meet again."

"Where did you come from?" Matthew asked, trying to put his body between the reporter and Ralph. Kevin picked up on Matthew's behavior and helped shield Ralph, despite knowing that his spymaster, Dr. Buckman, would want him to seek out the publicity.

"I'm here unofficially," said Eric Espinoza, looking at Todd for a lead but getting none. "I'm a friend of Todd's. He tried to get the station to cover Camille, but the producers think she's old news." Matthew didn't like Espinoza's sudden appearance, his eager rush through the crowd, or the look of anticipation on his face. He had been primed for this possibility. "Who's that behind you?" Eric asked.

"A man who's had a seizure." Matthew said. "He needs some room."

"I'm not an epileptic," Ralph said loudly enough to be heard above the crowd. "I'm also not a fool."

Matthew turned. "I didn't mean to suggest anything," he said to Ralph whose spasms continued, diminished but evident.

"I told you," Ralph said, "I felt something when you touched me." He began to slowly move his hand. "Jesus Christ…"

Kevin, feeling a hasty departure was in their best interest, decided Ralph was stable enough for him to hail one of Camille's ushers to take him to the vestibule. "We're leaving now, Todd," he said, leading the three of them through the crowd and out to Todd's car.

"I know Eric pretty well," Todd said as he drove. "I can handle him."

27

Kevin lay on his bed, his hands behind his head, his body damp as though he had broken a fever. The clock on his nightstand read 4:30. His eyes had traced what seemed like a million circular motions of the ceiling fan since he'd attempted to make love to Pam Benton, a young nurse he'd picked up at The Tourniquet. The bar, a run-down tavern near the medical center, was a favorite hangout of residents and nurses looking to get a great cheeseburger and get laid in the same evening. He had not been to the bar in over a year, absorbed in his duties as Chief Resident, but he went there after leaving Matthew and Todd, the night of Camille's service.

Medicated by Dr. Samuel Adams, he stumbled through what must have been the worst pick-up line in history. "This place is a shithole. Would you like to come home with me?" She just nodded and smiled slightly; and he knew they were part of the conspiracy of the lonely. She held her warm body next to his in the night air, walking the five blocks to his apartment.

"I've seen you around the hospital," she said. He noticed how much her figure and hair color reminded him of Eileen.

"I can't say the same in return. What floor do you work?"

"Post-op."

"I don't get there very often."

"I know."

They bypassed the usual social formalities and small talk, passed on wine, and headed directly to the bedroom where they tore off their clothes and abandoned themselves to the sheets. She was pliable and warm-blooded and exactly the medication he needed at the moment; she had even brought her own six-pack of condoms. She was also surprisingly understanding.

"This has never happened to me before," Kevin said, rolling off her body.

"I'm certainly *very* happy, Kevin. Don't worry about it."

"It must be the beer," he said, knowing that he had only had three and that was hours ago, more than enough time for the alcohol to have lost its effect on his sexual ability.

"Honey, I wish you could come, but that's your business. You certainly lasted long enough to please any woman. I just hope you had fun. Did you?" She kissed him hard on the lips, turned on her side, curled her body next to his and fell asleep, the easy tide of her breath a sharp contrast to his emotional squalls.

He called forth his inner doctor, telling the patient in him that sooner or later the same thing happens to all guys. It's worse for those who can't even get hard, like the article he once read about porn stars who hold up production for hours "waiting for wood." It's the stress of the job, he told himself, or a temporary hormone imbalance. But he knew his internal doctor was lying to him. He couldn't even release his own desire. He slipped out of bed and walked naked into the living room, over to the open window where he stared at the quarter moon in the cloudless sky.

"Fuck," he yelled at the top of his lungs into the darkness, pounding the wall repeatedly with the side of his clenched fist. "Fuck it all."

Kevin and Matthew borrowed Hector's van Sunday morning for the three-hour trip to Peoria.

"Do you think she'll be there?" Matthew asked.

"What matters is that she'll know *you* were there."

Eileen's childhood home was similar in general layout to Kevin's but light-years lower on the economic ladder. The furniture was as old as Rosie Summerfield's great-grandmother–shabby, not antique–the tattered edges of the couch and chairs covered with stained antimacassars. Plain pine shelves held a lifetime of tacky knickknacks–salt and pepper shakers, small china plates rimmed in gold leaf, and enameled silver-plate spoons purchased at truck stops from here to Nowhere, Nevada. Kevin grasped Eileen's obsession with her Limoges tea service–Martha Stewart would have had apoplexy in this place.

Eileen's mother, Phyllis, graciously offered them tea and home-baked cookies, responding with one-word answers to their awkward attempt at small talk as they sat at her drab kitchen table. Unlike the china used by her daughter, Eileen's mother's cups were the kind given as sales premiums in supermarkets, chipped and stained with years of use. She seemed distant and uncomfortable. Kevin thought it strange that she made no reference to Matthew and Eileen's problems. Perhaps she had been forewarned by Eileen to avoid the subject, was too embarrassed about the situation, or too preoccupied by her husband's illness.

Matthew broached the subject. "Where's Eileen?"

"Shopping," Phyllis said, her eyes avoiding his.

"Oh," Matthew said, disappointed. "I'd hoped she'd be here."

Eileen's mother made no reply.

Eileen's father, Bill, was a pale skeleton of a man. The strength behind his voice belied his physical appearance. "Thank you for coming,

Matthew." He pulled himself up to a sitting position in the bed. Matthew introduced Kevin.

"I'm sorry you're sick," Matthew said, taking his hand. Kevin watched in hopeful anticipation.

"How do you feel?" Matthew asked, his mouth set firm, small beads of sweat appearing on his forehead; he appeared to be straining, intentionally trying to make something happen. Kevin was rooting for him, hoping his efforts in bringing Matthew here today would be a partial atonement.

"Does my hand feel hot?" Matthew asked.

"No. Is something wrong?"

Matthew gently released his father-in-law's hand, a look of defeat on his face. "I hoped my visit would make you feel better."

"I do, knowing you cared enough to drive all the way from Chicago—especially with the problems between you and Eileen."

Bill looked tired. The visit had drained his energy. Kevin's father had looked the same as he neared the end of his life. Kevin choked back a flood of emotions, silently wishing for a way to jumpstart Matthew's hands.

"Give her time," Bill said.

28

The clinic had become swollen with patients as word of Matthew's ability spread throughout the city. He became inundated with work and refused no one his attention or time–except himself. It was as if critical mass for miracles had been reached and Matthew had no graphite rods to slow the reaction.

Matthew continued to pursue his search for enlightenment. He asked Susan and Todd to help him choose books and select seminars that might be helpful. But Matthew had little time to read or attend any of the programs suggested by his new brain trust.

"This is the one program you *must* attend," Todd said a few weeks after the ecclesiastical disaster at St. James. He had invited Matthew and Kevin to dinner at a local Italian restaurant. Matthew hadn't wanted to go, but Kevin convinced him that if they had to eat anyway, they should do it with Todd's credit card.

"Who is it?" Matthew asked, skeptically.

"Fanny Colwell."

"I know about her," Kevin said. "She's famous. And a doctor too."

Matthew was silent. Kevin noticed how much he had aged, thinking that every time Matthew cured someone he lost a small part of himself. Sometimes he thought he did too. "How's the search for a new residency going?" Kevin asked, uncomfortable with his own introspection. "You haven't said much about it lately."

Matthew frowned. "Buckman wrote an innocuous referral letter for my file, but I swear that he's calling the programs I'm applying to and telling them about me."

Kevin held his breath. "Do you want me to talk to him?' he asked.

"No," Matthew said. "He gave me his word. He knows that you're here. The less he connects the two of us, the better for you."

"What about Fanny?" Todd asked. "The program will be at my center. I promise you won't have any problems there."

"Is Eric coming?" Matthew asked, warily, "or Oprah Winfrey?"

Todd smiled. "If he tries to enroll, I'll personally bar the door."

"I think you should go," Kevin said. "Fanny's not my cup of tea, but from what I understand, she's no Camille either. Susan's said some nice things about her."

"Will you go too?" Matthew asked.

Fanny Colwell's program was Matthew's baptism into the world of weekend spiritual workshops. A former obstetrician, Fanny had recreated herself as an internationally recognized evangelist of new-age healing. Hector, warning Matthew that his expectations might not be met, told him to take the weekend off. Kevin made the arrangements, including a dispensation from his mother for his Sunday visit. Saturday morning, after riding two buses and a noisy "El," they arrived at Todd's center.

Located in Lincoln Park, home to Chicago's yuppie community, The Healing Place occupied two floors of a rehabbed building on north Clark Street. What Todd claimed to be a simple facility was actually a beautifully appointed clinic for alternative medical practitioners. The directory listed names and modalities of standard acupuncturists and homeopaths as well as a number of esoteric therapies with eastern names. On the second floor were small group therapy rooms and a large space for workshops. Todd was waiting for them at the registration desk with complimentary tickets. He watched as Kevin studied the lobby directory. "Most of them are part-time," Todd said.

"I don't see Matthew's name here yet," Kevin said.

Todd smiled. "I'm not recruiting Matthew. Ask him if you don't believe me."

"Of course not," Kevin said. He didn't believe him any more than he believed Eric Espinoza happened to charge through the church by chance and get to them just as Ralph Hurden was beginning his series of muscle spasms. Buckman's plan was becoming clearer.

"This is an interesting place," Matthew said. "Do you own the building?"

"My father does," Todd said–which provoked in Matthew more questions than answers. "But enough of that. It's time to start. Let me take you upstairs."

A hundred and fifty people attended the workshop. Unlike the horde at St. James, these were mostly standard suburban-looking people, a difference Matthew understood as he leaned over one man's shoulder while he wrote a check at the registration table–Fanny's crowd had to fork over two hundred dollars each to attend.

"I wonder what cut Todd gets," Kevin asked.

Three people were in wheelchairs–normal demographics for the size of the crowd, Matthew decided, comparing the smaller size of Fanny's audience to Camille's. Two additional physicians were present, the four of them embarrassingly forced to stand and receive enthusiastic applause for their courage in "coming out of the spiritual closet" when Fanny, a svelte, gray-haired woman wearing an expensive suit, asked in a thick Brooklyn accent if there was "a doctor in the house."

The first morning passed slowly. Matthew sat quietly as each participant in turn gave their name and shared the story of their illness, frequently turning to one of the four physicians as they lambasted standard medicine, often with Fanny's support. Kevin felt embarrassed when it was his turn to speak, having little to contribute besides his name. Matthew, like Kevin, gave only his name and profession.

Many of those attending claimed to have conquered cancer, multiple sclerosis, and AIDS using various non-traditional methods both Kevin and Matthew considered to be outright nonsense such as olive oil baths, drinking one's own urine, and coffee ground enemas—a return to medicine's dark ages when barber surgeons opened veins and studied patients' bowel movements for a proper diagnosis. While Matthew appeared to listen intently, Kevin tuned out.

Matthew and Kevin ate lunch with the other doctors. They were both family practitioners from small towns in central Illinois and said that so far, they were enjoying the program. Fanny spoke for the entire afternoon, her presentation filled with humor and simple wisdom Kevin and Matthew could appreciate. Some of what she said about positive attitude influencing the course of a patient's illness made sense to them. Other topics, like "taking charge of our own illnesses" offended Kevin, reducing his role as a physician to that of a technician. But clearly Fanny was not in the same league as Camille. Unlike Camille, the Brooklyn-born purveyor of body-mind healing was a doctor who had one foot firmly planted in the world of medicine. Her other foot, Kevin decided after checking out the display of books and tapes for sale, was firmly entrenched in the First National Bank.

Sunday was devoted to guided imagery, a process Fanny described as a healing meditation. Participants were required to shut their eyes while soft new-age music was piped into the room. Fanny read a script of an imaginary journey to the seashore that was to lead the participants into their spiritual hearts. "I have some good news for those of you here today who believe they've never done anything right in their lives," Fanny said, smiling. Kevin looked at Matthew and grinned. "You can't do a guided image the wrong way. Your experience will be valid no matter what happens."

Not wishing to venture inside himself–he was all too familiar with the demons residing in his inner darkness–Kevin did not play her game, but instead kept his eyes open in the dimly lit room watching Matthew and the other sheep float on Fanny's soothing words. After fifteen minutes, the session concluded with each participant writing a poem generated from his or her experience. Kevin scrawled as much as he could recollect of one of his old poems on the paper provided to him.

A few aggressive pilgrims were selected to read their poems aloud. Fanny, doing her best Sigmund Freud meets Dear Abby, analyzed the odes, interpreting the deep meanings within their words and images. One young lady burst into tears after reading aloud her two paragraphs. "I'm terrified by what I've written," she said, tearfully. "My words describe my own death."

"There are many types of deaths," Fanny said, handing her a tissue. "When we shed one of our negative beliefs, we often feel like part of us is dying."

Matthew raised his hand. Kevin would have cut his off before reading his work to a roomful of strangers.

Fanny called on Matthew, who raised his paper to eye level and read aloud. Kevin sat stunned at the beauty of Matthew's poetry:

I have been to Iowa and walked out in the corn where Costner could not go.
And listened to my Father asking me to play a game of catch.
Among the rows I once again remembered the short scene from *Last Temptation*
Where the sleeping Judas and his brother Christ woke up embracing in each other's arms.
And I'm not sure now if Iscariot got the lesser of the God-sent jobs.

But I would rather be the one who hung upon the cross
Instead of him that got the task to set it up–
A role as God-sent as the other had. Still no one understands.
And in that field my Father whispered softly all He's ever said to me:
"Let go. Embrace your name and dance with me.
Feel who you are but can't completely know."

Without a word, Fanny walked over to Matthew and hugged him, tears in her eyes. "You have the soul of a healer," she said. Kevin hid his eyes under the visor of his outstretched palm.

Matthew sat for the remainder of the afternoon listening with the ears of the converted to the poetry of others and, during the breaks, accepting the accolades of other participants who praised his poem, asking him where he practiced and if he was currently accepting new patients. Kevin watched the interactions carefully, silently praying that nobody would take Matthew's hand and seize, retch, or in any other way cast out their demons and evil humors. But Matthew kept his hands in his pockets, carefully avoiding even the slightest physical contact. At the conclusion of the afternoon, he picked up a flyer with a calendar of Fanny's future engagements.

Returning to the clinic, Matthew overflowed with praise for his new idol. Hector was unimpressed. "Did she give you the answers you wanted, Matthew?"

"No. But she was great. I want to see her again, to learn guided imagery so I can use it with my own patients."

"You can buy her books," Kevin said. "It's cheaper. Unless Todd has a connection for free tickets to her next show." Matthew caught Kevin's cynicism.

Hector sighed. "My grandfather had a saying: Don't jump off the cliff until you're sure there's a lake at the bottom. You're on a workshop high. Be careful you don't crash too hard. You will, you know."

"You and Susan convinced me to learn from these people," Matthew said. "Now you trash them."

"I'm not putting them down, Matthew. I understand what you're feeling. I've been through it myself. I just don't want you to get hooked by Fanny–or anyone else. You don't need her stories or her techniques. Use your own."

"I'm going to Fanny's workshop next weekend in Milwaukee. Do you want to go?" Matthew asked.

Hector declined, but Kevin agreed to accompany him if Susan drove. He called her and she consented to play chauffeur. Todd came through with complimentary tickets, as Kevin somehow knew he would; after all, his best boy was going.

Matthew stormed out of Fanny's Milwaukee workshop by mid-morning of the first day, barely reaching the car before beginning a series of angry outbursts. Kevin and Susan followed him to the parking lot. "Take me home," he said.

A pouring rain kept Susan's windshield wipers busy. The steely clouds matched Matthew's mood as he listened to the radio. "It was just a damn show," he said. "And don't say 'I told you so.'"

Susan smiled. "My mouth is shut."

"Everything was rehearsed," Matthew continued. "The jokes, the stories, every line and facial expression was repeated almost verbatim. The only thing different was the audience."

"We all wear masks," Susan said. "Fanny, me, and both of you." She turned her head to Matthew, her eyes compassionate.

"Watch the road, Susan," Matthew said. "What are you saying?"

"*Personality* is a Greek word that means mask," Susan said. "Sure it was a show. You saw Fanny in her spiritual teacher mask. But look at it from her point of view." A truck passed, throwing a sheet of water over the front windshield.

"She promotes herself as a healer," Matthew said. "Isn't there any part of medicine that hasn't become a business?"

"The soul of medicine is alive in you and Hector and even Kevin."

"Thanks," Kevin said. "I think."

"You're right, of course. She's doing her best." Matthew's voice dripped with cynicism. "They all are. Buckman and Eileen and the whole fucking world. You should have told me about Fanny when I asked you to drive us."

"Honor the teaching, not the teacher," Susan said. "Fanny does a lot of good. Much of what she says is valid. She gives hope to many people."

"At ten grand a weekend," Kevin said from the back seat.

"She puts on a show because she's frightened," Susan said.

"Of what?" Matthew asked.

"None of what she teaches is original; she borrows her material from others, even if she fails to acknowledge that fact. Fanny's found a way to package and mass-market elementary spirituality. There are lots of people seeking someone like her to cure them."

"It feels like another fraud to me," Matthew said.

"Spiritual truth doesn't *belong* to anyone, Matthew," Susan said. "The questions people ask demand deeper, more spontaneous replies. But it's the best she can do." According to Susan, all spiritual teachers face the same dilemma: The deeper the message, the less the masses will buy it.

Matthew sighed. "Someone must be out there with the answers I need."

Susan smiled broadly. "If the answers were on a billboard, you wouldn't see them."

"I suppose the wisdom of the universe hangs out in Nike ads," Kevin said.

"'Read the next billboard, Kevin. 'Just do it' is a profound message."

"Are you nuts?" Kevin asked.

"Over there, Kevin. Read it."

Kevin read in the flattest tone he could summon. "You've got a mind of your own. Do what's right for you."

"There's more."

"You are your own dog. Red Dog Beer."

Matthew laughed. "Maybe that is the answer," he said. "I am my own dog."

"Give yourself a Milkbone, Matthew," Susan said.

29

One Saturday morning Kevin decided to pay an unscheduled visit to
The Healing Place. Not completely clear about Todd's connection to
Buckman, Kevin hoped uncover their agenda and protect himself
should Buckman turn on him for failing to discredit Matthew. Todd
welcomed Kevin into his office and offered him a drink as if he'd been
expecting him since the day he was born.

"I came to talk about Matthew," Kevin said.

"I'm as concerned as you are about him. He's using work to escape
his pain," Todd said.

"What do you want from him?" Kevin asked.

Todd reassured Kevin that he had no interest in Matthew except to
support him. "Of course I wish that he would become more public, but
I honor Matthew's feelings and would never push him past his own
comfort level," Todd said. Comfort level? Kevin asked himself. He was
way past his with everyone: Matthew, Buckman, himself, and now this
therapeutic asshole who Kevin believed was lying through his capped
teeth.

Kevin wanted to take a closer look at the facility than he had been able to during the weekend of Fanny's workshop. He began with the bookstore. Along with a large selection of books, tapes, and video programs, the shop sold vitamins, homeopathic remedies, and nutritional supplements. He was examining a colorful display of Chinese herbal medicine boxes when he heard a voice he recognized.

Dan Stevenson stood on the stairs immediately outside the door to the shop, asking for directions to Todd's seminar. Kevin slipped behind a bookshelf and waited until he heard Dan's voice fade up the stairs.

"Do you know that guy?" Kevin asked the young man behind the counter.

"Dan Stevenson. He takes classes here."

"What kind of classes?"

"Todd's stuff. Self-esteem. Creating your future," the clerk said.

Kevin left the building, cursing Dan Stevenson, the newest addition to the ever-increasing list of people fucking with his life. He walked three blocks to a small coffee shop and sat at the counter, his face as hot as Matthew's hands. An elderly waitress in a stained uniform leaned her elbows on the counter. "You look terrible, young man," she said. "You want coffee?"

"Decaf please," Kevin answered. She poured a steaming mug. Kevin was so unnerved he spilled half of it. Dan's presence at The Healing Place might have been a coincidence. But as he sat and toyed with the remainder of his coffee, he feared the connection between Dan and Todd, and the even more sinister alliance between the two of them and Buckman. His terror worsened at the realization that he was an agent out in the cold, isolated from anyone he could trust.

Todd called Matthew two days after Kevin's visit and asked if he could see him. "It's about getting more money for you," Todd said. Matthew said he could come after clinic hours.

Matthew and Todd talked for an hour.

"I'm a guy with a vision," Todd said. "My dream is to find a healer like you and create a support organization so you can work freely without concern for petty details."

Todd unzipped a brown leather portfolio he had brought with him and removed a sheaf of folded papers. "Look at these articles."

Matthew saw his name fly out from several headlines. "Where did you get these?"

"Here and there. By the way, Ralph Hurden sends his regards. He's back at work. Look at this piece from an underground health magazine–three patients claim you cured them. Check out the part I highlighted, 'Doctor Gutierrez refused to allow our reporter to interview the young doctor with the healing touch.' And here's *The Free University Press*." The headline read "A Special Clinic with A Mystery Healer." "This is the Sunday supplement of the *Sun Times* with an article on Hector's clinic. Gutierrez discusses his charity work, completely ignoring your contribution to the clinic's recent growth."

Matthew was dumbfounded. "How come I've never seen any of these?"

"You tell me," Todd said, putting his arm around Matthew's shoulder. "You've been working like a slave. What bothers me is that nobody at the clinic has shown any of this to you."

Matthew thought for a moment. "Actually they have. Peter tried to give one of these to me. A few patients have said they've read about me, but I refused to listen."

"Are you listening now?" Todd asked.

"Yes."

"The entire city, maybe even the whole damn world, would like to beat a path to your front door. You've got to stop hiding here. You need your own clinic where nobody takes advantage of you. It's your pattern, Matthew. First Buckman and now Hector."

"Hector's been wonderful to me. He's protected me. And I help a lot of people here."

"You could help more."

Matthew looked perplexed. In his exhaustion and confusion, he began to wonder if Todd was right. He mused aloud, questioning whether his move to Hector's clinic had been a mistake, that perhaps he should have confronted Buckman and refused to quit, sued him if he had to. Eileen would still be with him.

"How about this one?" Todd asked. He reached into his jacket and pulled out a copy of a newsletter. The headline read: Widow's Cancer Goes Into Remission: Gives Clinic $50,000.

"Where did you get this?"

"The correct question is: How much of that money did you see? It says here that the cure was attributed to the 'other doctor' at the clinic. Hector is mentioned a dozen times but your name doesn't appear anywhere."

"Why would Hector keep this from me?"

Todd smiled. "Ask him. Matthew, let me help you to realize fully what's possible in your life." Like a magician pulling doves from his jacket, Todd reached into a side pocket and removed another newspaper clipping. He unfolded it to highlight and center a picture of a young mother and her infant child. Matthew gasped. He remembered the incident.

"I thought so. You met her at the zoo—under shocking circumstances." Todd handed the paper to Matthew.

Matthew read the article. The child had been born with a congenital heart defect, the major blood vessels incorrectly connected to the opposite sides of the heart from where they belonged. The diagnosis had been confirmed at the University of Chicago hospital.

"Keep reading, Matthew," Todd said, picking up the surplus toilet articles on the dresser one by one to examine them and dropping them back in their places disdainfully. "Especially the part about how the condition spontaneously corrected itself. The mother believes it was the shock from the 'handsome young stranger' that was responsible for the miracle. The doctors labeled her belief as nonsense."

"Why have you been collecting these?"

"I've always been good at detective work. I want to get you out of this sewer and into a clinic where you can reach your maximum potential, get the recognition you deserve, and make some real money—until you find a new training program, of course. Most people like me with management degrees become corporate bean counters who never contribute to the world. This is my way of making a difference."

"Money isn't everything, Todd. I'm overworked and exhausted, but that's because I'm doing what I love. I'm really happy here."

"All I ask is that you think about what I'm offering, Matthew. I'd like to open your office on January second. A five room apartment is waiting for you, fully furnished." Todd tapped on the cheap dresser. "Not this crap."

That night Matthew did not sleep well. Todd's offer percolated through his self-doubt and pain. He loved his life at Hector's and treasured his patients. But he knew that, hurt as he was by Eileen's behavior, he still wanted her back, and believed that a regular paycheck was the means to that end.

30

Buckman insisted that Kevin meet him at nine sharp the next morning, then kept him waiting until almost ten before he was ushered into his office.

"I'm disappointed in Matthew," Buckman said. "I had hoped he would have self-destructed by now. Are you quite sure that you're telling me everything you know, Kevin?"

"Yes, sir."

"I hope so. What about Todd Lawrence? Have you anything to say about him?" Kevin thought about stonewalling, but considered that if Buckman was involved in a conspiracy with Stevenson and Lawrence, he already knew that Matthew and he had attended Fanny's workshop. Kevin told him the minimum he could, carefully weighing his words to reveal as few details as possible. Kevin studied his face, hoping for some reaction.

"I would not recommend Dr. Colwell's program to my residents," was Buckman's stone-faced response. He smiled thinly. "Can we wrap this up soon, please?"

"I hope to accomplish your goal, sir."

"I'm sure that you do, Kevin." He picked up the phone and began to dial, dismissing Kevin with a wave of his hand.

"You look tired," Kevin said to Matthew as he sat on a corner of his bed.

"I'm beyond tired," Matthew said. He handed Kevin a thick manila envelope, "From Todd."

Kevin scanned the document. It was a contract for a position as a staff doctor at The Healing Place. Kevin felt his face redden. "When did you and Todd begin negotiations?" he asked.

"We talked last night," Matthew said. "I didn't think he was this serious or could move this quickly." He seemed awed at the prospect.

"You're going to tell Todd that you're not interested, aren't you?"

"It's tempting. But I can't stop asking myself how Eileen would react if I earned a decent wage."

Without knocking, Todd walked in. "Speak of the devil," Kevin said. "Your timing's impeccable. What do you want?" He could barely hide his hostility.

"Hello Kevin," Todd said. "I assume you received my packet, Matthew. I'd have delivered it in person, but I've been out pricing medical equipment for the clinic, cutting-edge technology for your office."

"Hold on, Todd," Kevin interrupted. "When did Matthew say that he was joining you?"

"Excuse me, Kev," Matthew said. "I don't need an agent."

Todd unzipped his portfolio and spread two dozen brochures on the bed. "The best of everything," he said. "EKG. In-house laboratory. Even a new computer system for record keeping and billing. We're expanding the clinic to include a number of physicians like you who'll work alongside the alternative practitioners.

"I see you managed to steal more than one concept while you were here at the clinic," Kevin said.

Ignoring Kevin's comment, Todd watched Matthew examine the brochures. "Did we discuss salary?"

"No," Matthew said.

"We'll limit your working hours. Eight until four, Monday through Friday. You need more rest than they're giving you here. You get five thousand a month to start. I'll hire an extra nurse and receptionist especially for you and, of course, the clinic will pay your malpractice insurance premiums. You'll concentrate on making people well."

"That's a great offer, Todd," Matthew said. "But I can't just quit here. It wouldn't be fair to Hector."

"I agree," Kevin said, as forcefully as he could spit out the two words.

"Of course," Todd said, coolly. "But you have to be fair to yourself too. I want you to get what you deserve, so I'll make the offer even fairer by adding a five thousand dollar bonus if you sign the contract today. You can do what you like with the extra money; if you choose, you can donate it to Hector as reverse severance pay."

"Come back at five," Matthew said.

"Don't sign," Kevin said as soon as Todd was gone. "Something feels wrong with this deal."

"Todd's an asshole, but it's a *lot* of money, Kevin."

"*On ne voit bien qu'avec le coeur*…It is only with the heart that one can see rightly. What is essential is invisible to the eye," Kevin said. "That's from *The Little Prince*."

"I read that," Matthew said. "In English."

"You're the first real break Hector's had in his dream to make this clinic a first-rate facility for the city's poor. Without you, he may not be able to make the payments on the building. He only took the risk of buying this place because of you."

"What about *my* dreams?" Matthew asked. "I have a few questions for Hector."

"Hector should have discussed the clinic's financial issues with you. But I have no doubt that he loves you. His only fault was trying to protect you from the wolves who would use your gift, chew you up, and spit you out. You have a short memory, Matthew. Hector offered you a job when you had no place to go."

"I'm not one of Hector's hopeless patients," Matthew said. "I'm a doctor, Kevin."

Matthew found Hector in the war room. "Todd offered me a job."

Hector smiled. "I expected he eventually would."

"I could use the money, Hector."

"I don't doubt that. Are you going to accept his offer?"

"The clinic's income is up significantly."

Hector looked puzzled. "What's this about?"

"A woman gave you fifty thousand dollars. That's true, isn't it?"

"Let me tell you the facts, Matthew. It's true that our income is higher, but nothing close to what you fantasize. And yes, I did get a gift of fifty thousand dollars. A wonderful woman whom you cured wanted to thank you by helping the clinic. I asked her for a straight-out gift for you. I explained that your resources were drained working here. She consulted her accountant and offered instead to make a down payment on the building. The so-called philanthropist who gave us the dollar-a-year lease was about to sell the clinic to an urban renewal project. We would have been history in less than a year. Her down payment saved us."

Hector walked over to a desk, opened a drawer and pulled out an envelope. "This is a partnership contract I've been working on for a month. You can call the attorney and make any changes you want."

Matthew picked up Hector's envelope and handed it back to him. "I apologize if I was rude, Hector. I love it here, but I want Eileen back and she needs a place to live where she won't be afraid. Todd's offering me a lot of money."

"This contract expresses my feelings," Hector said. "But you have to be sure of what you want. Work at Todd's. See if it's right for you, but take my advice–don't sign a contract with him. You're job will be here if you want it."

31

Todd agreed to Matthew's request for an open-ended position at The Healing Center. Kevin decided to continue his work at Hector's clinic despite Matthew's absence. Buckman was opposed at first, but Kevin insisted, convincing him that the days spent away from the Research would allow him greater flexibility to keep tabs on Matthew. "I'll grant you some latitude," he said, "but my patience is wearing thin."

Days became weeks. Matthew remained at Todd's. His phone calls to Eileen went unreturned. He wrote her and received no response. Weary from the repeated rejection and fearful that he might lose her forever if he pushed too hard, he stopped trying.

Just after clinic hours had ended on a particularly snowy night in January, Kevin heard the door to Hector's clinic slam open and looked up to see a woman rush past Carmen, directly to the inner sanctum at the end of the hall, sobbing as she dashed by. She wore no coat despite the cold and the snow that had been filling the clinic's windowsills for hours. Kevin couldn't see her face but he noticed that her dress was torn open in front.

He ran into the war room. It took a moment before he recognized Susan who stood there speaking in Spanish.

"Susan? In Christ's name, what happened to you?" Hector was aghast.

Susan rubbed her forearm across her face, smearing blood on her cheeks and chin. She fell onto the couch. Kevin's image of Susan as a pillar of inner strength crumbled seeing her so human and vulnerable.

Kevin and Hector moved to either side of her. Hector sat her up. From what they could see, she had only a few superficial scratches, nothing to account for the vast amount of blood. She would not settle down. Hector shook her violently.

"Relax, Susan," Hector said. "You're safe."

Susan's eyes darted back and forth between them. "Carlos," she stammered. "He escaped. He tried to...tried to rape me." Her face grew grim and hard–half anger, half suppressed hysteria. Kevin's gut twisted, his emotions see-sawing between wanting to hug his suffering friend and wishing to kill her fucking no-good husband.

"Susan, look at me." Hector ordered.

Tears ran down her face. She took a deep breath. "That bastard said the judge could not erase what God had joined." She wiped her face. "He said the divorce means nothing in the eyes of the Church. I hate him."

"Hold on a second, Susan," Hector said. He went to the door and asked Carmen to lock the clinic, then returned to Susan's side.

"I tried to kill him," Susan continued. "I wanted to kill him. Oh God, what did I do?"

She slid to the floor, Hector's strength unable to hold her. He knelt to face her.

"What *did* you do, Susan?" Hector asked gently.

"He pulled a knife on me. I got it from him…wrestled with him." She paused for a moment. "Oh Jesus, this blood isn't mine, is it?" She began to cry again.

"You did what you had to do," Hector said.

"I was so violent–everything I hated in Carlos. I acted like him, like an animal."

"Listen to me, Susan," Hector said. "You were defending yourself. He tried to rape you, probably kill you too. Can't you see the difference?"

"Yes, but I can't feel it here." She pointed to her heart. Several buttons had been ripped from her dress, exposing the delicate lace of her brassiere.

"I want you to stay here tonight," Hector said. "I'll talk with the police. You take Matthew's room. Until Carlos is found, you don't go anywhere alone, understand?"

"I don't care anymore. I can't stand myself. It would have been better if he had killed me."

Kevin helped her upstairs and returned to the war room. After phoning his wife to say he would be late, Hector called a detective who arrived in ten minutes and introduced himself to Kevin as John Novak. He was a dark, athletic man in his forties with chestnut hair and a thick mustache that he toyed with. Kevin knew him from his occasional visits to the hospital, a suspect in tow.

"Found your perp, Doc," Novak said. "He was getting stitched up at Cabrini Hospital. He claimed he'd been robbed. Somebody almost castrated him."

"His ex-wife," Hector said. "He tried to rape her."

"Where is she?"

"She's here."

"I'll send a squad car for her."

"Not yet, you won't."

"Hey, Doc, you should see this guy. Stay clear of her. She has to be one tough bitch. Hooker?"

"No. A doctor."

Novak paused and touched his upper lip. "Oh."

"She's a friend of mine, John. Doctor Olivera. She's a resident at the Research Hospital."

"Her? I know her from the E. R. She's a nice lady."

"She's a mess, John. How about cutting her some slack? She'll come in tomorrow."

"It's against procedure. It would take a big favor."

"Like last year?" Hector asked. "That young lady your wife doesn't know about. What was her name?"

Novak smiled. "You're right, Doc. We're too busy tonight to send anyone. You can bring her in yourself."

"Whatever you say, John."

"I always knew I liked you, Doc," Novak said. "Just don't give her any legal advice. Don't taint my witness."

"Sure." Hector asked Kevin to walk John to the door while he went to see Susan. When Kevin got to Matthew's room, she was lying on the bed, staring at the ceiling. Hector was explaining to her about Novak's visit.

Hector took her hand. "The police said you did quite a job on Carlos."

"I told you. I'm no better than him."

Kevin took a chair and sat in the corner of the room while Hector spoke to her. "There's nothing wrong with what you did, Susan. Should you have let him rape you? Or kill you? With all the spiritual work you do, you're still human. There's nothing right or wrong about a healthy survival instinct."

Susan paused. "But I could have killed...I wanted to kill him."

"Did you?"

"No."

"You had your chance, but you ran."

"Because I was afraid of what I wanted to do to him, Hector."

"Did you think you were a saint?" Hector wrapped his arms around her gently. Susan gave in to his embrace. Kevin saw that Hector expected nothing of her except that she accept his presence. And as Hector held Susan, Kevin thought of Eileen.

32

"What exactly does Matthew *do*?" Buckman asked. It was the first time he had ever posed the question directly. He had cornered Kevin in the classroom after rounds on one of the three days a week Kevin still spent at the Research, Chief Resident now in name only. Phil Edelstein had taken over the job that needed a full-time body. Because of Kevin's irregular schedule he was not assigned his own patients; he became a melancholy shadow man, a dowager emperor whose children now ruled his kingdom, aimlessly wandering the halls, bereft of any real power or purpose. He acted more the visiting consultant than senior resident, helping junior residents and medical students with difficult patients, assisting with procedures, hanging out in the E.R., and, despite his best efforts to avoid him, crossing Buckman's path more than he desired.

Buckman rose from his seat and checked to make sure that the door was firmly shut. "Don't fence with me, Kevin. Tell me the truth. Do patients' diseases simply melt away when he touches them or is it a gradual process?"

"I thought you believed Matthew was a fraud," Kevin said, the words bolder than he intended.

"I didn't ask for your commentary. I want a report."

Carefully coloring the story, Kevin told him about the cases he had seen at Hector's clinic, avoiding any details that Buckman could have twisted into an interpretation of unethical behavior on Matthew's part. He told Buckman about the diabetics who had discontinued their insulin and the cardiac patients whose angina had vanished; he kept the reports as general and unemotional as he could, emphasizing Matthew's natural ability to convince patients to improve their dietary and exercise regimens. Kevin left out the cancers that had disappeared, the arthritis that had become extinct, the dissecting aneurysm that had vaporized, and, of course, Ralph Hurden's new ability to run marathons. Buckman listened intently, stopping Kevin's narrative to ask for specific details. Padding his report with the cases Buckman already knew of or had access to, Kevin reminded him of Larry Trenton, and also told him about the young boy with the appendicitis, suggesting that Buckman contact the pediatricians who had treated him. "I already know about that case," he said. "I'm asking specifically, Kevin, if you have ever personally witnessed Matthew do anything that...well, that might defy the laws of science."

"Are you talking miracles, sir?"

"*Of course not*, Kevin. You know better than to ask me a question like that. Harrison's 'cures' can be attributed to spontaneous processes within the body. What I am asking is if *you* have ever *personally* seen anything that defied rational scientific belief."

Kevin looked down at the back of his hand. "No, sir."

"Let me know if you ever do." Buckman rose and left the classroom.

"Mrs. Summerfield's back in the house," the Cardiac ICU nurse said when Kevin responded to his pager. "You'd better get here this morning, Dr. Hargrove. She's in pretty bad shape." Kevin headed to Rosie's bedside.

No longer the woman he had met that night in the E.R., Rosie looked small and fragile now, her body a battered and well-worn suitcase that had carried her through more than seventy years. She had suffered another major heart attack and was connected to the regalia of plastic tubes and electronic boxes that are so often the last things to touch our bodies before we die.

Her voice was weak. "Dr. Hargrove, how sweet of you to visit me. Where's Dr. Harrison? The nurse says that he isn't here anymore."

"Dr. Harrison has a new job in his own clinic," Kevin said, moving her IV line away from her arm and taking her hand. "You would be proud of him." Rosie had the answer that Buckman was seeking. To hell with him, Kevin decided. "Would you like it if I could arrange for Dr. Harrison to take care of you? He might be able to help in the same way he did the last time."

Rosie squeezed Kevin's hand. "No, I don't think that will be necessary. My new grandchild was born last month."

"That's wonderful," Kevin said.

"Would you give Dr. Harrison a message for me?" Rosie began to cough and had difficulty catching her breath. Kevin wanted Matthew to help Rosie for her own sake, so she could spend a little more time with her new grandchild. "I wanted him to know that my grandchild is a boy."

"A boy?" Kevin echoed. "How nice."

"Yes," Rosie said. "We named him Matthew. Would you tell him?"

Kevin swallowed hard. "Yes, ma'am."

Kevin heard later that she died at 4:06 p.m., surrounded by her family, a different Matthew at her bedside.

33

Chicago's March wind chilled Kevin as he emerged from a cab at The Healing Place at nine p.m. It had been two months since Matthew had left Hector's clinic. Kevin had called, left messages, and had even faxed Matthew trying to be casual and cheery, so as not to put him off with heavy, serious, or judgmental conversation. Matthew's responses were vague and brief but always negative; he was absorbed in his new work and too exhausted to see his old friends. Kevin worried about him. He also missed him. Matthew had thrown Kevin's life into an uproar, but he found himself feeling incomplete without Matthew's daily presence, as if the course of mundane nature were not enough to keep him engaged with the world.

Kevin assumed that if Buckman were in league with Todd and was now receiving intelligence reports from him, he would let up on Kevin–but his demands for hard evidence of Matthew's supposed misdeeds only increased. In the past eight weeks, Kevin's weight had dropped; his face looked gaunt in the bathroom mirror as he mindlessly dragged his razor across his jaw each morning. From the worried look on her face each time he went home, Kevin was sure that his mother was half-convinced he was using drugs. Eileen's father continued to deteriorate; her voice was sad and desperate when Kevin spoke to her. On the bright side, Susan seemed to be doing well. With Carlos back behind bars, she appeared happier, no longer hiding her sensuous body under shapeless clothing–her new therapist's suggestion.

Hector had said nothing about Matthew since his departure, but Kevin knew that he missed him too. Kevin discussed his feeling with Susan. Matthew had been ignoring her calls too. Neither of them understood what Matthew had found at Todd's clinic–he was never motivated by money and if his plan was to win back Eileen with a positive bank balance, it wasn't working.

Kevin rang his doorbell and was happy to find Matthew home. Through the security speaker, Matthew's voice was flat with no sense of surprise at Kevin's unscheduled visit. They sat in Matthew's living room, drinking a nice French white. "You look as shitty as me," Kevin said. "How much weight have *you* lost?"

"About fifteen pounds. You?"

"Ten. I thought we both ate during times of stress," Kevin said. "I miss you."

"Thanks." Matthew stared into his wine, uncomfortable with Kevin's presence.

"What's going on?"

"I'm happy here. It's a nice apartment."

"I can see that." The floors were solid oak, the high ceilings, thickly draped mullioned windows, and dark furniture more suited to a Bavarian men's club than the apartment of a single guy still south of thirty. Kevin slid his leather chair next to Matthew's. "You want to come clean?"

Matthew sat silently, as if he were deciding how much of the truth he wanted to share. "My first few days here were miserable," he said. "The hot water in my apartment worked only occasionally and the windows leaked huge amounts of cold air. I went out for all my meals."

"What about the clinic?" Kevin asked.

"I saw just two walk-in patients the entire first week, both children of rich hypochondriacs, each with only a minor cold. Both mothers demanded antibiotics. Against my better judgment, I agreed. I thought it was strange that Todd wasn't here to welcome me, but sent the key to the apartment by messenger. I figured he must have been busy elsewhere, working to increase the patient load."

"I thought he ran this place," Kevin said, hiding his upset with both of them: Todd for lying and Matthew for ignoring his warnings.

"So did I," Matthew said, sheepishly.

"After a week, the nurse Todd promised finally materialized, an overweight, sloppy woman, slow both mentally and physically. She made me realize how much I missed Carmen's teasing and helpful suggestions. The schedule filled with patients but, honestly, I was bored with the parade of colds, flu, and minor sprains. My toughest call was whether to order an X-ray for a thirty-two year old racquetball player who had twisted his right foot. I ordered the film. There was no fracture."

"With what you're earning," Kevin said, "I would be happy to be bored, spending my free time shopping on Oak Street." Kevin paused, then asked, "No miracles?"

"Nope. I was hoping for one. Anything to cut the boredom. Things changed dramatically the last week of January. Patients flooded into the clinic, some of them with strange comments about miracles and spontaneous recovery from chronic illnesses. A week later, I found this ad for my office in a newspaper. Todd's promoting me like a Lincoln Park Lourdes." He tossed the ad into Kevin's lap.

Kevin read it. "What a fucking asshole," Kevin muttered. "Todd doesn't know the difference between you and that phoney-assed sister of mercy, Camille Whatshername.

"That's how I felt," Matthew said. "I called Todd at home. As expected, I got his voicemail. I realized I had made a big mistake leaving Hector's."

"Then why are you still here?" Kevin asked.

"Todd denied any knowledge of the ad. He claimed that he had hired an agency to announce the opening of my office. He said that somebody must have gotten mixed up but that every good medical practice advertises."

"Hector doesn't," Kevin said. "Where are all these dollars coming from?" he asked. "How can Todd afford the new equipment and your overhead?"

"The equipment never arrived," Matthew said. "When I ask him about it, he reminds me that I get my paycheck on time."

"Do you?" Kevin asked.

"No," Matthew said. Matthew was in deep shit and Kevin wanted to help. "You're holding something back."

Matthew swallowed hard. "I signed the contract."

"Why the hell did you do that?"

"He assured me it was just a formality and would terminate after thirty days. He claimed the malpractice insurance wouldn't cover me without a written agreement. I wanted the chance to get Eileen back so badly that I bought his argument. What I didn't realize was that the contract gave him a three-year option on my life."

"Why didn't you tell anyone?" Kevin asked.

"I told Todd I wanted out after the first week," Matthew said. "Two lawyers arrived at the clinic and painted a very unpleasant picture of my future if I breached the contract. I'm so fucking blind, Kevin. Patients believe I'm God's right hand, but I was too stupid to read the fine print."

"I brought you something," Kevin said. Taking a small book out of his coat, he gave it to Matthew.

Matthew sat quietly. Then he smiled, rose from his chair and hugged Kevin. "Thank you. I guess both Todd and Hector are in for a shock. Let's go."

Matthew retrieved his suitcase and hastily packed his belongings including the copy of *The Little Prince* that Kevin had brought him. He called Todd, correct in his assumption that his voicemail would answer. He left a message that he had moved back to Hector's and that Todd could direct his patients there.

Locking the door behind him and tucking the key under it, Matthew imagined Todd's anger when he discovered that he was gone, but he knew that he could no longer ignore the dictates of his heart. "Fuck the consequences," he said with a smile.

34

"Eileen's willing to talk about you," Kevin said. "To me."

"A second," Matthew laughed nervously. "Arranging a duel."

Kevin smiled. "At least I can discuss her choice of weapon."

Even on a Saturday, the drive from Chicago to Peoria took over three hours, four if you count the hour Kevin spent on North Michigan Avenue, purchasing a teapot at the Wedgwood store, a last minute idea he had not cleared with Matthew. Eileen, he believed, might respond to a small gesture of affection from her husband.

Eileen burst into tears when she opened the box. "It's beautiful, Kevin. But it's not from him." Taken aback, Kevin asked her how she knew. "Matthew hated the china," she said. "We had a huge fight when we registered for our wedding gifts. I only used it for company."

Eileen invited Kevin into the living room.

"How's your father?" he asked.

"He died two weeks ago."

"Why didn't you call? Matthew and I would have come to his wake."

"I wasn't thinking clearly. When you said you were coming to Peoria, I figured it was best to apologize in person." She lowered her gaze.

"How's your mother?"

"She's spending the weekend in St. Louis with her sister."

Eileen made tea for them—without the show or the silver strainer—using the new teapot. At Kevin's urging, she recounted the story of her life since she had left Matthew. She had lived for a few months with a sympathetic girlfriend in Elgin who was newly divorced and had been glad to share the rent. The friend abruptly departed for Arizona with her meager court-ordered settlement, leaving Eileen unable to afford the apartment herself. A series of equally unstable roommates convinced Eileen to move back to Peoria with her parents, the last place she wanted to be. The director of Eileen's pre-school in Chicago had been upset with her sudden departure, but a replacement teacher was found and Eileen's contract voided.

Despite a poor reference from her former employer, Eileen found work in Peoria as a teacher's aide in a private nursery school. She lost herself in housework and helping care for her father.

Eileen said the room in which her father lay dying had smelled of air freshener covering the stale scent of terminal illness. "Overripe fruit," she said. The odor made her gag; whatever dignity the man once had disappeared when he lost control of his basic bodily functions.

"I wanted to be anywhere but here," she said. "And yet I couldn't leave him."

"We all have mixed feelings about our parents," Kevin said, feeling angry with his father for dying without adequate insurance. Had he not been forced to moonlight to cover his father's medical bills, Kevin decided, he would not have become entangled in Matthew's mess.

"Your father didn't drink," she said, continuing her story, telling Kevin how living at home again triggered the same emotions she had felt in her childhood. Eileen said that she had pushed the feelings and sensations away. But the muscles of her neck and back had been in constant spasm.

Kevin's gaze wandered as he listened to Eileen's story. Her parents' house was tired. The brown siding and trim badly needed repairs and paint. Two of three windows facing the street had cracked panes. "Pretty shabby," Eileen said, noticing his focus.

The place, she said, was once bright and fresh, but her father's alcoholism had robbed the family of even a modest standard of living. "We've kept on, Mom and me, but right now even maintenance is a strain."

"Why didn't you call Matthew?"

"I was confused and upset," she said. "I saw the same thing happening to Matthew that happened to my father."

"Matthew wasn't drinking, Eileen."

"I know that, Kevin. I was blinded by fear and anger. To my mind, Matthew–and my life–were on a downhill slide. My standard of living went from bad to worse when he took the job with Hector. He loved it there. I believed that he might stay forever and I couldn't live that way. My mother helped me see that just recently. She said that she was no saint and pointed out to me that neither was I. She said I judge everything by how much money a person has. She wanted to leave my father many times, but he made a number of good faith attempts to quit."

"It couldn't have been easy with two children," Kevin said. "What happened between them?"

"They made peace. Or maybe they just got used to each other," Eileen said. "I was really angry and asked my mother how she let herself be such a victim."

"What did she say?"

"The one thing she knew would get me: that for all my father's faults she'd never deserted him–but I'd done that to Matthew."

"There's no comparison between your leaving Matthew and your father's drinking, Eileen."

"I agree. But when you think about it, there is a strange logic to what she said."

"People do hurtful things under pressure," Kevin said, feeling shitty, attempting to justify every rotten thing he had done in his life.

Eileen rose from her chair and paced the room, picking up random objects and putting them back down again. "I've been thinking a lot about Chicago. I did a lot of damage to my life. To Matthew's too," she said, wiping her eyes and sitting down next to Kevin on the couch.

Kevin reached over to hold her and comfort her but as he felt her warm and alive in his arms, he wanted to possess her, to make love to her with his body and his heart. And did she stir too? Realizing that what he was feeling and doing wasn't right, he awkwardly broke their embrace. "You know, Matthew still loves you."

"He never came here to take me home," she said.

"You never responded to his phone calls."

"Touché."

"That was the past," Kevin said. "I'd like to see what I can do to help you create a future."

"What's in this for you? Guys don't drive half a day to patch up someone else's marriage."

"I care for you both," Kevin said, lying, or at least simplifying. "I would feel great if I could help fix your relationship. I owe at least that much to Matthew."

"Tell me how he's doing. Matthew's had so many problems in his life. Do you know if he's back on Prozac?"

"Prozac?" Kevin asked.

Eileen looked horrified. "You didn't know? You can't tell him that I told you."

"I promise," Kevin said, shedding his shock and entering his spy-for-Buckman mode, "but only if you tell me what you're talking about."

"I feel so horrible, but as his friend maybe you should know. It's really nothing for Matthew to be ashamed about. He suffers from dysthymic depression. It started when he was eighteen and tried to commit suicide."

A chill swept through Kevin's body. Would he have behaved the same if had known that Matthew suffered from chronic depression, even more so that he had actually attempted suicide? Did Buckman know about this? Some vague memory stirred within Kevin, a blurry snapshot from the night he investigated Matthew's file in Buckman's office. "He never talks about it, but one of his cousins told me that it had something to do with a girlfriend of his who had leukemia."

"He recovered completely, didn't he?" Kevin asked, mentally flipping through Matthew's file at the Research.

"He's okay," Eileen said. "Except for the scars on his wrists."

"Scars?" Kevin asked, once more taken aback.

"Yes. His introduction to self-surgery–his dad's razor blades. Didn't you notice that he never takes off his watch?"

"I never gave it much thought," Kevin said, realizing that she was correct.

"You're a doctor–you understand there are lots of people like Matthew who function perfectly well without anyone knowing that they suffer from depression. He sees a psychiatrist when he needs a few months of treatment."

"How often is that?" Kevin asked.

"Twice a year. The medication works well. Fortunately, the depression isn't serious."

Actually the problem was quite serious, Kevin thought to himself as the picture of that night in Buckman's office came into sharp focus. In his haste to return home before the rain, he had almost bypassed the two pages of questions about past criminal convictions, drug abuse, hospital disciplinary actions, and malpractice suits that are routine to every professional application, thinking he would not find anything there. But, ever the stickler for details, Kevin had taken the time to scan the list. Matthew, as he had expected, had checked "No" to the entire series of questions including the one that had asked if the applicant was aware of any health impairment that could affect his ability to perform professional duties. Matthew had lied. He had answered "no" on the state license and the hospital residency applications, a dangerous and stupid falsification, precisely the ammunition Buckman needed to destroy Matthew's career.

"What do I do, Kevin?" Eileen asked.

"About what?" Kevin asked, lost in his thoughts. He wondered what he would do with his new information and, at the same time, wished that he did not possess it. "Oh, you mean about Matthew." He went for it. "How would you feel about meeting with him?"

"That would depend on the place and the circumstances. I'm scared that I might say or do something stupid."

Kevin suggested someplace public, perhaps for dinner. She agreed, on the condition that he be present as a referee in case things became unpleasant.

She smiled and put her hand on his arm. "And about Matthew's depression?"

"Depression?" Kevin said. "What depression?" But he knew he would never forget.

35

"Dinner with Eileen?" Matthew asked. "Whose idea was it?"

"Mine," Kevin said. "The restaurant choice is yours. But McDonald's isn't an appropriate spot for a reconciliation."

"I feel bad about her father."

"She knows it was wrong not to have told you."

Matthew and Kevin sat in his room at Hector's on a Saturday evening. "How does she look?" Matthew asked. Kevin said that she had lost some weight but looked lovely. "Why do you think she wants to get together now?"

Kevin told Matthew that Eileen had grown a great deal after she left, especially while caring for her father. "People don't really change," Matthew said. Kevin disagreed with him, telling Matthew everything that Eileen and he had discussed during his visit, including the story of the teapot, but disincluding the revelation of Matthew's depression and his lies about it.

Matthew laughed–a little coarsely, Kevin thought. "Eileen believes that serving tea properly is the mark of good breeding. I told you people don't change."

"Give her a break, Matthew," Kevin said. Since finding out about Matthew's depression, Kevin saw him in a different light. Matthew needed someone to watch over him. "Are you willing to talk to her?"

"Sure," Matthew said bitterly. "Why not?"

"I thought you wanted her back. Why are you so hostile?"

Matthew sighed. "Part of me wants to hug her and another part wants to cut her out of my life forever. My problem right now is Todd."

"Let a lawyer fix it."

"Todd's picking me up in half an hour."

"Why?"

"He's arranged for a crew to film me treating patients."

"Refuse to do it."

"It was in my contract. He showed me the clause that says I have to be available for a reasonable number of publicity appearances and promotional activities of the clinic. He said that if I do this one thing for him, he'd tear up the contract and release seven thousand dollars he owes in back pay. I thought about telling him to fuck off, but realized that I wouldn't win anything by refusing. And if Eileen's serious about coming back, I'll need that cash."

They made small talk–Bulls, Cubs, Bears–until Todd arrived. He ignored Kevin. "We're ready, Matthew," he said. "I'll take you to the studio."

"Kevin's going with us."

"Okay," Todd said.

"Seven thousand dollars," Matthew muttered to Kevin. "Don't worry," he laughed, "I'm not going to play Camille no matter what Todd wants. My contract doesn't specify a minimum number of miracles."

Todd's large conference room, the site of Fanny's performance, had been transformed into a television studio. A suite of exam room furniture had been carried upstairs and arranged in front of a professional looking backdrop of royal blue curtains and a large Healing Place logo. An audience of fifty–the scary kind of plastic people who fill late night television advertising with fixed smiles, untenable optimism, and articulate questions–sat on chairs arranged in semicircular rows facing the brightly lit stage. "It looks like a damn infomercial," Kevin said.

Todd coldly told Kevin to take a seat in the audience. Kevin watched with fascination as Todd and a young blond female director choreographed the show. The audience, he discovered, were participants in Todd's various seminars who had been "invited" as an "act of service" to The Healing Place.

Three patients had been selected for Matthew to work his miracles upon–an older woman with arthritis, a young child with a congenital deformity of his spine, and a middle-aged man with advanced heart disease. Kevin thought that, besides Matthew, they appeared to be the only authentic people at the event.

Todd, as moderator, halted the crew numerous times, delaying the taping each time Matthew responded to his comments and questions with standard medical explanations, neutralizing any reference to his healing abilities. Kevin enjoyed watching Matthew play so masterfully with Todd. And he wanted each of the patients to experience one of Matthew's miracles. But not here, he thought–later, perhaps at home–when Todd could gain no benefit from their recoveries. Matthew did a thorough but routine examination–one, Kevin realized wistfully, that would have made Buckman proud of him–of each of the patients, treating them with kindness and consideration.

"I don't feel anything at all," the arthritic woman said to the camera after Matthew was finished with her. "But Dr. Harrison is a nice young man."

Todd stopped the taping again and beckoned Matthew off stage but in full view of the audience. "Are you holding back?" he yelled. "Is this some kind of joke?"

Matthew calmly shrugged his shoulders in response to Todd's fury. "I'm doing the best I can."

"Do your fucking thing," Todd shouted. "*Heal* someone." Kevin searched the faces of the audience, astonished that none of them seemed to react to Todd's behavior. It was as if they expected him to act so cruelly. Were Kevin not Matthew's friend, he would have walked out.

After four grueling hours of repeated takes and Todd's abuse, the three exhausted patients were no more cured than they had been when they arrived. Matthew told the patients they should consult with their regular physicians to make sure they were on a proper course of treatment for their ailments and that they should work to live happy lives even with their illnesses. Matthew left the stage and joined Kevin.

"Let's go," Matthew said. "Todd and his contract are history."

"Did you do that on purpose?" Kevin asked.

"Honestly, no. I was having a great deal of fun making Todd angry, but I would have loved to have helped those people. I can't turn it on and off at will. You know that."

Todd finished talking to the director and joined them. "Do you know what that cost us?" he screamed.

"I'm not a circus act," Matthew said calmly. "You owe me seven thousand dollars, Todd, and one voided contract. At least Hector was honest about what he said he would pay me. I want my money. You have one week or my lawyer will be paying *you* a call."

"We'll see about that," Todd said as he stalked off, slamming the door behind him.

Matthew smiled. "Kevin, I think I'm ready to have that dinner with Eileen."

36

The luxury of the main room at Nick's Fishmarket reflected the upscale prices of the entrees. Eileen and Kevin had arrived within minutes of each other to find that Matthew had called to say that he was unexpectedly delayed and that they should begin without him.

"It's too dark to read the menu," Eileen said to the waiter, who smiled professionally and turned a rheostat discretely located at the side of the semicircular booth. A tiny halogen fixture in the ceiling flooded their table with blue-white light. Somehow, the place struck both of them as silly, and they found themselves giggling nervously.

Eileen fidgeted with her silverware and dishes, turning her plate over to check the mark. "I appreciate you being here, Kevin. I'm nervous."

"Maybe you should have something stronger to drink than water," he said.

In painful silence they watched a young couple sitting across the aisle from them. In a booth the same size as theirs, one that could seat six in comfort, the two clung to each other. "Did you spend any time in the city or drive here just for dinner?" Kevin asked awkwardly.

"I've been window shopping on Michigan Avenue," Eileen said.

The waiter brought a vase with a dozen roses to the table across from them, prompting the young man to slide from the booth and drop to his knees. He produced a small black box from his pocket. Diners at the adjoining tables caught on and stared as the young man slipped the engagement ring on the finger of his tearful fiancé. Kevin glanced at Eileen who just looked rueful.

Matthew arrived, agitated and awkward as he slipped into the booth and sat next to Eileen. "I'm sorry I was late," he said. Their bodies grew rigid alongside each other. He asked the waiter to bring him a double Scotch, which he downed in two gulps. Eileen just stared at him. Kevin noticed that Matthew was once again wearing his wedding ring, something he hadn't done for the past months.

"What's wrong?" Kevin asked.

"Todd's lawyer–again," Matthew said. "That's why I wasn't here on time."

"Are you in trouble?" Eileen asked, uneasy. Already this was not heading in the direction Kevin had envisioned: an initial period of the usual embarrassed small talk, followed by the two of them taking the first steps toward a reconciliation. Matthew had been the calamity man when she left; Kevin feared Eileen would get the impression he hadn't changed.

"I'm not sure," Matthew said, softening. Matthew, with Kevin's frequent interjections, told Eileen about Todd who was, contrary to his promise, refusing to nullify the contract.

"What are you going to do?" she asked.

"I hired a lawyer. I'm going to need your help, Kevin."

"What can I do?" Kevin asked. How quickly would the contract dissolve, he wondered, if Matthew lost his medical license due to the sudden disclosure of his falsified application? Matthew said that Kevin would be able to attest to Todd's fraudulent methods of coercion.

"I signed with Todd under duress," Matthew explained to Eileen. "He breached the agreement and owes me money."

"You better have a *really* good lawyer," Kevin said.

"Todd stretched the truth whenever *he* pleased. His new Lexus was leased from my patient revenues."

"Matthew, don't tell me you got involved with a crook," Eileen said.

Matthew's face went red. He turned to Kevin. "Remember Eric Espinoza?"

"Who's he?" Eileen asked, increasingly skittish.

"A news reporter," Matthew said. "Todd was Eric's therapist when Eric was still *Enrique* Espinoza, a mixed-up kid sent to jail for selling heroin. He's clean now, but Todd holds the key to Eric's closet."

"*Heroin?*" Eileen repeated.

"Maybe this isn't a good topic for you two to be discussing tonight," Kevin said.

Matthew sighed. "I apologize, Eileen. You drove a long way. Let's put my problems aside and talk about us."

"This *is* us," she said. "If we're going to talk about us, we have to talk about what's going on with you."

"I have to say *that's* a switch after the last six months," Matthew said. He realized how cold his words sounded. "I'm sorry. You didn't come here to talk about my legal problems. And I started out all wrong–I should have told you how bad I feel about your father."

The waiter approached for their food orders. None of them had yet opened their menus. "What do you recommend?" Kevin asked.

"Columbia River salmon," he said.

"That's fine for all of us," Eileen said coolly. Matthew asked the waiter to choose a bottle of Chablis.

After the waiter departed, Eileen said, "I'm glad he died. He was a shit, but I learned a lot from him."

Neither Kevin nor Matthew had anything to add to that. They made strained small talk until the food arrived. Matthew took two bites of his fish and put his fork down. "What do you want from me, Eileen?"

"I don't know," she said.

Kevin picked at his food, his appetite gone, unable to look at either of the two people he cared so much about. He regretted having encouraged the meeting.

Matthew pushed his plate away. "Maybe you're right about this not being a good time."

"You have good reason to be angry with me," she said.

"I'm beyond anger, Eileen. You abandoned me at the worst possible time."

"I did," she said, testily. "But did you consider that I might have been having problems too?"

Kevin felt like a child, helpless as his parents quarreled. "Time out," he said. "This isn't going to solve anything."

"That's easy to say, Kevin," Eileen said, "But the fact is that Matthew…"

Kevin interrupted her. "I think you should stop the accusations and focus on what you want from each other."

The three of them sat in silence. Matthew swallowed the contents of his wineglass in one gulp. "With all that's gone on, I still need you, Eileen," he said in a barely audible whisper. "More than ever."

She poked at her untouched fish. "I'm a different person than I was when I left."

"You hurt me. How do I know that you won't do the same thing again?"

"Life has no guarantees," she said. "We'll have to keep talking, to see if we can be human beings together, tell the truth to each other." She offered her hand and he accepted. Kevin was relieved.

"I want to be completely honest with you about the past months," Matthew said, collecting himself. "It was tough without you. I was tempted only once. But just tempted."

"*Not now,*" Kevin murmured. Wouldn't he have the sense to keep his mouth shut, just take baby steps at this first meeting?

"Matthew, I don't want to know the details," she said.

"I don't either," Kevin said, trying to stop him. This was the way he had spoken to Buckman the morning he made the intuitive diagnosis of Rachel Fremont's lymphoma; such a bright guy didn't know when to keep his mouth shut.

"No," he continued, ignoring both of them. "Let me tell you about it. Susan invited me to dinner recently. I was unaware that her ex-husband had attempted to rape her."

Eileen was becoming more upset. "*I don't want to hear this, Matthew.*"

"Matthew, shut up and eat your salmon," Kevin said.

He barreled past Kevin's admonition. "When Susan told me what had happened to her, she got hysterical. I guess she misunderstood my hug and asked me to spend the night. Eileen, I was lonely too. I spent the night with her. We slept together but nothing happened. Turned out neither of us wanted to."

"*You what?*"

"Eileen, it was something intimate and special that I shared with Susan. It was beyond anything sexual and I'm glad that I did it."

Eileen's volume increased. "I don't *get* it."

"I still heal people," Matthew said, pouring out his sins in an unbroken litany, hoping to be absolved for everything at once. He refilled his glass and swallowed it.

"Of course you do," Eileen said, reeling from the conversation. "You're a doctor."

"Do you understand what I've just said?" He took her hand. "Like your arm that night at Hector's."

She pulled out of his grasp.

"I healed Kevin's hand, too," Matthew added.

"Why didn't *you* tell me about this, Kevin? What does Matthew mean that he *healed your hand*?"

"I'm sorry—I didn't realize how shocking it must have been for you," Matthew said gently.

No longer able to deny what she had been so desperate to avoid, Eileen, pale and shaken, listened as Matthew explained about the broken mirror and the agreement to keep the episode a secret.

"Go on," she said quietly, her jaw muscles clenched.

He told her of the many others who left his office healed as if by magic. He began with Larry Trenton and Ralph Hurden, detailing a dozen more miracles at Hector's clinic. He shared his experience with Rosie Summerfield. "This is who I am, Eileen," he said.

Eileen paused for a moment to digest what she had heard. "You son-of-a-bitch," she said. "You say that you want me back but, in the same breath you tell me that you're a magician. You're lying. If you're not, *why didn't you heal my father?*"

"I tried."

"I guess you didn't try hard enough. Was this your way of punishing me?" she asked. "You bastard," she said. She slapped him hard across his cheek. Kevin backed away from her in case he was her next target. Eileen slid from the booth and stalked unsteadily out of the restaurant.

Matthew started to follow her but Kevin stopped him. "She needs help," Matthew said.

"Not from you."

Kevin caught up with Eileen outside the restaurant and asked her where she was staying.

"I didn't think that far ahead," she said, wiping her tears. "I thought that I might end up with Matthew tonight."

"You shouldn't drive. Let me get you a room."

"I can't afford a downtown hotel."

"You can stay with me."

Eileen exhaled and steadied herself. "Okay."

"Where's your car?" Kevin asked. Eileen reached into her purse and produced a ticket that she handed to the restaurant's doorman.

The streets changed from bright and noisy to dark and empty as they drove to the medical center in silence. Kevin looked at Eileen's face illuminated in the electronic blue of the dashboard lights. She turned and smiled, noticing his stare. "You've been very sweet, Kevin. Thank you."

Kevin shrugged. "I just want to help." Kevin's gut contracted with the lie, but he barely felt it beneath the sexual tension that filled his body.

The hunger between them slowly grew as they got closer to Kevin's apartment. "Let me see your hand," she asked when he had parked the car and turned off the engine. Her touch was warm and incredibly soft. "Is it true?"

"It is," Kevin said, hesitating for just a moment before placing his hand on her chest. She did not remove it, nor did she stop him as his hand moved over the curves of her body, pulling her close to him.

Neither of them knew when they decided it, when the touch became a kind of consummation. They got out of her car together, clinging to each other, and went upstairs, unblinking as they passed by the door to the apartment she had shared with Matthew. They entered Kevin's apartment, their clothes fell away, and they held each other like two people who were drowning. Neither of them remembered what they said to each other as they fell into bed, what explanations they groped for as they touched and hugged and moved their bodies against each other for what seemed like endless hours in the dark. Kevin did know that she gripped his healed hand so hard it hurt him. When they came, they were both crying.

37

Dan Stevenson's phone message the next morning was terse and mysterious. After Eileen left, wordlessly gathering her clothes, kissing Kevin on the cheek and stealing down the stairs before he could figure out what he felt or could say to her, he called Dan back, expecting somehow that Buckman already knew where Eileen had been last night. In the aftermath of what morning told Kevin was a sleepless, stupid, and sad act, every disaster seemed possible.

Dan insisted that they meet someplace outside the hospital. They settled on the observation deck of the Sears Tower at lunchtime. Kevin called in sick, something he had never done before, and stayed home from the clinic and the Research. He arrived early at the Chicago landmark because the day was clear and, like the native New Yorkers who had never been to the Empire State Building, he had never seen his own city from the Sears observation deck. He thought the view would give him the perspective it was sorely clear he lacked.

"I'm sorry to drag you up here," Dan said. His eyes moved like a frightened cat's, scanning the area around them.

"You're acting like a character in a spy novel."

"Chicago's smaller than you know."

"Cut to the chase, Dan."

"I'm leaving the Research in a few weeks," he said.

"That's it? That's what I paid six dollars to hear? Congratulations."

"Nobody knows yet that I'm leaving."

"I'm honored to be the first."

"This involves your friend Matthew Harrison."

Stevenson had Kevin's attention. He said that he had accepted an offer at a hospital in San Diego, but that before his departure, he wanted to clear his conscience. "I've done Buckman's dirty work for too long. He's part of the reason why I'm leaving, but I won't be able to live with myself unless I try to undo some of the damage I helped inflict on Matthew."

Kevin wanted to ask him if by chance he'd slept with Matthew's wife. If not, Kevin thought, he was far ahead of Dan in the body count. Something didn't feel right to Kevin. "What were you doing at The Healing Place?" he asked.

"Buckman sent me there to check the place out, to double-team Matthew. I don't think he trusts you. I don't think he trusts anyone."

"Why are you telling me this?" Kevin asked.

"Buckman's gone too far this time. He's hired a private investigator to destroy Matthew's career. So far, the PI has sent three patients to see him. One tried to purchase prescriptions for medications he didn't need—Percoset and Valium. The second was a woman who attempted to seduce Matthew. I don't know what the third tried, but Matthew didn't fall for any of them. Buckman's become so blinded by the pain of his daughter's illness that, in my opinion, he's using Matthew as target practice. He's become obsessed with finding a way to have Matthew's medical license revoked. Fortunately, it hasn't worked yet."

Goddamn. This had gotten bigger than Kevin had imagined it ever could. The web they had all woven had been knotted and reknotted. Was there any way out? "So go tell Matthew," he said.

"I tried to call him. He hung up on me twice and won't return my messages."

"Do you blame him?" Kevin asked. "What's with all the secrecy?"

"Buckman's smart," Dan said. "I don't want him to connect the two of us. That's good for nobody. You can't tell Matthew where you got your information. Just warn him to be careful."

"All I have is your word. Why should Matthew trust that? Give me something solid that Matthew can use against Buckman."

"Are you crazy? I'm the only one besides Buckman who knows the name of the agency. If I gave you that information, I would be slitting my own throat. Buckman has a long reach, Kevin. As far as San Diego."

A long reach, Kevin thought to himself, after Dan left him alone gazing at the city. And Buckman's not above *anything*–including sending someone like you to test my loyalty.

"Matthew *tried* to heal your father. I thought he would burst a blood vessel in the attempt."

Eileen stared at *La Grande Jatte*, the Seurat painting, one of the crown jewels of the Chicago Art Institute. Kevin saw nothing in it but a boring French picnic. After returning home from his lunchtime meeting with Dan, Eileen's call took Kevin by surprise, and delight. She had not returned to Peoria, but had remained in Chicago. She had decided the place and the time for their meeting. "I can't believe that Matthew can *just touch people* and they get well. It sounds almost Satanic. He healed me but I have no memory of it."

"Repression is a normal defense against terrifying memories. I did it myself for a while after he healed my hand. Mathew's power is a good thing, a gift that defies scientific explanation. There are people whose cancers have disappeared and others whose heart problems have vanished without drugs or surgery–all thanks to Matthew."

"Why didn't it work with my father?"

"He can't turn it on and off at will. He *really* wanted it to work with your Dad. We both did. You have no idea how much it hurt him."

She grimaced, turned her focus back to the picture, and seemed momentarily lost to Kevin. "How do you think he did it?"

"By touching people. Beyond that I can't explain. Who could?"

"I meant the painting. How do you think Seurat put millions of dots together to make something so beautiful?"

So beautiful, Kevin thought–just like her. As sad and wrong as their night together had been, it was the most pleasurable, passionate time Kevin could ever remember spending with a woman. He felt like a diabetic craving sugar. He wanted her again. "How long are you planning to stay in town?"

"I know why we slept together," she said, turning to him. "And in some ways you helped me, but we can't do this again."

Kevin wanted to yell at her, grab her and hold her, kiss her, run. She had chosen a public place to tell him and that was damn smart; had she returned to his apartment he would have found some way to get her back into his bed. But he was not going to let some Frenchman and his millions of fucking dots stop him from getting what he wanted. He could reason with her–for her sake, his, maybe even Matthew's. "We don't have to sleep together, Eileen. I don't think we should just end something as good as we had last night. We need to keep seeing each other. We owe ourselves that."

"Even if I never make it back with Matthew," she said, facing him square on, "I can't keep this kind of secret from him."

Her words swept him in a wave of nausea. "You can't tell him."

"Do you want to do it?"

"No, of course not. But why do you have to? Can't we still see each other? It only has to be as serious as *you* want. We can just be–independent."

"Either you tell Matthew the truth or I will."

Kevin wanted to ignore her words and just hold her, somehow *make* her body feel the same urgent pressure his felt, take her home and make love to her until they both were empty. He didn't care about the ring stashed in her dresser drawer in Peoria or how many lies he would have to tell himself and the world. "Please, Eileen."

"You're a good guy, Kevin, but I can be happy on my own—I need to be, right now. I'm going back to Peoria," she said, kissing him on the cheek. "You tell him or I will," she reiterated, turning and walking from the room.

Kevin remained for a long moment after she left him, staring at the happy couples in the painting, sitting on the grass during a sunny Sunday afternoon, no Buckman or Matthew fucking up *their* lives.

A few scotches later, the sun dipping below the skyscrapers of Chicago's Loop, Kevin went to Matthew's apartment, and told his best friend what he had done.

"You slept with my *wife*?" Matthew roared. His fist came out of nowhere, knocking Kevin to the floor.

"Excuse me," Kevin said, shielding his face from a repeat blow. He couldn't see straight; Matthew loomed above him as he tried to stand, the pain shooting through him like a hurt he deserved. "It just happened."

"We're married," Matthew said. "How could you do that to me?" He sounded plaintive, uncomprehending.

"Promise not to punch me again," Kevin said, blotting his nose with a handful of tissues. He wasn't bleeding too much, but it hurt to swallow. Matthew agreed and they sat on his bed.

"You can sleep with her when I'm dead," Matthew said.

"You didn't have to break my face."

"It's just a bloody nose. And the punch wasn't just about you," Matthew said. "It was for Buckman too."

"What about him?" Kevin said, warily.

"One of Hector's friends is a cop with connections to private investigators. He passed on a rumor that somebody hired a professional to trip me up. It's only a matter of time before he runs down the source, but we both think it's him. Who else would be after me?"

Kevin told Matthew that it wasn't a rumor.

"You know?" Matthew shouted. "What the fuck do you mean you *know*?"

Kevin backed away from him. "Stay in your seat and keep your fists down or I won't say one more word."

"You fucking know about this?" Matthew yelled. "First you screw my wife, then you tell me that you know about a plot to frame me and you have the nerve to sit there and admit that you didn't tell me about it?" Matthew rose from his seat and grabbed Kevin by the shirt collar. Kevin could smell the rage seeping from him. "If you don't tell me the truth, I'm going to beat you to a fucking pulp and leave you for the cockroaches."

Matthew was a wounded pit bull with enough muscle mass to make good on his threat. Kevin managed to pull himself out of Matthew's grip and, from a safe distance, admitted that he did know Buckman was spying on him. "I protected you. I didn't tell him anything that could hurt you."

"There wasn't anything to tell," Matthew said, his voice so low and crisp that all Kevin heard was menace. "Why did you do it, Kevin?"

"Buckman found out about my moonlighting and gave me a choice. It was either spy on you or lose my residency and my future."

"You sorryass Judas."

"That's not all." Kevin knew that it was time to come clean, or at least half clean, figuring Matthew might eventually find out and *really* hurt him. "It was either you or me in Buckman's office the day he fired you. He forced me to keep my mouth shut while he railroaded you or else *both* our careers were toast."

"You gutless fucking wonder," Matthew muttered. "You pretended to be my friend."

"I *am* your friend. I lied to Buckman for you. Everything I told Buckman was worthless to him. I deflected him every chance I could."

"You lied to *me*, Kevin. You watched my life fall to shit and you still lied."

"I ran all kinds of interference for you–I really did. And besides, you know I'm sorry, Matthew," Kevin said.

"You sure are." Matthew's voice had a new firmness. "You have a choice, Kevin. It's you or Buckman. I want solid proof that he hired a detective. I'm going to turn the tables on him and sue his ass out of medicine."

Kevin's blood went cold. "I can't do that. It would be suicide for the person who told me. And for me too. I need Buckman's stamp of approval for my position next year."

"Isn't that a shame. If you didn't get it, you just might have to work in a clinic among poor people. You're a clever guy," Matthew said, as stealthily as before, "but if you don't get me what I want, I'm going to tell Buckman about your hand. I wonder if he'll give his blessing to your future when he finds out that you've been lying to him when you were Exhibit Number One."

Kevin had to deal. "Isn't it enough for you to know what he's doing? Just be extra careful. You can catch the next fake patient who tries to trip you up. Or you can call Buckman and tell him that Hector heard a rumor about his plan. That should scare him away."

"That's not good enough, Kevin. I don't want to have to be 'extra careful.' Either you get me what I want or you can kiss your career good-bye. And if you ever go near Eileen again, I'll rip out whatever passes for your heart."

Matthew rose and opened his front door. "Get out."

Susan returned Kevin's call later that night. "Kevin, have you quit? Or retired? I haven't seen you anywhere. We thought you got lost."

"I need to talk."

"I'm really tired."

"Have you seen Matthew recently?"

"I've been spending my free time with Francie. She's going downhill. It's really sad, but she's got such *poise*. I'll talk to you tomorrow at the hospital."

"I have to see you *now*, Susan. Matthew's in trouble."

"I'll boil some water."

Kevin sat in Susan's den, ignoring a cup of chamomile tea, telling her what had happened. "Matthew doesn't understand that I've been trying to *protect* him from Buckman." Susan stared at him, speechless. "And the night with Eileen *just happened*."

Kevin half expected Susan, like Matthew, to punch him. He harbored a secret hope that she would understand his faults, especially after discovering her own humanness the night she tried to kill Carlos. He wanted her to provide some small amount of absolution—or at least talk to Matthew and attempt to turn him from his current course of action. "You have to help me."

"You got yourself into this, you miserable bastard. You get yourself out." She appeared tired. "What do you want *me* to do?"

"Talk to Matthew. Reason with him."

"How did you expect Matthew to behave? You betrayed him. You slept with Eileen."

"You slept with him."

"*Slept*, Kevin. Nothing else."

"It's the same thing."

"Is that why you came to *me*? Because we slept together? We didn't lie about it. And there was nothing to be ashamed of."

"Are you going to help me?"

"Here's the best advice you'll ever get in your life: Tell the truth. Take your lumps. I wouldn't blame Matthew for whatever he makes you do. And I'll tell him that if he calls me. Now get out of here, Kevin. I'm going to try to get some sleep and you're not going to stand in my way."

Three terror-filled days later, filled with dreadful hours Kevin spent avoiding both Susan and Buckman at the Research, Matthew knocked on his door. Kevin had already determined to present himself the next morning in Buckman's office with a first-strike defense.

Matthew walked into Kevin's living room, sighed, and collapsed into a chair. "I'm angry enough to beat your head in."

Kevin exhaled. "Go ahead. But only if you forgive me after you do it."

"Forgiveness isn't the issue, Kevin, but if it helps you, consider it done. I think you're a shit. I would never have fucked you over like you did to me. If you had been straight, we could have stopped Buckman."

"What are you going to do?" Kevin asked.

"I can't force you to do anything that would hurt yourself or anyone else. That would make me the same as Buckman. Just promise me that you'll tell me the truth. I don't need more lies or surprises. Is there anything else you need to tell me, or are we clean with each other?"

The man who had hit Kevin a few days before was now calm and generous as a nun. At least for the moment things were stable and there was no need to play the trump card Kevin had hidden in his back pocket.

"We're cool," Kevin said.

"You seem particularly quiet this afternoon, Kevin. Is everything going well at the hospital?" Kevin had been standing in the back yard, lost in his thoughts.

"Sure, Mom."

"The roses were beautiful last year," she said, looking at the plants beginning to send their early leaves out into the world. "Daddy loved them. Remember how you and he would prune them?"

"Mom, can I ask you a question?"

"Of course," she said. "But it's *may I ask.* I know it's tragic, having an English teacher as a mother." She smiled her little mothery smile. "First get some iced tea."

They sat on two ancient wicker chairs in the late afternoon shade. "Have you ever had to make a decision that hurt someone else?" Kevin asked.

"It's difficult to answer your question without the facts, Kevin. No matter what you do, you're going to displease someone."

"I don't mean displease, Mom. What if you were forced to do something to protect yourself and you knew that it would hurt someone else?"

"Hurt them physically, Kevin?"

"No, Mom. But sometimes you have to choose yourself over others, don't you?"

"Oh yes. My family was terribly opposed to my marriage to your father. My parents begged me to dump him."

"That's not the same thing," Kevin said. "They weren't hurt in any way by your choice. What if marrying Dad had meant that one of your parents would have become seriously ill? Or worse?"

She squinted at Kevin. "Are you in trouble?"

"No, Mom. I was asking for another resident in the program, someone who came to me with a difficult problem."

"Well, it had better not be you," she said with a smile. "Only a saint would to choose to suffer for the benefit of someone else. And, Kevin dear, much as I love you, you ain't no saint."

Kevin smiled weakly. "Thanks, Mom."

"Let me change the subject. I hope you won't be angry with me," she said.

"Angry?"

"I'm so proud of you, Kevin. I know that you said you didn't want any fuss over your graduation, but I planned a small party. Nothing extravagant. I sent the invitations yesterday."

"That's sweet, Mom. No, I don't mind."

She clapped her hands in delight. "Oh, good. I called Dr. Buckman's office and got the names of the doctors in Highland Park. I invited them, and Dr. Buckman too."

38

Kevin sat across the desk from Ben Listman in his sumptuous office in Highland Park. "Your work here has been excellent, Kevin."

"Thank you, sir."

"The staff and the doctors like you. We would very much like to see you join us next year. We have a slight problem, though, which is why I called you in."

"Sir?"

"Dr. Buckman promised to send your records and an official letter of recommendation to me weeks ago. I haven't received them."

Dr. Buckman, committing a sin of omission, Kevin thought. Why wasn't he surprised? "I'm sure he'll send the necessary papers, Dr. Listman. You have his verbal okay. Isn't that good enough?"

"If it were up to me, Kevin, I would hire you today. But we're a huge corporation with a book of official policy as thick as the Chicago phone directory."

"Maybe I could speed the process if I called Dr. Buckman myself, sir."

"Good luck. I called him a few days ago. Is everything okay between the two of you?"

"Of course. Why wouldn't it be?"

"I'm sure it's not a big deal, Kevin, but Buckman seemed a bit evasive. It was probably just a bad day for him, but he didn't want to talk about you. He can be a real S.O.B. at times, but I'm sure you can straighten the problem out."

"There's no problem, Dr. Listman."

"Good, Kevin." He added, "We need to have his letter in our hands within the week. Much as we like you, we can't hold off filling the position."

Kevin walked into his office. He sat at the desk and examined the beautiful wood beneath his hands, imagining his name on the door, engraved on a brass nameplate. I'm so close to what I want, he thought. I can't lose this. Matthew could indeed hurt him by telling Buckman that he withheld the story of his hand, but it would be Matthew's word against his. He could deny Matthew's story. But, Kevin argued to himself, what if Buckman believed Matthew? Kevin's weapon against Matthew, the blatant lie on his applications, was worthless if Buckman learned Kevin withheld information about Matthew's Achilles heel for an eleventh hour attempt to save himself. Kevin thought of his mother having to cancel her party for him, but, on the other hand, wondered how he could live with himself if he once more betrayed Matthew, who had just inconveniently refused to betray him. But beyond the push and pull of his internal and solitary debate, the one central unknown was Buckman. Why was he stalling?

Kevin phoned Buckman's office to see if he was still there, hoping to get him to write the letter he needed to secure his dream, but was informed that Buckman had taken a few days off and was at home.

"Would you like me to call him for you, Dr. Hargrove?" she asked.

He told her that he knew how to reach him and hung up to call a cab.

Kevin's taxi pulled into the gravel driveway of Buckman's Tudor home. The tulips and daffodils were in full bloom. He was disconcerted to see Susan's car parked in the driveway. What was *she* doing here? Had Francie's illness taken a downturn? The maid answered the door. Kevin explained that he had to see Dr. Buckman; it was an emergency.

Susan appeared from the top of the stairs and descended half way so she could speak to Kevin without raising her voice. "Kevin? What the hell are you doing here?" He shouldered his way past the maid, climbed to meet her, and quietly told her that he had to see the Chief.

"This is a bad time," she said. "Buckman went to the pharmacy for some codeine for Francie."

"How is she?"

"Near the end. You had better leave before he gets back. Catherine, call Dr. Hargrove a cab, would you?"

"I know her, Susan. I'd like to see her."

"All right," she said, looking warily at the front door. "Just for a second, though."

Kevin stopped at the door to Francie's room, taking in the scene: the canopied bed, the stuffed animals on the dressers—a woman dying in a little girl's room. Francie was sitting up in bed. Kevin almost didn't recognize her, but the fire in her eyes—the most beautiful feature of what was once a Hollywood-perfect face—still smoldered. "Dr. Hargrove." The color drained from her cheeks. "I was hoping that you were Dr. Harrison."

"Matthew?" Kevin asked. Why was she asking for *him*? Had Matthew been here? Was he on speaking terms with Buckman?

"Francie asked me to ask Matthew if he would come to see her," Susan said. "I was just telling her that he said he has too many patients. He's too busy to take another case."

A faint smile touched Francie's lips. "You're a worse liar than my father, Susan. He refused, didn't he?"

Susan dropped her gaze. "Yes. He was angry at me for even asking him." Susan shaded the truth. Matthew, incensed with Buckman's treachery, had all but thrown Susan out of Hector's clinic for daring to approach him with the request.

Francie's face barely changed expression. Kevin could tell she had seen entire bouquets of disappointments in her lifetime and could no longer summon the energy to respond to one more that was handed to her.

"I feel terrible, Francie," Susan said.

"You tried your best. Do you blame him for refusing?"

Why hadn't Matthew come? Kevin wondered. Didn't he have a responsibility—no matter *what* her father had done—at least to try?

"What are you doing here, Dr. Hargrove? My Chief Resident making house calls? Explain yourself, please." Buckman had entered the room on panther's feet. Kevin's heart skipped three beats. Buckman looked at Francie, then at Susan and Kevin, his face frozen into his departmental chief mask, not a father at all.

"Is that how you treat your residents? Don't speak to him in that tone," Francie said.

Buckman raised his brow. "What tone?"

"Your asshole chief-of-medicine tone. I'm tired of it. I have something to ask you."

Buckman softened. "Anything, sweetheart."

"Will you ask Doctor Harrison to come here and see me?"

Buckman stiffened as if he'd been shot. He glared at Susan. "Is this Doctor Olivera's idea?"

"No, Daddy. It's mine."

"What does Dr. Hargrove have to do with this?" Buckman asked.

"Nothing, sir," Kevin said. "I came here to discuss something else entirely."

"At home?" Buckman asked.

"I can assure you that it's critical, sir."

"Maybe later," he said, turning his back on Kevin and facing Francie. "You want me to ask that two-bit quack to see you? What good would that do? Besides, he probably wouldn't come. He hates me so much that he quit my program."

"He didn't quit, Daddy. You forced him out."

"Who told you that?"

"I did," Susan said. "It's the truth."

Buckman's face darkened. "Are you insane, Olivera? Are you calling me a…"

"The word is liar, Daddy. Are you going to fire me too?"

"Stop this," Buckman shouted. And then he caught himself.

"Forget it, Daddy. You already fired me. Round about the time you were writing that paper on cholesterol and I had this little melanoma thing going on. Do you ask your residents questions about how melanomas metastasize?"

Kevin saw what he thought he'd never see: tears in Buckman's eyes. He gently took his daughter's hand. "I love you, Francie."

"Which is why you're going to ask Doctor Harrison if he'll make a house call." Francie had grown slurry, drowsy. Buckman stood and watched her labored breathing.

Susan touched his shoulder. "We better let her rest, Dr. Buckman."

He said nothing.

"Come with me." Susan took his hand, led him down the stairs to a small paneled library filled with medical journals, none of which could help his daughter. The three sat facing each other. "I know these last few weeks have been hard on you."

"I won't call Matthew," Buckman said.

"You have to," Susan shouted.

Buckman stirred himself into a grimace. "Except for the fact that Francie likes you…"

"What are you going to do to me, Dr. Buckman?" Susan's voice crackled. "Fire all of us because we know the truth? I put my husband in jail for rape. I almost killed him when he attacked me. Do you think I'm scared of you?"

"One more word, Doctor Olivera, and you can go back to passing out thermometers and medications."

"Back to nursing? Do you think going from nursing to medicine was a vertical move?"

"Then you can join your wannabe doctor friend Harrison in his clinic. Matthew's a carnival performer. Why the hell should I see him? The finest doctors in the world can't help." Buckman spat out his words, more in anger than in explanation.

"It's not what he can or can't do; it's what Francie believes he can do. It's what she needs," Susan said.

Buckman sighed. Kevin heard Napoleon just east of Waterloo, Nixon on the White House lawn, Mobutu fleeing. "Please, Susan," Buckman asked, pleading, "could you ask Doctor Harrison again, perhaps as a personal favor to you? He wouldn't appreciate a visit from me."

"Matthew threw me out," Susan said. "If you want him to come, you'll have to go yourself."

Buckman was crushed.

"Dr. Buckman, may I add something?" Kevin asked.

Buckman blinked wetly. "Please do."

"Dr. Harrison is the real thing."

"How do *you* know?"

"If I tell you and go with you to see Matthew, may I ask a favor in return?"

"Whatever you want."

"Ben Listman needs your letter. As soon as possible."

39

Buckman agreed to let Kevin talk to Matthew first, to test the waters before the two of them faced off.

Matthew was alone, collapsed in a chair in the war room at ten a.m. "What the hell are you doing here, Kevin?"

"Why aren't you seeing patients?" Kevin asked.

Matthew had tears in his eyes. "I killed a little boy. A beautiful little child."

Kevin pulled a chair next to Matthew's. "I'm sorry. Tell me about it."

"It happened about a week ago. I was having a bad day. My lawyer was having a problem with my contract and I couldn't get Buckman off my mind. The boy's mother seemed really concerned. She said that Noah had been up half the night complaining about his head and neck hurting and that he hadn't eaten. While I was examining him, she talked non-stop, telling me about her employer, a woman I remembered, one whose breast cancer disappeared. I couldn't focus. Everything was gray inside my head except for the voices that kept telling me what a loser I am. I kept thinking of Todd and Buckman and how I've messed up my life with Eileen." He sighed. "I rushed the examination. I didn't pay attention and missed the signs that were clearly there. I told Noah's mother that he had a good case of the flu."

"And then?" Kevin asked.

"Carmen pointed out the boy's stiff neck and photophobia, that perhaps a spinal tap would be in order, but I cut her off. I told her that she was just a nurse."

"You're only human, Matthew."

"I was arrogant. Carmen was right. A third year medical student can recognize meningitis. Noah died last night at the Research. Buckman's finally found a way to destroy me."

"One mistake doesn't end a career, Matthew. And Buckman's here."

"Here? Why?"

"He's in as much pain as you. Will you see him?"

"Sure," Matthew said, defeated.

"Good morning Dr. Harrison," Buckman said, his big frame tentative in the doorway. "May I come in?"

"You already are. Sit down."

"Dr. Buckman…" Kevin said.

"It's okay, Kevin. I can handle this."

"I've come to ask a favor," Buckman said. Matthew sat silent.

"Matt…Dr. Harrison, I would like you to come to our home and treat my daughter, Francine." The clock ticked louder. "Please."

"You're not here about the boy?" Matthew asked.

Buckman squinted. "What boy? Francine wants to see you." He chuckled inappropriately. "Isn't this when they say it's a matter of life and death?"

Matthew sighed. "Life. Death. They're both the same, only death's easier."

Buckman ignored the comment. Knowing what he did about Matthew at age eighteen, Kevin could not. But he kept his silence, at least for the moment. "If you need an incentive," Buckman continued, "I could see my way clear to take you back into the program. Next July."

Matthew rose from his chair. He began to pace the room.

"Are you all right, Harrison?" Buckman asked.

"No."

"Please don't let your anger stop you. Don't try to hurt me through my daughter."

Matthew took a deep breath. "I'm not angry. I don't hate you. I just can't do it."

"Don't you mean won't?" Buckman asked.

"No," Matthew said emphatically. "I've lost the right to be a doctor. I killed a boy. He was four, maybe five. I was so careless, I didn't even ask his age. He had all the classical symptoms of meningitis. Your residents wouldn't have missed it. But I did."

"Every doctor makes mistakes," Buckman said.

"Not like this one."

Buckman persisted. "My daughter wants to see you. Susan's told her you're special, that you're a healer."

"I told Dr. Buckman about my hand," Kevin said.

"Maybe I was a healer once. I'm not now. Did you expect a miracle? Have you finally decided to come to Church?"

A flash of the old Buckman appeared. "To Church? Who the hell do you think you are? That's been your problem, Harrison. You think you're God."

"*I* think *I'm* God?" Matthew said. "Who ran the residency program like he was the fucking Pope?"

"Did it seem that way?" Buckman asked without rancor.

"Are you kidding?"

Buckman took a deep breath. "Do you know any German?"

"Is this a question from morning rounds?"

Buckman managed a small smile.

"A little," Matthew said.

"Do you know what '*Ich kann nichts anders,*' means?"

"It means 'I can't do anything else.' Or something like that."

"More properly, 'I couldn't do anything else.' Do you know who used those words historically?"

Matthew shook his head. "Stop the games, please."

"It was Martin Luther. He was explaining why he started the reformation. The meaning goes deep. It refers to a driving compulsion, an inability to act any other way, as if your very existence depends on it, because of what's inside here." Buckman pointed to his heart. "I ran the program the best way I knew how. I couldn't see any other way to do it." The next words stuck in Buckman's throat, requiring every ounce of energy he had left to get them out, "I'm sorry if I was unfair to you. I didn't know better. I do now."

Buckman rose from his chair, tall, vulnerable, and tattered. "Is there any way I can convince you to see my daughter? Is there anything I can do?"

Matthew shook his head no. "I can't. I'm sorry."

Buckman walked to the door. "I'm sorry I disturbed you. Francie appealed to me to ask you to see her, to touch her. She knows I threw you out, knows that's why you refused Susan's request. My daughter is dying. I gave her my word I would do whatever I could."

"There's nothing I can do anymore," Matthew said as Buckman departed.

Rounds at the Research were summoning Kevin. He had mundane promises to keep and couldn't stay with Matthew. He wasn't sure he could bear his own despair. Would Buckman keep his promise about Kevin's practice? He would, probably, but Kevin felt drained, an empty bottle. "I'm coming back after I finish this afternoon," he said, summoning up some cheer, a measure of ordinary feeling. "You'd better be here."

"I will be."

40

When Matthew Harrison was eighteen years old, he had a girlfriend, Anne, who developed leukemia. The two of them had grown up almost as brother and sister, three houses away from each other. The girl and boy next door became young adults and fell in love, but the standard storybook romance was shattered by Anne's cancer. Matthew feared that his first love would die. Then he discovered an even deeper terror when Anne experienced searing heat come from his hand as he touched her. Two days later, the doctors announced their confusion over Anne's unexplainable spontaneous remission.

Anne believed Matthew's touch had healed her and, to his horror, told anyone who would listen. Her doctors and her priest politely scoffed at the over-enthusiastic teenager. Anne continued to insist that Matthew had performed a miracle. When she told her parents she intended to marry him, they sent her to cool off in a Swiss boarding school.

The attempt to separate the young lovers was successful—and permanent. Anne suffered a relapse of her illness while in Switzerland and died within a week. When he heard she was sick, Matthew wanted to save her. He withdrew his savings from the bank. His parents found his airline ticket to Zurich and confiscated it. He asked his friends for money to purchase another but they could not lend him enough. In his grief, he decided he didn't want a power that he couldn't use to save the people he loved.

In the afternoon after Buckman's visit, Matthew sat in his office thinking not only about Noah, the boy who had died from his misdiagnosis, and Francie, the daughter of his enemy, who stood at the brink of death, but also about Anne.

Matthew became more depressed and unhappy. He refused to see patients and sat alone in his room, listening to the voices within him, the dark ones that had whispered to him his whole life. His inner demons, feasting on Noah's death, voiced their poison louder than they had ever dared. Matthew listened to them more seriously than he had since he was eighteen.

The voices had concrete evidence to back their claims. Matthew thought hard about his life and decided it would be easier to be dead. He had made Buckman a powerful enemy, lost Eileen, legally entangled himself with Todd, and, worst of all, had killed Noah. He had destroyed his career and ruined his life. He would just go to sleep.

Matthew peeled back the paper cover from a scalpel and felt the green plastic handle in his hand. He sat for hours, growing increasingly numb as he played with the knife, running the blade lightly over the scars that ghosted his wrists.

Then another voice, a soft one from underneath the others began to whisper. "Put down the knife." It was Noah's voice. The child spoke again, this time louder. "Embrace your name and dance with me." Matthew started to cry. He told Noah how sorry he was.

Noah came to Matthew as a voice that flowed through him and swept away all the other voices except its own. Noah's voice told him one simple thing. "Embrace your name. It means God's gift." It was more like a knowing than real words heard. Matthew slipped the scalpel back in its protective sleeve and sat quietly. No more voices came to him.

It took three kicks before the lock on Matthew's door gave way. "Are you all right?" Kevin asked. Susan and Eileen rushed into the room hard on his heels.

Something profound had happened to Matthew. The three of them could tell by the way that he held his body and how clearly he looked at them.

"I was in town with my mother," Eileen said. "I stopped by the Research to find Kevin and ask how you were doing when I ran into Susan. Kevin and she were worried about you." Eileen picked the scalpel from off the desk.

"You know what they say. He who lives by it." Matthew smiled at her, eerily calm, a lake after a storm.

She put the scalpel down and knelt next to him. "Matthew, please help Francie. It didn't work with my father, but I know your heart. You can't refuse somebody who needs you."

"I spent the afternoon thinking that I'd rather be dead than be me," Matthew said, his eyes lowering to the ground.

"With the gift of healing that you have?" Susan asked, "Are you crazy?"

"A lot of people probably think I am," Matthew said, a smile crossing his face. "If you know how to transfer this so-called 'gift' to yourself, you're welcome to it. My ability to heal people is a love-hate relationship. Sometimes I wonder why God chose me and there are other moments when I want to know what horrible thing I've done to have been cursed with this power."

"You can get therapy," Susan said.

"What would I say?" Matthew laughed. "That I can heal people and it pisses me off? That I've spent a lifetime feeling different from everyone else? I *am* different."

"Maybe you can find some kind of balance," Eileen said.

"Susan's already suggested that," Matthew said. "But it's just an illusion."

"Is that so?" Susan asked, listening carefully.

"Remember your bicycle metaphor, Susan? It doesn't work. If you watch a motion picture of a balanced rider frame by frame, you'll see he's actually making a series of tiny deviations to either side, coming back to center so quickly it only looks like the bicycle's moving in a straight line."

Kevin frowned, "I don't understand."

"Look at it from a medical point of view," Matthew said. "Blood sugar and insulin levels are in constant flux across an average value that we call normal. Sodium and potassium too. The dance goes on non-stop. Everything's in motion–seeking balance by going out of balance. We appreciate day by comparing it to night, good to bad, life to death. We have to keep moving in order to feel anything."

He handed the scalpel to Kevin. "Get rid of this for me, would you?"

He held up his wrists. The scars were gone. Matthew appeared to gather himself in his own center. "*Ich kann nichts anders,*" he said.

"It's a Buckmanism," Kevin explained to Eileen. "It means he'll do it."

41

An unusually warm spring rain covered Susan's windshield. The wipers danced with the water, out of sync with a Mahler symphony on the radio. The drops not cleared by the wiper reflected the head and tail-lights of other cars. They drove north up Lake Shore Drive with Matthew staring at the lake, black except for the light reflected from the high rises and the street lamps. The smell of trees awake from their winter sleep blended with the rich scents of the lake and the rain. Susan and Matthew sat in front, Eileen and Kevin in back. There was enough space in the back seat for the two of them to sit far enough apart not to touch. As they rounded a curve at Oak Street, Eileen reached over and squeezed Kevin's hand. He didn't know what it meant, but he appreciated it.

Matthew broke the silence. "Take the next exit. Montrose Harbor."

"Why?" Susan asked.

Matthew smiled. He was too relaxed, Kevin thought. "Trust me," Matthew said.

"It would be nice to get there before Francie dies," Kevin said. "What are you going to do?"

"Swim."

Kevin laughed. "That's why God made YMCAs with olympic-size pools. The lake will be freezing."

"I know, Kev. Do you want to join me?"

"I didn't bring my Speedo."

He smiled. "Neither did I."

Susan parked in the deserted lot. They all got out of the car, and watched as Matthew strode across the grass to the breakwater, twenty feet or so from the car. He removed his shoes, peeled off his shirt and pants, and dropped them as he approached the ten feet of large, flat rocks leading to the water's edge. The three of them stood by the car, dumbfounded. The rain fell harder.

"Are you sure you won't join me?" Matthew called back, gleeful.

"You can stop now, Matthew. It's dangerous," Eileen yelled.

"Nope." He stripped off his underwear and socks, the sure white form of his body luminous in the mercury vapor lights of the parking lot, and raised his head and arms into the rain which had by now become a downpour. Walking to the edge, he jumped into the water and shouted, "*Yes*." Eileen ran across the grass. Kevin followed. They watched, side by side, as Matthew played in the cold water like an otter.

Matthew looked up at Kevin, whipping the water from his hair.

Kevin looked hard at the pure joy reflected on Matthew's face. He wanted to jump in with him, but he stopped short, too frightened. He walked back to the car while Eileen gathered Matthew's clothes. Matthew scrambled out, dancing across the rocky breakwater, got dressed, and jumped back into the car. The rest of them looked at each other, mystified. At least the guy was alive. They piled into the car and returned to the traffic on North Lake Shore Drive.

The car windows fogged with their breath and heat as they continued the drive to Glencoe. Buckman's street was lined with ancient trees, towering over the large, expensive homes that had been there for fifty years, representing the good life for the attorneys, doctors, and businessmen who could afford to pay more in annual real estate taxes than three month's of a resident's salary at the Research. The crunch of driveway gravel under their tires scattered a gray cat.

The rain had stopped: a few stars dared to appear among the dissipating storm clouds. The air was heavy, fertile with the perfumes of flowering crab apple trees and lilacs. The night was a promise of life and a comment on its ironies.

"I'll go with you," Kevin said, opening the car door.

"You're all coming," Matthew said, opening the door for Susan.

"Aren't you terrified?" Eileen asked.

"Of course."

The four of them walked up to the heavy oak door with its shiny brass dolphin's head knocker and rang the bell. The door opened.

"I'm Matthew Harrison."

"Yes." The maid was somber. She led them through the foyer with its dark stone floors and oak paneling. They followed through the den, a lighter room with white stucco walls, pale blue ultrasuede couches, and a large screen TV.

A sunroom adjoined the den. It was constructed completely of glass, even the ceiling. Sliding doors opened onto the backyard where floodlights bounced off the trees. Despite the open doors, the room smelled of antiseptic and death.

Buckman and his wife sat on white wrought iron chairs, on opposite sides of Francie, who slept fitfully in a hospital bed. A middle-aged nurse ten feet away knitted something green. She raised her head and smiled.

Mrs. Buckman rose from her seat. A stately woman with silver hair, she wore a floor-length purple velvet robe. "Thank you," she said. She put her hand on Matthew's shoulder.

Buckman rose from his chair and directed Matthew back into the den. "Thank you for coming," he said. Buckman fidgeted. "About the residency position…"

"Later. I'm here for Francie."

"She's asleep. I'm sure I know your answer. You can start in July."

"I'm sorry, Doctor Buckman, but I'm not going to accept your offer."

Buckman's mouth dropped open. "Who do you think will take you, Matthew?"

"I don't know. Something will work out. You were my third choice, you know." Matthew gave him a grin.

Buckman was dumbfounded. "Do you think Mass General is going to welcome you with open arms?"

"Maybe. Maybe not."

Francie stirred.

"It's your decision, but the subject isn't closed."

"It is for me." Matthew returned to the sunroom. Buckman followed him.

Francie had changed even since Kevin had seen her that morning. She was little more than a burnt-out shell of a person, her upper lip trembling with each breath. The yellow-gray hue of her skin was a sign ancient physicians would have understood without the benefit of computerized technology. The nurse put down her knitting to fluff Francie's pillow, gently smiling as she stroked her patient's forehead. "Dr. Harrison's here, sweetheart."

Francie's voice was husky, her breathing labored. She made an effort to smile. "Thank you for coming, Doctor."

"Please call me Matthew."

Kevin stood beside Matthew at Francie's bedside, looking into her soft brown eyes. Matthew moved a strand of her hair away from her face.

"I have faith in you. My father's eyes..." Francie said with great effort, "blind."

Matthew looked puzzled.

"Macular degeneration," Buckman said from behind Matthew. "I was a few years away from legal blindness. I felt something the night of the reception at the Union. Then the disease disappeared. Eventually, I knew it was you."

"Then why did you hurt me?" Matthew asked, turning to face him.

Buckman took a breath. "I hated you," he said, choking on the words. "You could do what I can't." He looked at Francie. "You cured the wrong one," he said in an anguished whisper.

Matthew's heart opened. "I feel so sorry for you," he said gently, putting both of his hands on Buckman's shoulders. Then he turned back to Francie and lightly touched the side of her face. "Your hand," she said.

He pulled it away. "Too hot?"

Francie reached out and grasped it–a movement that took all her strength. "No. Warm…alive."

With one hand Matthew held Francie; with his other, he took Kevin's. Kevin saw the light from the trees and the yard and the very stars themselves carry Matthew over the rocks and into the lake. The light flowed into Matthew, through his hand and into the dying girl on the bed. It was indefinable, the passion and human presence which is the assurance against the loneliness and isolation of suffering–the shared strength that allows each of us to let go of life when we must. Kevin felt it surge though Matthew's hand into him and was a different man.

Francie opened her eyes from the momentary sleep that had taken her. She looked at Matthew and tried to speak, but could not find the energy. Instead, she squeezed his hand with a strength that defied understanding and slipped into the embrace of the Universe.

Epilogue

Kevin heard that Matthew was in the Mission District of San Francisco with the winos and the hookers. Rumor was that he was living in a section of town as rundown as Hector's neighborhood. But in each story that drifted back to Chicago, Matthew was reported to be happy.

After Matthew left, Kevin finished his residency and got the position in Highland Park. Eileen returned to Peoria and found a job teaching. She and Kevin don't call each other. Kevin sees Buckman at Department of Medicine meetings and Grand Rounds at the Research. Buckman treats him like a peer, as his confederate in the adult world of loss and remorse. Buckman's clear and healthy eyes never fail to unnerve him. And day after day Kevin treats the ills—some serious, some absurd—of the white, scared, and well insured.

But something makes Kevin return to the rocks where Matthew jumped in the water that rainy spring night.

He sits there, staring across the lake at the tall buildings reflected in the dark water. He sees Matthew splashing in the lake, happy. And sometimes he cries—for his life and his unborn poetry.

Sometimes Kevin gets as far as unbuttoning his shirt. Once he actually took it off, letting the sun warm him. But he always buttons it back up and drives home carefully—not, however, before he makes sure he has the washcloth with him, the one from that night at the residents' party. On those days he doesn't carry it with him, he keeps it in the bottom of

his desk drawer, wrapped around the mandarin yellow Duofold that
Matthew gave him the night before he left. Matthew pointed out the
tiny engraved letters on the pen's barrel: *Primum, non nocere*. First, do
no harm–the ethical basis of medical practice and of life itself. Matthew
smiled as he stuck the pen in Kevin's pocket and said that Kevin needed it more than him.

   One of these days Kevin might actually get the courage to fill the
damn thing.

About the Author

Michael A. Greenberg practices dermatology in Elk Grove Village, IL. He is an anchor columnist for *American Medical News* writing on issues of medicine and humanism.